freedom for joe

freedom for joe

Lee Burns
www.leeburns.net

This book is a work of fiction. Names, characters, businesses, organizations, places, events, and incidents either are the product of the author's imagination or are used fictitiously. Any resemblance to actual persons, living or dead, events, or locales is entirely coincidental.

Copyright © 2013 by Lee Burns
All Rights Reserved.

Published in the United States by *Persistent 1 Publishing*
eISBN: 978-0-9893082-1-2

Without limiting the rights under copyright reserved above, no part of this publication may be reproduced, stored in or introduced into a retrieval system, or transmitted, in any form, or by any means (electronic, mechanical, photocopying, recording or otherwise) without the prior written permission of the above copyright holder of this book.

Edited by Stacee Lawrence
Copyediting by Nada Kaidbey
Front Cover design by Tristan Burns
Jacket design by Melissa Burns

freedom for joe

LEE BURNS

Persistent 1 Publishing

ACKNOWLEDGEMENTS

I would like to extend a very special acknowledgement to my *house of artists*, also known as my wife, Melissa, and my children, Tristan, Megan and Grace, while also inclining my father, Gary, for all of their unwavering support and sacrifices for me, in the long journey to bring the *freedom for joe* story to fruition. I love you all.

I would also like to extend a very special acknowledgment to my Mom, Toni, for inspiring me to break the mold. I love you Mom.

Additionally, I would like to especially acknowledge David Paladino, Clifford Woods, Craig Mooneyham, Ark Sardarov for their longtime, invaluable support, advice, encouragement and feedback.

Also to my brother, Chad, for his support, help, and for the inspiration for Johnny's "pellet gun story."

And lastly to the many, many other supporters, such as, my friends Jessica Drolet, Michael Pollack, Chrissy Speir and the numerous producers, directors, writers and actors, as well as the "joe's" on the street, who have given me feedback, support or simply maintained interest in the project and belief in my intention to complete it and share it with the world – Thank You! You all mean the world to me! *freedom for joe* is for you...

For the "joe's" worldwide.

Chapter 1

Young Joe Gilmore's knees were slightly bent as he leaned forward, his hands outstretched beneath the imaginary backside of the football teammate supposedly crouched in front of him: the massive blocking center who readied to hike Joe the oblong leather ball. Joe's hands thrust forward and down, as though he was preparing to receive the snap from the center, despite the fact that his hands were already clutching his most prized possession, a weathered and worn youth football.

It didn't matter that the leather of that pigskin was already in his hands, or that there was nothing between that football and the ground but empty space. For Joe, that center was crouched right there in the middle of his fellow guards and tackles—the offensive line of his football team. His mom, Sarah Gilmore, stood about twenty feet to his right. But when Joe looked in that direction all he saw was the most sure-handed, fleet-footed receiver in the entire league.

Joe squinted his brown and green, hazel eyes as he turned them forward once again and peered over the backs of his offensive line.

Even at the young age of nine, Joe's piercing eyes revealed the passion and perception of an old soul. At least that's what his grandma always said to anyone who was listening, and even to some who weren't. But those who took the time to look a little more closely, or perhaps a little more perceptively, usually ended up agreeing with the proud granny.

Joe's wild and wavy dark-brown hair moved gently in the breeze, in contrast to the intensely focused look on his face. He was a good-looking kid, with tanned and freckled cheeks that reflected the amount of time he spent outdoors—doing *what* didn't really matter all that much to him, so long as he was outside with his friends and moving.

He was already a bit taller than most of his buddies. And while he was very good at all the sports played by the kids in the neighborhood, none evoked his passion quite like football; a fact that was very evident from the fire in his eyes as he peered over his crouched center at the middle linebacker of the imaginary defense standing across from him.

The linebacker squinted back at him with an opposing glare.

"I'm coming for you, Gilmore!" he shouted across the line, bending down into his stance, legs poised to fire at the snap of the ball.

Joe brought his right hand to his mouth to give his fingers a lick, for better grip on the ball.

"Bring it!" he fired at the linebacker, ready for the challenge.

The linebacker's face oddly began to morph from an intense stare to a playful grin as Joe's dad, James Gilmore, could no longer hold his role as the menacing opposing defender.

"Bring it?" he asked Joe, the grin continuing to grow in admiration of his son's focus and determination.

About six feet two inches tall himself, and only in his late thirties, James still had an athletic physique. And even if his boyish, outside-all-the-time looks were now more of a rugged handsome appearance, it was still very easy to see exactly where Joe got many of his features.

"Daaad!" Joe huffed back at his father, "You're supposed to be serious."

"Oh," James answered as though he was totally unaware, the grin still plastered on his face as it usually was. "Sorry," he replied. "I thought it was about having fun."

"Daaad, it's the last play," Joe tried again.

"James Michael Gilmore," Sarah piped in with feigned intensity, barely keeping her own face straight. "You knock that off and get serious right now or we are going to kick your butt."

Sarah had the presence of a fighter and an angel all mixed into one. Not to mention the looks. Athletic and tall herself, or at least tall enough that James was in the continual habit of telling her that her legs went, "all the way up to heaven."

Her auburn hair cascaded around the silky smooth skin of her face and hung down just below her shoulders. Her brown and green hazel eyes, just like Joe's, were filled with the joy only a mother in the midst of play with her boys can know. But just now she was doing the best she could to hide that joy for the demanded seriousness of the moment, as she made her lips into a thin line and glared at James.

"Ooooh?" James retorted to the threat and the look with a smirk. "Well alright, then," he said, beginning to return the intensity to his own face, but only after a quick wink at Sarah.

Joe, tired of his parents' flirting and always looking for any weakness in the defense, took advantage of the distraction.

"Hut, hut!" he barked, jumping back from the line while cocking his right arm up to position, ready to fire out the ball.

"You little turkey," James yelled, losing the battle with his grin once again as he started his countdown to rush a moment late. "One-one-thousand, two-one-thousand..."

Sarah had already sprung from the line and was now cutting across the field behind the defense. Luckily for the defense—James—the "field" was only their suburban front lawn.

The lawn was a bit larger than the new housing additions' lots that were being churned out in other parts of the city. The Gilmore house, like the rest in the neighborhood, had been built in the sixties, on lots big enough that you could look out your side window without looking directly into your neighbor's. And while the yard was large and filled with the bark and leaves of the majestic oak trees that covered it, it still wasn't too big for James to be able to both guard Sarah and threaten Joe with a rush.

"Five-one-thousand!" James finished the required countdown before he could charge for the quarterback. He immediately rushed forward from Joe's left, on the street side of the yard, leaving Sarah behind him as he closed in on the small quarterback.

Sarah and Joe both broke toward the right side of the yard, the house side, as Joe tried to avoid the oncoming linebacker, James, in order to throw or run and Sarah tried to give Joe a better angle to pass the ball to her.

The famous number eight, Texas Cowboys, authentic jersey of the prolific superstar-quarterback Troy Johnson that Joe was wearing probably didn't give the little guy the best throwing opportunity, seeing as how it hung on his body like an oversized coat. But that didn't matter to

Joe; he always loved to throw more than run. After all, "That's how quarterbacks win championships," James had told him. And that's exactly what this was: the championship game.

So even though James was bearing down on him, Joe fearlessly stopped, planted his feet, and yanked his arm back to release the ball. As he did, everything slowed.

This always happened for Joe. It was part of the reason he loved the game so much. Not that he had anything in his life that needed escaping. He loved his parents, felt safe in his home, his church, and school. He had lots of rambunctious friends and, really, just an ideal all-American upbringing. It didn't hurt that it was in a neighborhood where it still felt more like the mid-sixties than the early-nineties it currently existed in. Everyone on the street knew your name, who you belonged to, and even cared whether or not you made it home for supper without too many scrapes on your knees.

No, it wasn't escape he needed or wanted. The love of the game just made the most intense moments slow down a little. The details of everything became clearer and more focused. To Joe this was just a normal part of the game, or at least normal for the way he played it.

He saw the linebacker diving for him in the peripheral vision of his left eye, and at the same time, he saw the wide receiver breaking open across the middle of the field. His eyes zoomed in on her hands, and he fired the ball toward her.

Now, he wasn't Troy Johnson just yet, even if you couldn't convince him of that. So he didn't quite see that the linebacker, James, was exerting himself only slightly less than all of his athletic abilities would allow, or that that Gilmore grin was still just below the surface of his father's overtly straining face as he crashed to the ground just short of Joe's feet.

Instead Joe saw the ball in flight. Laces, leather, laces, leather, as it spun through the air like a bird making its arc toward Sarah, just clearing the outstretched arms of the defensive backs that Joe was sure were there.

Sarah snatched the ball out of the air as it reached her, and then turned and ran the length of the field, as everything returned to normal speed for Joe.

It was only about a twenty-five-foot jog for Sarah to reach the end zone, otherwise known as the Gilmore driveway. And by the time she crossed into it, Joe, his little legs tearing across the yard, was already halfway to her.

"Touchdoooowwwwwwwn!!!" Joe yelled as he sprinted after her with his arms in the air, leaving the spent foe, James, lying on the grass behind him.

Sarah waited for Joe to reach her, then she raised her arm, spiked the ball, and threw her hands in the air like Joe's. They both began wiggling their hips and pumping their arms in unison; their practically patented touchdown dance.

"We're the world champs! We're the world champs!" they chanted as James rose and made his way toward them, the seriousness of the moment gone and all of them able to let their beaming smiles now run free.

When James reached the celebration he joined in with as much fervor as if he himself had made the winning score.

He grabbed Joe and hoisted him up onto one of his broad shoulders, between him and Sarah. All three of them raised an arm, their hands signaling the familiar "number one" sign of champions worldwide.

Joe was on top of the world as the surging crowd in the stands took up the family chant. He looked up and around at the large oak trees—the stadium as he saw it—enjoying the celebration of a goal achieved with the throngs of fans above him and his team below.

Atop one of the trees, another fan had joined in the stadium celebration fantasy. In fact, he had actually been there from the beginning of the game. Only this fan had an unusual cheer. It was a screech really, albeit a magical one: the piercing cry of a red-tailed hawk.

Sarah and James were too enraptured in the celebration—or perhaps it was each other by this point—to notice the feathered fan. But Joe saw the regal hawk.

He saw the hawk and it made him feel good. He liked the idea of something up there that could see over the whole yard, heck, over the whole neighborhood. And that was without even stretching its wings. *Why, it could probably see the whole world when it was flying high up in the sky*, Joe thought.

It was a good thought, a thought that left him feeling bigger for some reason. But his mind didn't stay in that world of lofty ideas for long. The chant of "world champs" below him had now turned to "ice cream, ice cream" instead. And that was enough to pull any nine-year-old boy's attention away from the heavens and back to earth in a hurry, or perhaps it was the other way around...

Chapter 2

The slick surface of a seventy-two-inch flat screen television reflects the moonlight, which intermittently pours into a room through the cloudy night sky. The sheer curtains that hang over floor-to-ceiling windows lightly sway in the vented, warm air of a dark, luxurious penthouse apartment.

On the screen of the TV, an early thirties, pretty news anchor, with her handy plastic smile, issues the news of the day; her straightened, jet-black hair lies perfectly over her shoulders.

"Opening statements were given today in the trial of Reyben Muñoz, the nineteen-year-old male accused of the murder of Detective James Gilmore," her manicured voice announces.

A picture of James in uniform appears on the screen next to her. The salt-and-pepper hair around his temples reveals him to be about twenty years older than he had been when he was playing in the front yard of his house with Joe and Sarah.

In the bedroom of the penthouse a late twenties, beautiful, slender blonde with porcelain skin—super model Cindy Robinson—lies under silk sheets and a down comforter on a massive bed. She sleeps on her side, her face turned toward the large windows.

Behind her, on the edge of the bed's other side, sits a shirtless male. The ambient light of the TV illuminates his back, revealing the tattoo across his right shoulder—a buffalo with snow sprinkled over the top of its furry hide. He holds a beer in his hand as he stares off blankly in the direction of the indulgent space's stylish Italian-tiled bathroom floor.

On the flat screen to his left the news anchor continues. "Detective Gilmore was slain nearly a year ago, while off duty, when he was shot in the head from behind as he sat in his personal car at a traffic light."

The male figure raises his right arm, bringing the soothing liquid to his lips. He gulps it down and then sets the can on the nightstand, next to two additional empty cans. His hand grabs a black iPhone lying next to them.

"Police have speculated that the unexpected and seemingly random attack was an initiation act for the infamous One Blood inner-city gang." The woman's voice drones on.

The male absently thumbs through his address book, stopping on the name Trace Lassiter.

"Detective Gilmore is, of course, the father of the star quarterback of the Rattlers football team, Joe Gilmore," the news anchor adds.

The male glances in the direction of the TV.

"To this point Joe has refused to comment on the proceedings, other than to say that he would not be attend—"

The voice is cut off as the TV screen goes black.

Barely visible in the darkness, the male holds the TV remote in his left hand, still pointing it at the screen. After a moment he quietly places it back on the nightstand. He looks down at the glowing screen of the phone in the palm of his other hand. He stares at it until it goes dark, before looking back over his shoulder at the sleeping Cindy.

Appearing to have decided against the call to Trace, he tosses the phone onto the shag-carpeted floor and spoons in behind Cindy, wrapping his muscled arms tightly around her and burying his face into the back of her neck and her silky blonde hair.

Cindy rouses slightly from her slumber.

"Not tonight, baby. I'm still not feeling right," she mumbles, misinterpreting his intent for one of a sexual nature.

Silently, the male pulls himself away from her, rolling onto his back and staring at the ceiling as Cindy drifts back off to sleep.

After a few restless minutes he rises, picks up his phone from the floor, and grabs a pair of crumpled-up jeans off of a covered chair that sits against the bedroom wall.

As he exits the room with his gear in hand he passes by a painting on the wall.

On the gold-framed canvas is a beautiful picture of a mountainous landscape. In the soft blue sky between two of the peaks there is what, in the darkened atmosphere of the room, at first appears to be some kind of dot. But the night moon, momentarily breaking through the cloudy sky, illuminates the picture further, revealing the blot to actually be a red-tailed hawk soaring through the air. From the hawk's position in the sky, its motionless black bead of an eye almost seems to be surveying the room.

Chapter 3

The chilly, bubbly, auburn liquid in the crystal glass lightly sloshes over its rim and down the slender fingers, hand, and then arm of the stunning, twenty-three-year-old Jennifer Ames as she climbs into a king-size bed in an expansive, posh hotel suite, wearing only a small heart tattoo on the top of her firm left buttock. She giggles as she plops down between the pillows and rolls onto her back, her perky breasts jiggling as she tries to keep her glass aloft with little success in her intoxicated state.

At the dresser, the brunette hair of Trace Lassiter falls across the nape of her neck as she stands, in a thin, pink-stringed thong, facing the mirror and downing her own glass of the scintillating champagne elixir.

The bubbly gone, she sets down the glass and grabs a black credit card off the side of a silver tray that lies on top of the mahogany dresser. She then begins expertly handling the card, using it to separate a sizable pile of fine white powder, sitting on a square piece of white paper, into lines across the tray.

A fit, attractive male appears behind her, his face split in two by the beveled edge of the mirror, causing half of him to look disfigured, like the turmoil spinning inside him.

But even in only half of a steady reflection, however, his features still reveal him. The wavy, messy brown hair, the rugged, outdoorsy face that resembles James Gilmore, and those soulful, brown and green, hazel eyes can only belong to the same Joe Gilmore who used to toss the pigskin with his parents every Saturday morning of his youth.

The lines on his face paint the aging of the last twenty-one years, and the pain in his eyes reveals the loss and confusion of the most recent one. He downs his own glass of the memory escaping potion and then reaches for the gold bottle over Trace's shoulder to pour another.

While he fills his glass once again, Trace picks up a slick silver tube off of the tray and inhales one of the lines of coke. As she goes back down to fill the other nostril, Joe, clad in a pair of tight white boxers, presses himself against the pink string thong splitting her buttocks.

Trace finishes her line and then grips the dresser with both hands. She spreads her legs farther and pushes back against him, peering up at him in the reflection of the mirror with her sexy and inviting smile.

"Happy to see me?" she purrs.

Joe grins and tips the champagne bottle toward her arched back. Trace squeals in delight as the cold liquid hits her hot skin and runs down her spine and along the fabric of her thong.

On the bed, Jennifer laughs as Trace spins around and pulls Joe in for a passionate, animalistic kiss. Joe drops the empty champagne bottle to the carpet and grips Trace's ass, hungrily pressing her body against his.

Trace slides her hand down inside his boxers, her caress arousing him further.

"You *are* happy to see me." She grins as she pushes back from him. She stoops down and strips off his boxers, running her tongue along the ridges of his rock-hard abs and up to his neck as she rises back up. She pulls back, playing the tease, winks at him, and heads for the bed—her pink thong sliding to the floor along the way.

Joe catches his reflection in the mirror and, almost in avoidance of it, quickly downs his bubbly and places the glass on the dresser next to the cocaine. Then he reaches out and grabs the white paper that holds the remaining mound of powder—along with the accompanying silver tube—and turns for the escape of the bed and the girls.

On the pillowed surface of the mattress, Trace has already climbed on top of Jennifer. Their mouths devour each other, each grinding against the other's leg in pleasure as they grasp the soft flesh of burning bodies.

Joe reaches the corner of the bed and grabs one of Trace's ankles, pulling her toward him and twisting her over onto her back.

Trace laughs and opens her legs in anticipation.

Joe creases the paper and sprinkles a strand of coke along the line of her hip and down across the inside of her inner thigh.

"What are you doing now, QB?" Trace breathes excitedly.

Joe gives her a charming, devilish grin.

"Lie still," his voice sexily gravels as he kneels down, placing the cocaine and the silver tube on the thick carpet next to the bed.

Anxious to be part of the action, Jennifer grabs the rest of her glass of champagne off the nightstand and crawls over toward Trace. Leaning over her head, she pours a little of the sweet, cold liquid on each of Trace's firm breasts and then begins sucking it off, teasing her nipples with the light flick of her tongue.

Kneeling on the floor, Joe leans forward between Trace's legs. He slowly snorts the powder off her body and then licks up the remains.

The powder gone, his mind and conscience further numbed, and the beat of his heart increasing, Joe stands, turns his back to the bed, and spreads his arms. The back of his right shoulder wears the snow-frosted buffalo tattoo.

The girls separate and Joe flops back onto the bed; both hungrily climb on top of him.

Joe's eyes find the squares of mirror that cover the high ceiling above him.

The ceiling's vain decoration becomes surreal reflections of the three entangled in a tryst of drug-and-alcohol-fueled ecstasy and escape: slender legs, a muscular back, ravenous faces, taut stomachs and buttocks, hungry mouths, arms and eyes fill the mirrored squares above.

The escapade over, the three lie spent among the fluffy pillows now scattered across the crumpled, fine sheets; the comforter somehow having found its way to the floor.

Jennifer slowly sits up and slides off the side of the bed. She surveys the white pile of cocaine on the floor next to her, which she had avoided to this point.

Screw it, she thinks to herself; the promised god-like experience of its powder tempting her.

She picks up the silver tube of off the floor next to the cocaine, buries it into the center of the pile, and inhales deeply through her nose.

"OH! That burns!" she exclaims, sitting up sharply, the chemicals tearing at the soft lining of her sinuses.

Trace, snuggled up under Joe's arm as he absently stares off into the space above the bed, leans over and looks in Jennifer's direction.

"Was that your first time, Jen?" she questions with a condescending smile.

Jennifer's head bobs up and down, indicating that it was as she scrunches up her nose.

Trace giggles as Joe breathes a frustrated sigh.

"Rookies," he mumbles, only partially joking.

Jennifer takes a deep breath, trying to calm a heart that now feels like it is beating outside of her chest, as the betraying drug fuels its pounding.

She places both hands over her nose and rubs it vigorously.

Trace slides over to the edge of the bed as Jennifer looks up at her with fear in her eyes.

"Jesus, your pupils are totally dilated," Trace announces to Jen and Joe alike. "Take it easy, girl," Trace advises, trying to calm her as she reaches for her with growing concern.

As Jennifer pulls her trembling hands away from her nose, blood trickles out of her nostrils.

Joe sits up just in time to see Jennifer's body give a subtle shudder before she collapses back onto the floor in convulsions.

"Oh my God!" Trace screams, falling onto the floor next to her.

Joe leaps from the bed, grabbing the comforter off the floor, and rushes to Jen.

He wraps Jennifer in the blanket and looks to Trace.

"Hold her," he orders.

Trace just stares at him; fearful tears beginning to race down her face.

"NOW!" Joe yells.

Trace reactively opens her arms as Joe passes Jennifer to her.

Having no idea what to do next, Joe bolts up and rushes over to his phone, which lies in the chair by the front door. He grabs the device out of its holster and quickly thumbs to his Favorites list, presses one of the names on the screen, and places the phone to his ear. After a few tense moments of pacing, the person on the other end of the line answers in a groggy voice.

"B.," Joe says, "I fucked up, man." He looks toward Jennifer and Trace, his face filled with genuine concern. "I need your help."

Chapter 4

A red-tailed hawk circles high above the oval-shaped coliseum of the gladiators of modern day.

Over eighty thousand screaming fans are packed into the multilevel seats of this ode to their football heroes; making this monolith the Rattlers football team home stadium.

The roar of the crowd, celebrating the game in progress, drifts up into the heavens and past the circling hawk.

The hawk spots its empty seat and descends through the sky, wings spread against the wind, until it silently alights atop a bank of dormant lights that hangs over one of the two end zones.

From its perch high above the field, it peers down at the white-striped green grass below, which is speckled with the two teams of combatants.

Inside the television commentator's suite nestled between the top two sections of stadium seating the traditional, conservative, suit-and-tie-clad Chris Pennilton—mic in hand—sits in his elevated chair overlooking the field.

"Is there another player in the league that is more important to his team?" Chris offers up to his partner, the tightly wound and curly-haired former-player-turned-commentator Samuel Juarez.

"Oh, there's no question that he is the leader of this team," Sam excitedly replies, always happy to be asked his opinion. "They feed off his energy and focus," he explains. "The only real question is, does he have another miracle comeback in him today." Sam finishes, somewhat proud of what he considers to be his spot-on and insightful analysis.

The twenty-two players on the field are separated into opposing teams of eleven on either side of the ball, on the rectangle-shaped football field. The combatants are huddled into separate groups across from each other just to one side of the boldly marked fifty-yard line, toward the observant hawk.

The blue-and-brown uniforms of the Bears adorn the massive athletes breaking their huddle and spreading across the field on the farthest side of the ball from the hawk, while the slick black and red of the Rattlers covers the players nearest it, as they move toward the line of play and the readied Bears defense.

The sunlight glints off the top of the black helmet of the Rattlers quarterback as he steps behind the crouched men of his offensive line, while the noise of the crowd settles to an anxious murmur in anticipation of the coming play. The red-outlined, white number eight on his back wears the tarnish of the green-and-brown stains from the day's field of battle.

Through the black bars of his facemask, the quarterback surveys the alignment of the defense of the Bears with a steady calm.

The mouth of the Bears' defensive middle linebacker works in slow motion as his head turns from side to side, spitting out last-second adjustments to his team.

The quarterback's view moves from the linebacker and down across the backs of the six men crouched in front of him to the receiver in the slot position to his right, several steps beyond the end of the line.

Looking back at the quarterback are the clear eyes of the light-skinned African-American receiver, Brian Taylor.

The look was all it took for the embattled veterans of the game; the quarterback and Brian have seen the same flaw in the alignment of the Bears' defense and know exactly how to attack it.

"The Rattlers trail the Bears thirty-five to thirty-one, with twenty-seven seconds left in the game," Chris informs the millions who sit glued to their television screens at home, as he looks out over the field. "On their own forty-three-yard line, they have a long way to go. But if they can pull out a touchdown here, they will lock up that number-one seed and home field advantage throughout the playoffs."

The quarterback's eyes swing from Brian back to the Bears linebacker.

There is a momentary stillness as the two lock eyes, brothers by bond of battle and mutual respect of talent, enemies this moment by opposing wills bent toward opposite goals.

And then the moment is gone, shattered by the quarterback's commanding voice.

"Blue twenty-two!"

He pulls his left hand in, licking the bottom side of his fingers, and then follows with the right as the butt of the center, the red-haired and bearded Big Tom Saltzgiver, comes into his view just below the bottom of the black bars of the quarterback's mask.

He kneels in behind Big Salt, reaching his readied hands under his crotch in preparation for the snap of the ball.

"Blue twenty-two," he repeats as his foot shifts, cleats digging into the ground, preparing to fire off.

Big Salt's mangled, tape-wrapped, muddy fingers grip the oblong ball beneath the face of his large, marred helmet.

"Set, hut!" the quarterback's voice rings across the field.

The ball crashes into the quarterback's open hands and the coiled muscles of twenty-two men fire as they explode from their positions like thoroughbreds before an open starting gate.

The mammoths of the offensive and defensive lines crash against each other with the force of battering rams; no concern for the limits of bodies, only the will to win their individual battles matters.

Ripped-up chunks of earth fly from the cleats of the Rattlers' receivers as they launch from their stances and into their routes. The Bears' defensive back counterparts spring backward from their crouched positions, mirroring the moves of each offensive player.

The quarterback's feet bound across the grass with the grace of a dancer as he sprints back from the line, spinning the ball to the perfect grip in his hands at the apex of his cocked arms.

The offensive line bends into a horseshoe shape around the quarterback as the organized chaos of the orchestra of the game plays out around him; the score of the scene rising though the throats of the erupting fans standing in front of their seats in the packed stadium.

Brian's legs are churning at full tilt pace, fifteen yards down the right side of the field, when he deftly performs a stutter-step and cuts across in front of the defensive back covering him to shift his route toward the middle of the field. The defensive back's footwork encounters a momentary stumble as he tries to mirror Brian's moves, and he loses a step in his pursuit of the speedy receiver.

In the protected pocket created by the offensive line, the quarterback, surveying the left side of the field, jerks the football toward the Rattlers receiver running there.

The defensive safety deep in the middle of the defensive field—the last line of defense for the opposing Bears—breaks toward the expected throw. But the quarterback pulls the ball back down.

He turns his head to the area of the field that the safety has just vacated. Feeling, but never seeing, the outstretched arm of a defensive lineman reaching past his offensive blocker and grasping for his back, the quarterback slides forward and to his right, setting his feet to throw the ball.

The Bears' defensive middle linebacker, who had started to the quarterback's left, reverses his path and breaks toward the hole between the two offensive linemen in front of him, both already engaged with formidable foes. He has a clear path to the quarterback and is rapidly taking advantage of it.

The quarterback spots Brian exactly where he knew he'd be: flying down the middle of the field, still a step ahead of the Bears' defensive back trying to catch up to him.

Everything slows as his eyes zero in on Brian's hands and he turns his cannon of a right arm loose, launching a bomb just before the defensive middle linebacker buries his helmet into the quarterback's chest and knocks him backward, driving him into the turf.

The sound of the crowd goes silent in Brian's ears. He hears only the panting of his own breath and the pounding of his flying feet as he watches the spiraling pigskin arching down from the sky toward him.

His gloved, outstretched fingers make contact with and then grasp the spinning ball just before the defensive back smashes into him and they both crash to the ground at the Bears' eight-yard line; the crescendo of the crowd once again ringing for Brian to hear.

Sam springs from his seat in the booth, revealing his somewhat short stature.

"He caught it! He caught it!" he exclaims. "Oh my God, what a pass!"

"They don't have any time-outs left," Chris observes, excitement in his voice as well as he stands next to his partner. "They'll have to hurry to the line to spike the ball and stop the clock," he notes for the television fans also jumping to their feet in their homes and bars.

The quarterback runs down the middle of the field like a general in battle. Seemingly immune to the vicious blow that had been delivered to him by the linebacker, he directs his troops to hurry to the ball and into formation as he jerks his right arm up and down, signaling that he is going to spike the ball.

The game clock on the scoreboard steadily ticks down.

Twelve seconds.

Eleven seconds.

Ten seconds.

The zebra-striped official hurriedly sets the ball as both teams line up.

Seven seconds.

Big Salt grips the ball.

Six.

"Hut!" the quarterback barks.

Big Salt smashes the ball into his hands and the quarterback fires it into the ground.

The clock stops with four seconds left.

"Four seconds. Oh man, what a finish!" Sam blurts, beside himself over the arousing events of the game.

"We had this one marked on the calendar at the beginning of the season and it has certainly not disappointed," Chris studiously adds.

The Rattlers begin to gather in their huddle with an excited anxiousness for the coming final play of the game.

The quarterback, his back to them, looks to the sidelines where a headset-adorned, middle-aged black man with a powerful presence, Coach Osborne, covers his mouth with a laminated play sheet as he calls in the final play.

The quarterback turns to face his gathered troops. His brown and green, hazel eyes, filled with confident fire, reveal him to be the raucous stadium's hero, Joe Gilmore.

Joe notices the team's nerves as he kneels into the circle of his huddled men. He takes a deep, affected breath.

"Whew, I'm so nervous I could shit," he quips.

Brian blurts out a laugh.

Joe's best friend since he came into the Rattlers fold as a rookie eight years ago, Brian is used to Joe's timely humor and appreciates his leadership on the field—even if he often has to play the role of big brother to Joe off of it.

Joe gives the guy standing next to him, the rookie running back Larry Patterson, a shot in the arm as the team chuckles, relaxing into the moment.

"Holy crap this is fun," Joe declares with a twinkle in his eye.

"You got that right, baby," the grinning Big Salt responds.

This is why they love this guy. This is why they would follow their leader through hell and back. He still loves the spirit of the game above all else and still plays it with the carefree passion of a kid trying to get in just one more play before his momma calls him home for dinner.

Joe's eyes turn serious and determined, the competitive fire inside him ever-burning, but the smile never fades.

"This is *our* house," he reminds his teammates.

The boys all nod in agreement.

"Now let's go win this damn game," Joe adds. "Spread right, twenty-two black panther. On two, on two. Ready...break."

The team gives the customary one clap and shout of "Break" in unison as they turn toward the ball and the opposing Bears.

Both teams face off over the ball at the Bears' eight-yard line.

Big Salt points and shouts out blocking assignments to his linemates.

The defensive middle linebacker sways back and forth as he barks out directions to his team once again.

Joe licks his hands, his engrained pre-snap routine, as he steps toward the line, surveying the defensive alignment of the Bears.

Up in the stadium seats to Joe's left stands the faithful, gracefully aging, and still beautiful Sarah Gilmore. Her stomach is in the usual knots from holding her breath while she watches her baby play the combative game of modern titans.

Cindy is next to her, grasping her hand, with Trace wrapping hers around Cindy's opposite arm.

The three are surrounded by other Rattlers family members, all anxiously looking on as well.

Joe looks to the middle linebacker.

"Hey Evans," he calls with a smirk, "What do they have you in for? Don't they know the game is on the line?"

Evans grins back at him, up to the challenge.

"I'm comin' for ya, bitch," he shouts back.

Joe eases in under Big Salt as his grin fades.

"Red one-three trap! Red one-three trap!" he calls into the momentary quiet of the stadium.

"Set..."

Joe stops as he catches one of the Bears' safeties easing down toward the line.

He steps back from under Big Salt into shotgun position while turning from side to side, giving hand signals to the receivers and then to Larry behind him as he changes the play, adjusting to the opponent's movements.

"Buffalo nineteen! Buffalo nineteen!" Joe barks out the new call.

"Hut! Hut!"

Big Salt jerks the ball back into Joe's open hands as the two teams spring into battle once more.

Joe turns and fakes a hand off to Larry, who crashes into the line, sealing the hole the safety had lined up for his blitzing attack—exactly the reason Joe had adjusted the play.

Joe's feet dance in the pocket behind his offensive line once again as his eyes scan the field for an open receiver.

One of the Bears' defensive linemen, to Joe's back, breaks free and zeros in on him. He races forward, launching himself into the air like a massive torpedo aimed at the Rattlers' quarterback.

Just as he dives, Joe catches sight of him out of the corner of his eye and spins out of his grasp as the lineman flies over.

The mammoths in front of Joe part slightly, revealing a hole in the line of massive men locked in contest.

Joe pulls the ball down from its apex in his hands and tucks it tightly under his arm. He's going to run for it.

The volume of the crowd rises as Joe heads for the narrow hole in the offensive line, toward the victory-laden end zone.

Big Salt waylays a defensive lineman as Joe passes by him, a clear path to triumph now within his reach.

The defensive middle linebacker sees Joe breaking for the end zone and rushes toward him from the left side of the field, his comrade closing just as fast from the right.

The three meet at the two-yard line with a horrendous collision that seems to reverberate throughout the stadium.

The crowd's initial cheer immediately becomes a collective inhale of concern.

The three combatants bounce off each other like three cars rebounding from a sandwiching crash in the middle of an intersection.

Joe, totally limp, falls face-first into the end zone as the other two warriors sling out to his sides.

The stadium goes silent as Joe's body crumples to the ground.

The ever-observant hawk steps from its perch on the bank of lights and swoops down to the top of one of the goalposts below, for a closer view. It cocks its head as its eyes zero in on Joe, face down in the end zone at the opposite end of the field.

Sarah's knuckles go white as she squeezes Cindy's hand, watching the one remaining man in her life lying in a heap on the field.

Cindy doesn't even feel the squeeze or the grip Trace has on her other arm; she, like Sarah, has suddenly forgotten how to breathe.

On the field, Big Salt drops to his knees next to Joe as Brian runs toward them. The team's medical trainers race for the field as another teammate anxiously waves them over.

Overcome by the moment, Big Salt grabs Joe by the shoulders and starts to turn him over.

Unexpectedly, Joe pushes off with his hands and assists in flipping himself over onto his back. He looks up at Big Salt, grinning.

"Did I make it?" he asks casually, covering the pain in his ribs.

"You son of a bitch," Big Salt replies, shaking his head.

Joe laughs as Brian arrives at the twosome, relieved to see his buddy conscious and moving.

Big Salt reaches down and grabs Joe, hoisting him up off the ground in a giant bear hug as the trainers make it to the group, relieved as well at the sight of the stadium and team's risen hero.

The hawk leaps from the goalpost and takes back to the sky as Sarah, Cindy, and Trace find the use of their lungs once again.

The fans in the stands erupt with vigor, their previously delayed celebration now free from the fear that had trapped it in their chests moments ago.

The Rattlers have won, and their idol is intact to fight another day.

Joe's laughter becomes an unbridled yell of exhilaration as his teammates slam into him, all celebrating a hard-fought victory in the game they love. They may be paid a king's ransom for their services, but in their hearts they're still the little boys who are in love with the thrill of the game.

In the commentator's suite, Sam and Chris wrap up the day's events.

"Wow, what a game," Sam begins, "I tell ya, Joe Gilmore definitely has my vote for the most valuable player trophy, hands down."

"I'd say he'd certainly have to be considered to be in the lead for it, when you combine what he has done this entire season with this amazing comeback today," Chris acknowledges. "There's no doubt that he has brought an incredible level of precision and fight to his game this year."

The game over, Joe and his teammates make their way toward their locker room among the sounds of a jubilant crowd.

A pretty female sports reporter, Jessica Drolet, runs up alongside Joe. "Joe, Joe," Jessica calls, trying to get him to slow down.

Joe stops at the edge of the field, in front of the tunnel leading under the stadium. He knows what's coming next and what his team obligations are, but he still hates this part of his job.

The fans—the sane ones at least—he's glad to sign autographs for, toss them a souvenir or something. They participate in the game; they're invested, at least emotionally. But the reporters Joe felt he could do without. People who made their wages by commenting on the lives that others were living, or digging to get you to react so they could create their contrived controversies, were useless as far as he was concerned.

Jessica quickly adjusts her hair for the camera as she waits for her cameraman to line up his shot. Joe readies himself to do his duty.

The cameraman gives Jessica a thumbs-up, indicating he's now rolling.

"Great game today, Joe" the reporter begins, looking up at him.

"Thanks," Joe replies. "Yeah, the team played great today."

"You guys were down by eleven points with less than three minutes left in the game. You know you need two scores, and you know the kind of season that the Bears have had. Not to mention the rivalry—their defense always plays you so tough," Jessica says, setting up her question. "Tell me, was there ever any doubt that you would be able to pull off this amazing comeback?"

"Well listen, it was a total team effort," Joe responds, honestly. "I'm really proud of the way these guys fought out there today. And you have to give the Bears a lot of credit as well. We have a lot of respect for their organization..."

Joe pauses as the Bears middle linebacker, Evans, walks by. He and Joe grab each other's hands, pat shoulder pads, acknowledging each other out of their mutual respect for the other warrior's commitment to the game. Each tells the other to "Stay healthy," as they part and Joe brings his attention back to the reporter.

"Sorry about that," he apologies. "Yeah, as I was saying, we have a lot of respect for them. They play the game the right way. And we wouldn't be surprised to see them again in the conference championship before the big dance, if we're fortunate enough to make it that far."

Behind Joe fans hang over the railing, chanting "MVP, MVP!" Many of them have painted faces and a few hold up signs: JOELICIOUS, THE COMEBACK KID, MARRY ME JOE!, JOE IS GOD.

"Well I think we would all welcome the excitement of that rematch," Jessica acknowledges. "Joe, on a more serious note," she adds, filling her face with concern as she shifts gears, "We know you haven't spoken very openly about this, but as the fans behind us remind everyone, you are in the running for the MVP trophy. Also, your team is being picked by everyone to win it all this year; but we also know this has to be a painful time for you, with the murder of your father last year and now the trial of his suspected murderer beginning this week. How are you coping with all of this?"

Joe just stares at her, refusing to respond.

"Joe?" she tries again, innocently holding the microphone up to him.

It's everything Joe can do to not reach out and slap her. But his team public relations training kicks in.

"As you said, I haven't spoken very openly about it," he replies flatly and then turns and jogs off, escaping toward the stadium tunnel.

Jessica turns back to her camera.

"Obviously, despite the victory, the star quarterback is still in understandable turmoil," she observes. "Chris, back up to you."

The fans go crazy as Joe nears them, leaving the digging of the reporter behind.

He doesn't stop for autographs this time, but he does manage to pull off a sweaty armband and toss it into the stands toward a young boy before he disappears into the tunnel.

Out of sight of the fans and media for the moment, Joe jogs through the tunnel toward the locker room and his team.

He passes various stadium personnel along the way, each giving him a high five, a "Good game, QB!," or "Great win."

As he passes by an adjacent hallway, there is a man leaning against the wall.

The man is about Joe's height, a little more round around the waist and in the face, but he has that same outdoorsy, "real man" quality about him—only he carries his with a gentle, jovial air.

He wears a big smile, along with a Rattlers ball cap and a big foam hand stenciled with a white #1.

"Hello, Noble One," the man calls in a friendly voice, as Joe passes by.

Joe doesn't even glance at him. "Hey," he responds halfheartedly, slightly increasing his pace toward the privacy of the lockers.

The man cocks his head to one side, a playful grin on his face as he watches Joe disappear down the hall.

When Joe is gone, the man turns in the opposite direction and begins walking toward the field. He slowly increases his pace to a jog as he rounds a bend and the passageway to the field comes into sight.

"And here he comes, ladies and gentlemen," the man begins; beaming, as he plays announcer to his own role as the star quarterback of the Rattlers. "Your quarterback, Joe...Gilmoooooooore!" he finishes as he sprints out of the tunnel, both arms in the air.

Chapter 5

Joe hurries into the massive Rattlers locker room, feeling a little relief as the large black doors close behind him, locking at least some of his pressures outside. There is something about the sound of that *click* behind him that just means safety. The rest of the world is barred from entry—only the family called the Rattlers can gather on this side of the closed doors.

The team's home locker room is large and luxurious, to say the least. Spacious, doorless mahogany lockers with nametags and player jersey numbers line the perimeter. Each also has an electrical outlet and a small, silver-plated lockbox built into one of the shelves. In front of some of the lockers are black and red, leather-covered chairs. A number of flat screen TVs hang in different places around the room.

The floor is carpeted in black, with the large red emblem of the Rattlers, a coiled rattlesnake with mouth open and fangs exposed, filling the center of the room.

The emblem is covered with players just now, as they gather for Coach Osborne's post-game speech. They squat or kneel down amid celebratory yells, high fives, and special handshakes.

Joe slips down beside a couple of his boys. They all bump fists, grin.

"Alright, alright, settle down," Coach's strong voice overrides the quiet murmurs of the players. Coach waits for total silence and complete attention, like a kindergarten teacher before a rambunctious class. It doesn't take but a beat longer for this class to put their entire collected focus toward the powerful man.

"Congratulations on a hard-fought victory today, gentlemen." The coach acknowledges them, the corners of his mouth ever so slightly upturned.

The group responds with a cheer.

"We set a number of goals when we began the journey of this season," Coach continues as the boys settle back down again. "The first was to win the division, which we accomplished last week."

More cheers from the team.

"The second was home field advantage throughout the playoffs, which we accomplished today," Coach builds.

Even bigger cheers.

"Now that we have secured our position in the dance, we will turn our focus to accomplishing our next goal: making it into the final dance pairing, the Championship Bowl!!" Coach finishes, sharing one of his rare but always perfectly timed and perfectly motivating moments of excited passion.

The room explodes.

Coach waits for the excitement to die down somewhat, replacing the smile on his face with the more solid look that usually reigns there.

"Alright, alright," he says, gaining their attention once more. "Let's maintain the same level of focus, the same level of preparation, and the same level of attack as we prepare for the Coyotes next week."

"Everybody bring it in," he adds, raising his right arm, "Let's have our QB send us off."

The boys all cheer as Joe makes his way to the center of the group. He raises his arm to meet Coach's, and the group all does the same.

"We fought like a team out there today," Joe begins, "Like a family. I'm proud of ya. I'm proud to be part of this family. Now let's finish this journey together. 'Focus,' on three. One, two, three..."

"Focus!" the team shouts in unison, before breaking off toward their individual lockers, all yelling and celebrating once again.

Coach leans into Joe.

"My office. Now," he quietly commands, and then turns and heads toward it.

Joe takes a subtle breath and follows him.

The players, still in celebratory mode, pat Joe on the shoulders, throw high fives and congratulatory acknowledgments his way as he moves through them.

Coach Osborne enters his office with the stride of a tiger on the prowl. Joe is in tow, and getting the feeling that he may be the meat on this hunt.

"Close the door and have a seat," Coach Osborne commands as he rounds his large desk, heading for the high-backed chair behind it.

In back of him, the shelves on the wall are strewn with trophies, pictures of earlier Rattlers teams celebrating championship wins, special game balls—the storied success of the Rattlers organization.

Already seated in the room, to the left of Coach and also facing Joe, is the bespectacled team doctor, Dr. Paul Adams.

"Doc," Joe nods, taking his seat in front of Coach's desk while trying to hide his resentment toward the doctor.

The best Joe can figure, Dr. Adams must have told Coach what happened in the hotel, after being roused and rushed to the scene by Brian in the middle of the night.

"Joe," Dr. Adams replies, his own resentment evident from being pressed into that position due to Joe's reckless actions.

Coach has settled into his chair. He takes his time looking Joe directly in the eye, then assumes a calm but very stern and deliberate tone.

"Son, I don't care if you *are* the face of the franchise." He indicates the wall behind him, "There have been plenty before you and there will plenty more to come."

He pauses for a moment, making sure the point is getting home.

"I will not allow you to destroy the reputation of this organization, myself, or your teammates," he continues. "We clear where we're startin' from here?"

"Yeah," Joe answers amid a tense breath.

"Good," Coach responds without softening his demeanor. "Now you damn well better be straight with me. Whose drugs were they?" he asks, not even referencing the hotel room—the time for beating around the bush having long since passed. Everyone in the room already knew why they were in there. There was no use pretending it might be for any other reason, and Coach wasn't one who had much patience for small talk anyway.

"Not mine," Joe answers, his poker face covering his quickening pulse. "I didn't even know they were there until it happened," he lies, his eyes subconsciously flicking in the direction of Dr. Adams.

Joe still doesn't know how much the doctor has said to Coach, or how much the quiet man in the corner even knows himself. The whole evening after Jennifer's collapse was nothing but a blur—not that much before it was incredibly clear in his memory, either.

While Paul suspects that it's highly unlikely Joe was unaware of the drugs, he has no hard evidence to the contrary. And, being a man of science, he is always more inclined to only report what is physically provable.

When he arrived at the hotel room, the only evidence of drugs that remained—besides the amount that had obviously sent Jennifer's body into shock—was a square, white piece of paper on the nightstand above her, with only traces of cocaine visible on it.

His attention had been so focused on saving the girl that he hadn't even thought to do any kind of examination of Joe or Trace at the time.

"You better be damn certain," Coach insists to Joe, interrupting the doctor's rapid retracing of his memory of the evening in question.

"I am," Joe responds.

"Did you use?" Coach fires the next question on his list, right on the heels of the conclusion of the first.

"No," Joe lies again.

Joe had already checked with an outside source: he knew that he was well past the forty-eight to seventy-two hours that the drug could have been tested for—and found present—in his system. This wasn't a habitual thing for him, more an occasional when-the-pressures-of-the-world-become-totally-unbearable kind of thing.

Coach also knew that a test would show nothing at this point, having been informed of such by Dr. Adams. And if he was completely honest with himself, there was a part of him that did experience a moment of relief once he knew that his star quarterback was, at least by league rules, in the clear.

But no matter the relief at not having to replace the most valuable player on his team, Coach was not in the mood to accept or turn a blind eye to any of this type of behavior.

"That still doesn't excuse you putting yourself in that kind of position in the first place," Coach admonishes, still pissed. "What about your own..." he trails off, stopping himself from going into areas regarding Joe's personal relationships.

He takes a breath, trying to calm himself, trying to take into account the life factors that Joe is dealing with at the moment, while at the same time still maintaining his own integrity and the organization's.

He'd become a friend to the Gilmore family from the moment he drafted Joe. He had enormous respect for the man that James was and the strong unit their family had been. It hadn't taken long for him to develop a close relationship with Joe during the hours they had spent together dissecting opposing defenses. And he saw a lot of James' responsible and conscious manner in Joe, not to mention Sarah's heart and fight.

Since James' death, he had watched those qualities shrink in his quarterback somewhat as he became hard. While he had shown up to camp that year with even more focus than usual, Joe had continued to keep everyone at arm's length during *any* attempted personal conversation.

This was an additional source of frustration for Coach. Although he had an exterior as tough as a grizzly bear's, on the inside the fact was he was a lot more teddy than grizzly, even if few players ever got to see it.

With these factors in mind Coach tries to soften his tone, without losing his position of authority with his player.

"Do I need to get you help, Joe? You need to talk to someone, son? Help you get through this..." he asks.

Relieved that this hadn't turned out worse, but still unwilling—or maybe even unable—to lower his guard, a terse, "No, I'm good," was all Joe could manage to reply. "Sorry I disappointed you," he adds, without much feeling, "Won't happen again."

Coach's foul mood resurfaces quickly.

"Well then keep this shit cleaned up. I don't want to hear about it on *Sportsnews*!" he barks.

"Yes, sir," Joe responds, rising. "We done?"

"Yeah." Coach gruffs, waving him away as he spins his chair from the desk.

Joe exits the room, guilt and frustration mixing with the anger and blame in his gut.

Walking back through the locker room, lost in the thoughts of trying to undo regrettable deeds, Joe is barely even aware of the guys in various stages of cleaning up around him. Most are out of their gear, some making their way toward the showers, others coming from it. Towel snapping, music, and jovial voices fill the rarely subsiding frat-boy vibe of the room as Joe arrives at his space.

Brian is at his locker, next to Joe's. Already showered and dressed, he is waiting for him—a somewhat common occurrence.

As solid a teammate and friend as anyone could ask for, there was no doubt that Brian was the team's backbone and moral compass, even if Joe was considered its leader. The two teammates were close enough that they, and others, commonly referred to the twosome as brothers.

"How'd it go?" Brian asks, concerned for his friend.

Joe just shakes his head as he begins stripping off his gear.

"How's the girl?" he questions Brian.

"In the hospital; she'll recover," Brian responds quietly, not wanting others to overhear the conversation, or Joe to pick up on the feeling of guilt he had over his limited involvement in the event.

Joe continues to undress, trying to replace thinking with routine.

"You want to grab a bite? Talk about it?" Brian offers.

"I'll get through it," Joe responds, now removing his pants.

Stripped down, he grabs a towel out of his locker. "Gotta grab a shower," is all he'll give the supportive Brian.

"Yeah, you do," Brian agrees. "'Cause you smell like a load of ass," he cracks, trying to lighten the mood.

Joe turns for the showers, not going for Brian's joke.

"Hey," Brian calls, waiting for Joe to look at him before he'll continue.

Joe stops. He turns to him.

"What?" he asks with a blank face.

"You do know we won, right?" Brian asks with a grin, refusing to give in to Joe's sour mood.

The ridge Joe has put up shows a crack as he softens slightly.

"I'm just sayin'," Brian adds, his arms and shoulders turning up to match the corners of his mouth.

"Good game today, B.," Joe acknowledges him, still not fully giving in to the smile Brian is offering.

"I know that shit, baby," Brian fires back, his smile growing. "That's how I do, when I have to carry yo' ass."

A grin finally creeps onto Joe's face as he shakes his head, Brian's persistence breaking through the wall; he's the one person who always seems to be able to pull off the feat, which is usually accomplished with the guerrilla tactics of jokes or perfectly timed, lighthearted insults.

Joe steps back toward Brian, reaching for his extended hand.

They do their intricate handshake, which ends with them flipping each other off in jest.

Joe, his mood a little lighter, turns for the showers once again.

"Hit me if ya' need me kid," Brian calls after him.

Joe answers with a wave of his hand as he walks off, Brian watching him go.

Joe out of sight, Brian takes a deep breath and exhales. Then he plops on his cap and exits the room.

All cleaned up now, Joe is at his locker buttoning up his tailored dress shirt as the running back, Larry, walks up.

"How's that knee?" Joe asks him.

"Good to go," Larry answers, "Got my treatment."

"Good," Joe responds as he grabs his duffel bag out of the locker and throws it over his shoulder.

The two of them head for the door as Larry gets to what he wants to discuss.

"Hey, I was looking at getting a jump start on protection against the Coyotes," he tells Joe.

"Yeah, they have a lot of blitz packages," Joe acknowledges, proud of the rookie for being proactive in his preparation for next week's game. "You obviously have to key on their linebackers primarily," he explains, "But the strong—and even the weak—safeties like to creep down late."

The two exit the room in discussion.

In the hallway outside the private locker room, only the remnants of the player's privileged entourages still remain. Sarah, Cindy, and Trace wait among the stragglers.

"We can get into it more Tuesday in the film room, if you want to come in early" Joe finishes.

"Sounds good to me," Larry responds as he and Joe reach the three ladies.

Trace steps toward them, glancing at Joe before embracing Larry. The two share a quick kiss.

"Great game, baby," Trace says to Larry.

"Thanks," he replies with a smile.

"Congratulations Joe," Sarah says, giving him a hug. "Just glad you're okay."

"Thanks, Mom," Joe replies, hugging her back.

He turns to Cindy and gives her a kiss.

"How are you feeling?" she asks, her hand on his chest.

"Yeah, you really had us worried," Trace adds.

"No worse for the wear," Joe assures them, putting his arm around Cindy. "Just part of the job," he grins.

"Hell, he was faking the whole time—just loves the attention," Larry jokes.

Everyone laughs.

"Alright. Well, I'll see you in the film room," Joe says to Larry, ready to head out.

"Oh, wait," Trace interjects. "You guys are coming to the party, right?"

She looks at Cindy.

"I don't know," Cindy answers, turning to Joe.

"Oh come on, you guys have to come," Trace begs.

"Ain't a party without you, QB," Larry adds.

"I don't know, guys. We'll see," Joe says, putting them off. "The only thing I know right now is I want some of my momma's home cookin' and a nap."

"Well, that I can do," Sarah answers with a smile, always happy to have Joe and Cindy in her empty house.

"Okay, well, I'll call you," Cindy says to Trace, not disappointed at the idea of skipping the party.

"Okay," Trace gives in, trying to hide her disappointment as Joe, Cindy, and Sarah turn to go.

Larry throws his arm around Trace and turns her in the opposite direction. She glances back over her shoulder as the groups go their separate ways.

Chapter 6

Joe and Cindy step out of the elevator and into his expansive penthouse apartment, the lights automatically coming on in the darkened space.

The modern apartment is very open, with high ceilings throughout, fine paintings, and décor; all arranged with a sense of strength and manly flair.

Cindy's heels click across the polished hardwood floors as she heads for the bathroom.

"That was fun," she calls to Joe as she turns down the hall, referring to the happy and relaxing dinner they had just shared with Sarah.

"Momma makes a mean chocolate pie," Joe calls back, heading for the kitchen.

He tosses his car keys on the marble countertop of the island and reaches for the brushed-chrome door of the in-wall refrigerator. He pulls it open and grabs a beer, still looking for a little assistance in easing his troubled mind.

He closes the fridge and pops the top off the bottle with an opener from the drawer on the island. He sets the top and opener on the counter and walks toward the sliding glass doors in the living room.

Joe sits on the balcony, staring out at the twinkling lights of the city and drinking his beer while trying to turn off the many thoughts running through his mind.

It's a problem that seems to have gotten worse and worse since the passing of his father. And it didn't help matters that he kept making what he considered to be really stupid decisions, especially in regards to Trace.

His phone buzzes on the inside pocket of his tailored Hugo Boss overcoat, interrupting the berating he was silently giving himself.

He pulls it out. There is a text from Trace.

I want to see you, it reads.

His jaw muscles clench as he deletes the text, turns off the phone, and slips it back in his pocket.

The glass door slides open. Cindy pokes her head out into the night air.

"Oh wow. It's always so much colder up here," she observes with a shiver. "Aren't you cold?'

"Little bit," he admits.

"Well come inside and make a fire," she requests with a smile as she hugs herself, rubbing her sweater-covered arms. "I'm freezing."

Joe gives a light chuckle, her cuteness getting to him.

"Alright, I'll be in in a second. Just let me finish my beer," he promises.

"Okay," Cindy replies, happy to see him smiling again. "Just don't freeze to death."

"I'll try," Joe jokes as she slides the door closed.

Cindy sits on the custom leather couch under a fuzzy blanket, talking on her phone.

She has muted the flat screen television hanging above the fireplace, which flashes the depraved images of the latest reality competition show.

"Yeah. I know, I know," she says to the person on the other end of the phone.

Joe sets his empty bottle on the brushed-chrome-and-glass coffee table, carrying wood from the balcony with his other arm.

He kneels in front of the fireplace, looking back at Cindy.

"It's Trace," she mouths.

Joe nods and starts to prepare the fire, wishing Trace would just leave them alone.

"Well, let me talk to him. I think he's just pretty wiped out," Cindy offers into the phone.

Joe takes a frustrated breath as he arranges the wood across the metal grate.

"I know, yeah," Cindy answers Trace's persistence. "Yeah, I want to, let me see," she lies.

Joe turns around to her as Cindy presses the mute button on her phone.

"What do you think? Should we go?" she asks him.

"I'm really not in the mood," Joe tells her.

"I know. Me either," Cindy admits. "It's just that she's my best friend and I feel bad leaving her there by herself," she adds.

"She's not alone, she's just needy," Joe says, disgusted. "She's got her boyfriend and a hundred other people there for Christ's sake!"

"I'm sorry," Cindy apologizes, "I didn't mean to get you upset."

Joe rises and comes over, sitting down next to her on the couch.

"Hey, no, I'm sorry," he begins, taking her hand. "I just don't feel like being around other people tonight, okay?"

"Okay," Cindy replies.

"Tell you what—why don't we just pick a movie and I'll open a bottle of wine? You can stay the night again tonight, if you want," Joe offers. "You can even pick the movie."

"What if it's a chick flick?" Cindy asks, brightening.

"Good luck finding one," Joe grins.

"Okay," Cindy agrees, accepting the challenge as she rises and heads for the DVD-filled armoire in the bedroom. "You better not have gotten rid of *The Notebook*," she warns him, only half kidding.

"Uugh," Joe breathes, flopping back onto the couch. "Just no stupid vampire movies," he calls after her as she makes her way down the hall once again.

"Okay," Cindy replies over her shoulder with a laugh as she unmutes her phone and goes back to Trace.

"I don't think we're going to make it…" Joe hears her tell Trace as her voice trails off, disappearing into the bedroom.

Joe brings his hands to his forehead and across his hair as he exhales a frustrated breath and tries to rub his mind to silence.

He rises up and leans back into the couch, looking in the muffled direction of Cindy's voice. The pensive look on his face reveals the inner turmoil of guilt and pain that he is trying so desperately to avoid. After another breath, he forces himself up and heads for the kitchen and the promised wine.

Chapter 7

Joe sits in a tall director's chair on a studio sound stage as the crew stands around, waiting to wrap up. Brian, also a part of the shoot, relaxes in the chair next to him.

The two wear their black Rattlers uniform pants with the red stripe down the side, along with the latest long-sleeve, black, Under Armour ColdGear compression tops over their chiseled torsos.

Brian turns to Joe.

"Hey, have you tried those Phillips' Stool Softeners?" he asks, breaking up the parade of jumbled thoughts in Joe's head.

"What?" Joe replies, totally confused by the odd, out-of-the-blue question.

"Well, by that last look you were giving to the camera, I thought you must be constipated," Brian says, feigning genuine concern until his furrowed brows begin to wiggle and he busts out with laughter.

Joe laughs too. Good one.

"Okay, okay," he acknowledges, nodding. "You have your fun, old man," he slings back. "You know, I thought you were going to tear a bicep holding up that kid," he jabs, referring to one of the young boys that had been part of the "Keep Kids in School" shoot.

"Old man?!" Brian cries, "Hell, I'm only two years older than you, kid!"

The photographer, Tristan Chad, walks up, interrupting the jokesters' banter.

"Shots look great, fellas," he tells them, "I think we're done here."

"Sweet," Joe replies, rising out of his chair and reaching for Tristan's hand.

"Thanks for your work today," the photographer offers as they shake. "The ad is going to be amazing."

"Hey, it was my pleasure," Joe assures him with a smile. Getting a chance to influence kids in a positive way was one of the few perks of celebrity he actually enjoyed.

"Yeah, mine too," Brian adds, shaking Tristan's hand as well. "Always enjoy working with the young ones."

"I think they quite enjoyed it as well," Tristan replies with a smile, remembering how wide-eyed the five young boys were when they had first come in to meet Joe and Brian.

He turns to the crew.

"Alright everyone, that's a wrap for Mr. Gilmore and Mr. Taylor," he announces to the group.

The crew applauds as Joe and Brian nod and then clap back; having been a part of teams since their youth, they appreciate all of the combined efforts of this one as well.

The moment of acknowledgement over, the crew goes to work breaking down the set as Joe and Brian head for their trailers outside in the lot to change back into their street clothes.

The sun is starting to hang low in the late autumn sky as Joe exits his trailer, his duffel bag looped over his shoulders.

Brian patiently waits sitting on the steps at the foot of his trailer door, his own bag lying on the ground by his feet.

The group of ten-year-old boys from the photo shoot go running by Brian and Joe, a football in hand as they head for the grassy field next to the stage.

"Great shoot, guys," Brian calls after them.

One of the boys gives a quick little wave in response as the crew speeds for the field, on a mission to get in a game before dark.

Joe and Brian look after the group, smiling at their carefree exuberance at the prospect of play.

As the boys reach the field, Brian turns to his bag and picks it up, standing from his seated position on the steps.

"So you're staying in tonight, right?" he asks, turning back toward Joe.

But Joe isn't there; he's already taken off after the boys.

Still a kid at heart, he wouldn't mind joining them in a little football before the light fades from the sky.

Brian smiles as he watches Joe catch up to the boys.

"Whose team am I on?" he hears Joe ask.

"You're gonna play?!" one of the boys excitedly shrieks, not believing their luck. "Awesooooome!" he yells, not waiting for Joe's answer.

All the boys hoot and holler their own version of excitement; their football hero is one of them.

"I guess there's not too much chance of injury for him," Brian jokes to himself with a chuckle.

The worry in his "big brother" shoulders relaxes and the smile still plays on his lips as he turns and heads for his car, leaving Joe and the boys to their game.

Joe, his two-hundred-dollar jeans now fashioned with grass and dirt stains, carries the ball as the night air turns cool and dusk falls. One of the boys hangs from his leg as Joe dramatically drags him forward.

"I can't be stopped, I can't be stopped," Joe jokes.

"Help me!" the boy yells to his teammates.

One of the boys springs onto Joe's other leg, and a third teammate wraps himself around Joe's waist.

Joe continues on, grinning from ear to ear.

"I can't be stopped, I can't be stopped," he insists, with a chuckle.

Their team having little luck on their own, the boy around Joe's waist yells to Joe's two teammates now.

"Help us!" he pleads.

The two boys look at each other, one shrugs as if to say "What the heck," and then they break for Joe as well.

"Dogpiiiiiile!" the bigger one yells as they both jump onto Joe's back.

Joe struggles forward for another step or two.

While it's quite likely he possesses the strength to carry on, he instead feigns terrific strain and drops to his knees, then tries to crawl forward with the ball cradled in his arm—just like James used to do with him when he was the boys' age.

"I can't be stoooooopped!" he yells out, in between emphatic grunts of effort.

The first tackler turns loose of his leg.

"Aaaaaaaaahhh!" he yells as he jumps up and dives onto Joe's back with the others.

Finally, the mighty Joe flops to the ground.

"Well I guess I *can* be stopped then," Joe mouths into the ground, seemingly completely defeated by the horde of smaller, happy foes.

All the boys roll off his prone body, laughing and grinning. One of them jumps up and begins doing a celebration dance.

"Oh yeah, oh yeah," he sings as he slings his hips around and around like he's working a Hula-Hoop.

Joe rises up onto his elbows and turns to the two boys who were his teammates.

"I thought you were on my team!" he exclaims, now laughing with them.

All the boys find this beyond hilarious, as they roll about on the ground in glee.

Joe slowly makes his way to his feet as he chuckles, the jubilant boys beginning to get up as well. He tosses the ball to one of them.

"Alright fellas," he says, still grinning. "That's it for me."

"Awwww," the boy that was initially yelling "Awesoooome" complains. "You're not leaving, are you?"

"Just five more minutes," another begs.

"I would if I could, guys," Joe tells them, "But I gotta go see my mom."

Another opportunity for the boys to laugh at him, which they definitely take full advantage of.

"You're not busting my chops now, are you?" Joe asks, the smile still on his face. "You're never too old for moms, right?"

"I guess not," Mr. Awesome replies.

"That's what I thought," Joe laughs, tousling the boy's hair.

"Well, thanks for letting me play with you. Stay in school," he says, turning toward his car.

"Okay," a couple of the boys answer.

Joe looks back at them as he breaks into a jog, headed for the duffel bag he had dropped by the edge of the field.

"Who are you rooting for on Sunday night?" he calls to them.

"Rattleeeeeeerrrrrs!!!" all the boys yell in unison.

"Yeeeeaaahh!" Joe yells back, pumping his arms.

Joe reaches his bag and snatches it up without breaking stride, feeling much more alive than he has in the past several days.

It had been the perfect salve for his troubled mind. Football, just for fun. The joy of the game, his salvation once more.

Chapter 8

Joe pulls into the driveway of the old Gilmore home in his blacked out Shelby Mustang GT 500. The chrome-framed license plate reads *QB*.

The car rumbles to a stop behind his mom's more conservative, six-month-old Honda Civic.

It had taken a lot of coaxing from Joe just to get her to let him buy it for her.

"My car runs just fine," Sarah had told him, in reference to the eight-year-old Civic he had had to get his dad to talk her into letting him buy for her when he got his pro football signing bonus of millions. "It still gets me wherever I need to go perfectly," she had insisted.

Joe had finally convinced her that he needed to purchase her a new one so that he wouldn't worry about her when she was driving alone. Of course this was after he had completely failed to talk her into going with a red Mercedes S600, despite the spirited test drive that had left her laughing.

"There's only so much a person needs, Joseph," she had lectured him, "The rest is just for showing off."

So he had finally had to agree to the more *reasonable* white Civic.

The lights are on in the big, old, two-story house. It is still in pristine shape, as are most of the houses on this block, where the neighbors still take pride in the care of their homes.

The massive oak trees that line the lots are in the process of spilling the last of their leaves onto the generally well-kept lawns. There are cars parked here and there along the street.

Joe grabs his bag and heads for the house, planning on grabbing a quick shower and a bite with his mom before swinging by Cindy's apartment on the way home.

Joe opens the front door of Sarah's house and walks in.

He hears the chatter of happy voices coming up the hall from the kitchen.

"Mom?" he calls out.

The voices stop.

"In the dining room," he hears her respond.

Joe drops his bag by the door and heads down the hall; the aging—but still sturdy—pier-and-beam wood floor creaks in response to his feet as he makes his way toward the back of the house.

He passes framed family pictures on the walls that hang along with Bible verses and other Christian trinkets.

The Christmas tree he and Cindy had recently decorated with Sarah sits in the living room he passes by.

Joe steps into the dining room to find his mom sitting at the table along with Pastor Roman, the leader of her church—the one Joe used to attend, prior to his father's death. Also with Sarah and the pastor are three other widowed women from the congregation and the pastor's nephew. They have open Bibles laid in front of them on the table.

"Hi, sweetheart," Sarah smiles up at Joe.

"Hey, Mom," Joe responds, offering a smaller grin back, not exactly comfortable in this company.

"Hello, Joseph," Pastor Roman acknowledges Joe.

Pastor Roman had tried to counsel Joe after his father's murder, but "Sometimes we just have to trust in God's will," was not the answer Joe was looking for, regardless of how much the kind pastor was trying to help. And Joe's leaving the church had only furthered the disagreement between the two men—not to mention hurt Sarah, who continued to find her strength there.

"Pastor," Joe replies with a nod.

It was all he could muster up for a response to the man whose answers to his struggle he still resented.

"Sorry, Mom," Joe continues to Sarah, "I forgot about your Bible study. I'll just come back by tomorrow."

"No, no, don't leave, Joey," Sarah quickly replies. "We were just wrapping up."

"Yes, please don't leave on our account," Pastor Roman adds, not wanting to interfere with Sarah and Joe's time, which he knows is so important to the mother.

"Well…" Joe isn't really sure how to respond.

Sarah notices the dirt and grass stains on his pants and arms.

"Why don't you just clean up here? I have some of your clothes washed and folded in the bathroom closet," she offers. "We can wrap up and I'll make you a sandwich or something with that leftover brisket."

"Okay, that sounds good," Joe gives in, the leftover brisket too good an offer to pass up.

"Good seeing you all," he adds to the rest of the group, politely, before exiting the room.

"Good to see you, Joe," Pastor Roman responds along with the similar acknowledgments from the group.

The sound of the shower running in the downstairs bathroom echoes in the hallway behind Sarah as she shuts the front door, having just seen her guests out.

She notices Joe's duffel bag next to the door and picks it up, carrying it down the hallway with her. She's sure he has more sweaty clothes in there somewhere.

Always looking for a chance to still be a mom to her baby boy, she happily heads for the laundry room.

She hums a hymn as she makes her way through the house to the washer. She always enjoys having Joe in the house. No matter how much comfort and strength she finds in her church and her pastor's teachings, she still hasn't been able to get used to her home being empty of both her men.

She pops open the lid to her dated washer—Joe hadn't been able to convince her to let him upgrade the laundry machines, either.

"They do the job, so there is no need," was her concise and firm assessment.

She pulls out the knob, and the washer begins to fill with water. She sets Joe's bag on top of the dryer, unzips it, and begins to pull out dirty clothes.

She tosses a crumpled gray T-shirt into the wash along with a couple of pairs of shorts. She reaches back into the bag and moves a rolled-up, clean white T-shirt to the side, revealing a small black leather pouch. She pays it no mind, still humming her song, as she pulls out the last article of clothing, a dirty pair of jeans.

She checks the pockets. The first one is empty. She reaches into the second and her fingers find what feels like something soft, in a small plastic bag. She pulls it out and suddenly realizes that she is now holding a baggie of cocaine in her hand.

Sarah's humming abruptly stops and she just stands there, stunned, her heart beginning to race as if she had just ingested the white contents of the small plastic bag herself.

Her eyes slowly make their way back to the black pouch in Joe's bag. Terrified, she reaches in and takes it out, unable to resist the pull of her mother's intuition.

Sarah peels open the black pouch, her hands beginning to shake. There are two more baggies inside and a white piece of paper tucked into the slot along the back of it.

"My God…" is all she can utter.

Joe is out of the shower and toweling off. He pulls on a clean pair of jeans from the linen closet.

"Joe?" he hears Sarah call through the door.

"Yeah?" he responds, looking toward it.

Sarah stands in the hallway, in front of the bathroom door.

"Your sandwich is on the table," she tells him, grateful for the wooden barrier's help in hiding her troubled face.

"Thanks, Mom," she hears Joe respond.

Sarah starts to say something else but then stops herself, not sure how to get it out. She turns back toward the front door and the stairs to her room on the second floor, carrying the black pouch in her hand as she ascends the steps.

Sarah enters her room quietly, the gravity of her discovery weighing heavy across her slumped shoulders.

She forces herself over to the side of her bed and sinks down onto the cushioned surface.

On the wall above her is a picture of James Gilmore in a police officer's uniform. Below that hangs an encased American flag, folded in memoriam. On the nightstand next to her sits a radiant, earlier picture of a young, happy Gilmore family.

Sarah looks up at the picture of James, her eyes begging for advice. None coming from the silent, kind face staring back at her, her gaze drifts down to the black pouch she holds in her lap. She can no longer stand the feel of it in her hand yet finds herself unable to release it completely.

She pounds the clenched fist of her free hand into the bed beside her as frustrated tears stream down her cheeks.

Joe sits at the dining room table. Unaware of the drama unfolding upstairs, he quietly munches on the sandwich and chips that Sarah had prepared for him.

Her open Bible still lies on the table in front of him. He reaches over, flips it shut, and slides it over to the side before taking another bite of his sandwich.

Whuump.

Joe's black pouch lands on the table in front of him with a thud.

His head snaps up to find Sarah standing in the doorway, holding his duffel bag. Her tears are gone, chased away by the anger that has replaced them.

Joe looks back down at his plate, *his* heart now the one that is racing.

After a tense, silence-filled moment of Joe trying to collect the thoughts that are racing to keep pace with the pounding in his chest, he places the remains of the sandwich in his hand back onto the plate.

He spits what was in his mouth into his napkin, and drops it onto the plate as well before grabbing the black pouch and standing to leave—without uttering a word.

"Sit down," Sarah sternly commands.

Joe just stands there, looking down at the table, avoiding her stare.

"Sit down!" she repeats with force.

Finally Joe looks back at her, barely able to conceal the shame behind his eyes.

"I'm a grown man," he tells her.

"Then act like one!" Sarah shouts.

Joe looks away from her, his initial fear now shifting toward defensive frustration.

Sarah softens ever so slightly, aware of the struggles the two have faced together over the past year.

"I realize that these are trying times, Joseph," she admits. "But—"

"Mom...back off, okay?" Joe cuts her off.

"You don't get to bring drugs into my house and then tell me to back off!" Sarah's anger explodes again.

"It was only one night!" Joe fires back. "I didn't even know that was in there. Besides, what are you doing going through my stuff?!" he demands.

Sarah resists her urge to return the shout and instead tries to pull herself together, not wanting the situation to get any more out of hand than it already is. She takes a deep breath.

"Don't you dare try to turn this around on me," she admonishes her son.

They both just stand there for a moment again, each at a loss for words. They may be angry at each other, but they are both aware of their need for the other's support and love, so neither of them is sure how to proceed.

Finally Sarah speaks. "What are you doing, Joey?" she asks with sincerity. "This isn't you…"

Joe takes a pensive breath. He shakes his head, biting his tongue.

"Honey, I'm sorry your father is gone—" she tries to continue.

"Don't! Just don't…" Joe says, cutting her off again.

Sarah's tears begin to return.

"How do we fix this, Joey? We have to stay together. You can lean on me, I'm here. If you'd just open up…"

Joe shakes his head again, refusing to meet her eyes as Sarah continues.

"You can't do these sorts of things. I mean, my God, can you image what would have happened if someone had caught you with this stuff? You could end up in jail, Joey! And right in the middle of your father's trial," she pleads.

Joe can't take it anymore.

"I'm leaving," he announces as he steps toward her. "Give me my bag."

Sarah stands her ground.

"No," she tells him, shaking her head.

"Mom, just give me my bag," Joe tries again.

"No. Not until we finish talking about this," Sarah refuses, remaining strong.

"GIVE ME MY GODDAMN BAG!!" Joe screams at her, exploding.

Sarah's free hand instinctively jerks out and slaps him hard across the face.

Joe just stands there boiling over, his hands beginning to tremble as the adrenaline starts to course through his veins.

He reaches out and snatches the handle of the bag in Sarah's hand.

Sarah throws her punishing hand onto the bag next to her other hand and yanks back.

The two struggle against each other. Sarah pulls with all her might as Joe tries not to use all of his. But finally he snaps in his frustration and yanks the bag from her grasp.

With the resistance suddenly gone, Sarah loses her balance and stumbles backward, her momentum spilling her onto the floor.

Joe freezes.

Neither of them can believe what just happened.

Sarah looks up at him with tears in her eyes.

"I'm your mother, Joey...I'm...I'm your mother..." she mumbles, in shock.

Unable to face the betrayed look in her eyes, Joe looks away, fighting back the gamut of horrible emotions that collide inside him.

He's torn by the guilt that rips at him for what he has just done, accidental or not. He's embarrassed about what she has discovered, but still fighting with the anger that's been eating away inside him ever since he watched his father's casket being lowered into the ground, due to the mindless act of a coward.

Still unable to meet her gaze, Joe simply steps past Sarah and down the hall to the front door.

When his hand grips the doorknob he finally stops, staring at the floor.

"I'm sorry," he mumbles, then pulls open the heavy door.

Joe steps out of the house, shutting the door closed behind him. His feet can't carry him fast enough to his waiting car and the escape from the nightmare of events inside the house.

Reaching the driver's side, he flings open the door, tosses the bag inside, and plops into the seat. While pulling the door closed he places the key in its slot and fires up the engine. He puts his foot on the brake and then stops.

He just sits there staring out the window, hands on the steering wheel, his world coming apart inside him.

"Aaaaaahhhhhhh!!!" he screams as he begins pounding on the steering wheel. Then as abruptly as he had started, he stops again.

His knuckles turn white from gripping the steering wheel as he stares straight ahead. His eyes are a thousand miles away, and yet, inescapably, here. Always here. Always in the yard to his right and to the home in front of him.

He looks over toward the front door.

For a moment he thinks about going back inside, but he doesn't know what to say, how to make it right. The image of Sarah on the ground looking up at him is already ingrained into his soul. So, he slowly puts the car in reverse and backs out into the street.

Chapter 9

Game commentators Chris and Sam stand in their press box, mics in hand, addressing the television camera and the millions watching on electronic screens around the nation. Outside their booth rain falls in sheets through the night sky.

"Welcome to wet and cold Rattlers stadium and our final game of the season here on *Football on Sunday Night*," Chris begins. "Partner," he continues, turning to Sam, "What can we say about this game? The Coyotes come in to face the Rattlers, needing a win to secure their place in postseason play. And while some may think that the

Rattlers would basically be taking this game off, having wrapped up the number-one seed and home field advantage last week, that's not quite how Joe Gilmore saw it when you spoke to him earlier today."

"That's right, Chris," Sam begins, so excited over this final game that he had barely slept the night before. "When I spoke with Joe this morning, he was fired up. He said that this game is just as important to the Rattlers as the previous fifteen. That the team has to remain focused and playing mistake-free football to achieve their goal of making a run all the way through the playoffs and into the Championship Bowl. They want to win this final game and head into the playoffs hot. It's forty-two degrees outside, the rain is coming down, and I'm expecting a hard-hitting, hard-fought game!"

On the field the pageantry of the pregame kickoff is in full swing.

The Coyotes, already having received their boo-filled welcome from the Rattlers fans, stalk their wet sideline, anxious for battle to begin.

The Rattlers players stand facing each other in two lines that stretch out from their tunnel and onto the field. A large gathering of the offensive players is in a bunch at the end of those lines, having already been introduced to the crowd.

After the customary dramatic pause, the stadium announcer's voice rings out across the arena.

"And now, Rattlers fans, get out of your seats..." he calls to the crowd.

The crowd didn't need the encouragement. They're already standing and screaming through the rain, knowing the entrance of their hero is imminent.

"Your quarterback, Joe...Gilmooooooooore!" the announcer booms across the powerful speakers, still only barely audible over the exploding voices of the crowd.

Joe comes sprinting out onto the field between the lines of players, who slap hands with him as he races by.

He crashes into his offensive group at the end, all of them yelling and jumping up and down as the adrenaline flows in anticipation of the challenge of the coming battle of opposing wills and strength of spirit and mind.

Joe's heart is full, his eyes are clear, he is ready for the game of titans once again—the game he was born to play.

In the safety, warmth, and luxury of one of the premiere private suites in the stadium, Sarah and Cindy sit in high-back leather seats, looking through the glass and down at the field.

Seemingly comfy and warm, the ladies converse idly as Sarah tries to hide the distraction of the swirling thoughts in her head.

She hadn't spoken with Joe since their fight earlier in the week.

Although she had been disappointed every time she had picked up her phone to see if maybe she had missed a call from him only to see the blank screen staring back at her, or peeked out her living room window at a sound on the street only to see a passing car, it had never crossed her mind not to be at the game to support her son.

Her heart ached for him despite the painful way they had parted. It wasn't right for a boy to lose his father, regardless of whether or not that boy had already grown into a man. While Sarah had managed to find the strength to carry on, to her, it seemed more like Joe had only found the anger to. Although she did a pretty good job of hiding it, she worried about him constantly and even more so since their fight.

Sarah glances over Cindy's shoulder at the milling group of the other key players' family and entourage members that fill the pristine stadium room, failing at keeping her focus on Cindy or her spinning thoughts.

Trace, who has been making her way through the small crowd, arrives next to Cindy. She has brought bottled spring water back for Cindy and Sarah and a mixed drink for herself.

After the customary "Thank you's," regarding the water, Trace and Cindy begin to chat.

Sarah shifts her gaze from the field to the rain on the glass, lost in thought. She looks up to the sky and the raindrops coming down.

High in the sky above the stadium, the red-tailed hawk circles through the rain. Its beautiful wings cut through the air as it makes the descent to its reserved seat atop the bank of lights that turn night into day on the field below.

Back in the commentator's suite, Chris and Sam make final remarks before kickoff.

"The Rattlers have won the coin toss and elected to receive. Apparently Joe Gilmore is anxious to get to work," Chris informs the television audience.

"And I can tell ya," Sam quickly adds, doing his best to sound astute, "Another strong performance like last week and he will almost assuredly lock down that MVP trophy."

The Coyotes line up across the field in their burnt-orange uniforms, behind a ball that stands on a tee on their thirty-five-yard line.

The Rattlers, in their traditional black and red, are spread across their side of the field, ready to receive the coming kickoff.

The voice of the crowd builds to a crescendo as the Coyotes' kicker jogs forward and smashes his foot into the ball, sending it end over end, up through the falling rain.

The Rattlers' kick returner catches the ball, three yards deep in his own end zone, and quickly heads up the field toward the charging Coyotes team as he tucks the ball safely under his arm.

He sees a hole in the wedge his players have set before him, blocking the oncoming Coyotes, and tears through it, expecting to continue flying up the field.

Unfortunately, his sight partially obstructed by the size of his blockers, he does not see the Coyotes player coming full blast for him until it's too late.

The Coyotes player smashes into the Rattlers runner, laying out his full body in the air to increase the force of the collision.

The sound of the hit rattles through the stadium, reaching all the way up to the commentator's booth as the Coyotes' player drives the Rattlers' kick-returner into the ground.

Sam is beside himself.

"Whoa! What a hit!" he yells, rising up on his toes in excitement. "And I can tell you from experience, even when you're the one giving it, WHAP, when it's that good sometimes it even rattles your own bones. A real slobber knocker," he adds, turning to Chris with an ear-to-ear grin.

"Weren't you a kicker?" Chris asks with a playful smirk, taking a shot at his partner.

"A kickoff specialist." Sam quickly corrects him, somewhat deflated but covering with false bravado. "Besides, kickers are a vital part of the game," he adds, turning his face back to the field.

"Uh-huh," Chris replies, smiling despite himself.

Kickers, unless they were winning a game in its last seconds, were still considered second-class citizens to the other gladiators on the field, apparently even post career.

The Rattlers offensive players gather in a huddle on the field. Joe leans into them with the play call.

"It's football weather today, boys," he grins, his breath turning white in the cold, wet air.

"Hell yeah," Big Salt agrees, "Pigs in the slop, baby."

Brian grins.

They all love this shit.

"Trips right, thirty-one slash, raven, on one, on one," Joe calls out the play, "Let's start this thing with a bang, gentlemen. Ready…"

"Break!" they all shout in unison with a clap of their hands as they turn and head for the ball and the readied Coyotes defense.

Joe steps to the line, licking his hands as he assesses the Coyotes' alignment. Their middle linebacker shouts to his teammates, getting everyone adjusted to the Rattlers opening formation.

Satisfied with what he sees, Joe eases in under Big Salt, reaching for the snap as the rain continues to fall.

"Blue thirty-one," he calls, "Blue thirty-one. Set, hut!"

Big Salt smashes the ball into Joe's open palms.

Massive muscles fire across the two squads, the gladiators in battle once again.

Joe glides back from the line, angling to his left while holding the ball out for Larry with his right hand. However, as Larry opens his arms for it, Joe pulls the ball away and Larry crashes through the line—a fake.

Joe looks up toward the left side of the line, where Brian is flying toward him. Joe shifts the ball to his left hand to hand it off to him; on the trick play reverse of direction from where Larry had initially drawn the rushing Coyotes defense.

Brian opens his arms and Joe slips the ball in. But as Brian passes him, accepting the hand-off, the slick, oblong pigskin doesn't stay in place.

Maybe it is too wet, maybe Joe doesn't put it in the right spot, or maybe Brian just doesn't close his arms quickly enough. Whatever the reason, the result is the same—the ball comes out, falling to the soaked ground.

Brian tries to stop and reverse his path, but his momentum carries him past the ball. His outstretched hands claw the air just beyond it as his cleats slip in the wet grass and he crashes to the ground.

In a seemingly fortuitous twist of luck, the ball takes just the right bounce and comes up on its end, spinning in place.

Joe, who has already made a break toward it, scoops it up on the run, out along the right side of the backfield. He continues past Brian, who quickly scrambles to recover.

Disaster avoided, Joe rolls to his right, scanning the field for an open receiver.

Behind him, however, the momentary blunder has put undue pressure on his blocking linemen. The defensive end on the left side has broken free and unbeknown to Joe he is coming for him full blast, with only the fallen Brian in his way.

Joe, his attention still focused forward, continues to his right, outside the protected pocket created by his blockers.

The Coyotes' outside linebacker several yards in front of him now has a free path directly to Joe and rapidly begins taking advantage of it.

Joe, ignoring the danger, spots one of his receivers breaking open in the field behind the advancing linebacker in front of him.

Behind Joe, Brian has scrambled back to his feet. But at a dead standstill, Brian is no match for the massive defensive end coming full tilt. All he sees is a blur of burnt orange as the monstrous Coyotes player smashes right through him, sending him flying through the air and onto his back while barely breaking his menacing stride toward Joe.

Unaware of the events to his rear, and prepared to take the punishment of the unavoidable hit of the linebacker now bearing down in front of him in exchange for a positive play, Joe sets his feet and cocks his arm to throw.

The defensive end is already laid out in the air behind him; before Joe can release the pass, he slams full-force into the lower part of his back, bending Joe in half.

As Joe's body recoils forward from the blow of the Coyotes' defensive end, he comes face-to-face with the linebacker, whose dive has brought his helmet into the direct trajectory of Joe's.

Their heads viciously crash together with a thunderous crack, which reverberates throughout the stadium.

A white light flashes in front of Joe, before the nothingness takes him over.

His body is ripped violently to the ground by the opposing forces of his combatants as the ball falls from the grasp of his hand, his muscles losing their command to contract.

Joe is immediately lost in a pile of bodies as both teams go diving for the fumbled football.

Whoosh. Whoosh.

The hawk's strong wings press against the wet air as it finishes its descent to the top of the goalpost at the other end of the field, landing a little closer to the covered Joe.

"Oh my God!" Cindy's scream rings through the suite as she springs to her feet. Sarah and Trace rise with her, their collective hearts momentarily forgetting how to fire.

"Fumble! Fumble!" Sam yells, excitedly leaning closer to the field. "Wow, I heard that hit all the way up here!"

From their view in the booth, the commentators can see one of the black-and-white-striped officials pull his head out of the pile of players.

The official signals that the Coyotes have recovered the ball and the crowd responds with a quiet groan, now focused less on the outcome of the play and more on the condition of their quarterback.

"And the Coyotes have recovered the ball," Chris informs the viewing audience, "But the bigger concern to these Rattlers fans may be the condition of Joe Gilmore."

"Yeah, I still haven't seen him get up," Sam adds, calming himself after his outburst.

The outcome of their scrum already having been announced by the official, the players continue to unravel from the pile until finally they all are back on their feet—all except one.

Acknowledged by the gasp of the crowd, Joe Gilmore still lies face-down on the field, pretty much the way he had initially fallen.

Brian is the first one there, dropping to his knees next to him.

"Joe! Joe!" he calls as he leans closer to the quarterback's prone face.

But Joe's eyes are closed and he isn't moving.

The guilt of having been unable to block the rushing lineman is already crushing Brian as he raises his arm, frantically waving the trainers over from the Rattlers sideline.

Sarah can't breathe again, no matter how hard she squeezes Cindy's hand.

And Cindy can't feel the grip that Trace has on her arm because she can't feel anything.

It's like a replay of the end of the game from the previous week.

At least that is what they are all hoping, praying...

Surely, Joe would get up. Any second now, Big Salt would flip him over and Joe's laugh would ease their concern. After all, he was the hero, and although heroes are sometimes flawed and sometimes fall, everyone one knows that they always, always get right back up.

But this time Joe wasn't getting up and they all knew it.

They knew it before the initial first trainers that arrived to check Joe out sent one running back to the sidelines for more serious equipment.

They knew it before Coach Osborne himself had hurried onto the field to see him. Before Brian and Big Salt and Larry, who knelt with other Rattlers and even Coyotes players, began bowing their heads in a circle of prayer.

They knew it just like the players on the field and the fans in the stands knew it, as the rain lines on their faces became mixed with their tears.

This time was different; this time was bad. This time, their hero's invincibility was showing a devastating crack.

The hawk peers down at Joe through the sheets of rain as beads of water drip from its poised beak.

The trainers, having obviously assessed the seriousness of the situation, already have Joe's body securely strapped to their medical board. All the proper spinal immobilization restraints are in place and the facemask of his helmet has been removed.

The three of them lift the board in unison to transfer Joe onto a stretcher as the ambulance they have requested backs its way across the field.

Cameramen, security guards, event staff, and cheerleaders that line the back of the end zone find themselves instinctively ambling ever so slightly forward toward Joe; everyone wants to help.

Among them is the seemingly odd fan who had run out of the tunnel, emulating Joe, after last week's game.

Minus the foam hand and Rattlers cap at present, he is now clad in a black jacket with bright yellow lettering that reads Event Security.

The man stares at Joe like an innocent child holding a hurt puppy.

The hawk's shrill cry from above sounds like it's coming from another world.

The man looks up toward the sound to see the hawk leap from the bank of lights and take back to the dark, wet sky as the back doors of the ambulance that now contains Joe Gilmore swing closed and the rain pours down through the heavy air of the devastated stadium.

Chapter 10

An oval drop of water with a pointed tail falls through the air. This one, a mixture of the oils and water of a body, the loss of a mother expressed in chemical form, crashes onto the clenched fist of Sarah Gilmore.

Pastor Roman sits to Sarah's left. Cindy is to her right, holding hands with Trace in the sanitized air of the emergency waiting room at Park Memorial Hospital. The women stare blankly in the direction of the receding doctor; his white coat flutters behind him as he retreats back through the closing doors of the Emergency Room, which separate patient from family and friends.

Having waited for what seemed like an eternity to hear the specifics of Joe's condition while holding onto hopes with fragile psyches, they now feel only the numb dregs of despair—having just received the crushing news from the doctor.

Each one's mind now races with inner dialogue and flashes of scenes past.

Why did I let him leave that way?! Sarah kept demanding of herself, her thoughts returning to their fight. *And why was I so stubborn? I could have picked up the phone, I could have called...he's just a boy. He wasn't trying to hurt me...*

And as quickly as those thoughts came, and would come again, her mind shifted to another memory stored in the vault of her mind that found a relation to the present—the first time Joe had been taken to the hospital for an injury resulting from the game he loved so much.

Joe had been tackled by a much bigger boy and, when he had fallen, his arm had landed across the root of a tree in the yard that had been anointed their football field for the day.

Sarah was out buying groceries when she had gotten the call from James to come to the hospital.

Although James clearly and calmly assured Sarah that it was only a broken arm and that they would be home soon, her usually conservative driving style had flown right out the window as she had raced through traffic to the ER with little regard for speed limits or red lights along the way.

At the hospital she had rushed into the room to find seven-year-old Joe, his left arm already in a cast, happily recounting the story to an attentive nurse of how he had completed the pass and his best friend Tommy had scored the winning touchdown as "the fat guy tackled me."

"I didn't cry, Momma," he had told Sarah when she reached the end of the bed.

Sarah had made up for his lack of tears right then and there, regardless of how hard she had tried to smile through them or how much it had helped to have James walk over and wrap his strong arms around her.

But there was no smiling this time, and no James to squeeze her tight; only pain, confusion, and loss.

The glass doors of the hospital slide open as Brian leads the charge of Big Salt, Larry, and Coach Osborne into the room.

Brian's eyes catch Cindy's as his head swings in her direction. The tears cascading from her lost eyes reveal that the news is dire.

With the other men in tow, Brian's feet somehow carry him toward her, despite the pain in his chest.

Cindy rises to be caught in his arms and the two embrace.

Coach Osborne eases toward Sarah, leaning down to her.

"How is he?" he asks, breaking the silence in the room, which had held only Cindy's sobs since their entrance.

Sarah blinks at him, unable to speak. The caring pastor slowly stands in her stead and relays the news from the doctor to Joe's Rattlers family.

The recounting of Joe's condition causes Cindy's stomach to feel like it is going to spill its contents; she covers her mouth and breaks for the bathroom. Trace rushes after her.

Brian spins and punches the closest wall, the guilt of the missed block erupting from inside him.

Tears wet Big Salt's red beard as he stands in the center of the room staring at nothing, unable to process the damage that has been done.

Larry sinks into a chair.

Coach Osborne watches his men suffer, unable to help as he fights back tears of his own.

Pastor Roman coaxes Sarah out of her chair and leads her from the room and down the hall toward the hospital chapel. Prayer is the only solace he knows to offer at a time like this.

The compassionate wooden face of the crucified Christ peers out over the hospital chapel as Pastor Roman's prayer drifts up to him.

"Though this woman suffers the pain that only a mother's heart can know," Pastor Roman beseeches in a compassionate voice, kneeling at the altar below the carved statue of their Savior, his head bowed, "We know that you too, Father, know this pain. But that you also know the joy of re-embrace and for this we humbly pray, if it be your will. We forever trust in your all-knowing power and grace, Almighty God. In the precious name of your holy son, Jesus Christ, we pray. Amen."

His prayer finished, Pastor Roman opens his eyes and lifts his head, rising to his feet. He turns to Sarah, who has been kneeling beside him in silence.

Her blank, tear-stained face stares up at the wooden Christ.

"Sarah?" Pastor Roman says, to what might as well have been an empty room. "Sarah?" he tries again, leaning toward her.

Sarah slowly turns her bewildered face to him, still pleading for answers.

"What did I do?" she begs. "What did I do?"

Pastor Roman drops to a knee, placing a hand on her shoulder.

"He's a fighter, Sarah," he tries to assure her. "And he got that fight from you," he adds sincerely. "There may be weeping in the night, but we know that joy comes in the morning. We cannot lose our faith—it's the only hope he has now."

Sarah's eyes fall to her lap. Her head nods in agreement, but her mind still frantically races from despair to guilt and back again.

Chapter 11

It is late the following night when Sarah is finally allowed to enter the ICU room containing her son. But only a few steps inside the door, her legs refuse to carry her forward any farther when her eyes find the bed where her son lies motionless, in a coma induced by the trauma of the collision with the linebacker.

Various medical equipment is attached to Joe's body: IVs are in both arms, a pulse oximeter—for reading the oxygen content of is his blood—is on his right index finger, EKG wires are under his gown and on his chest, and a white tube is down one of his nostrils. His neck is supported by a white C-collar and his torso is wrapped in a tight brace to protect his damaged spine. A catheter bag hangs from the side of the bed, its tube snaking under the sheets toward Joe's groin.

The plump ICU nurse who brought Sarah to the room watches the frozen mother with kind eyes.

"He is stabilized and breathing on his own now," she begins softly. "So you may visit with him quietly. You can speak to him and even hold his hand. But please don't make any loud noises or touch any of the machines in here or his brace. Okay?"

Sarah nods, never taking her eyes off Joe.

The nurse waits, her experience and compassion alerting her to the fact that this mother isn't ready to be left alone just yet.

After a moment or two, Sarah speaks.

"Excuse me, nurse?" she quietly begins.

"Yes?" the nurse replies in kind.

"Is he…is he paralyzed?" Sarah has to know, her eyes now locked on his cumbersome brace.

"We really won't be able to determine that until he wakes up," the nurse answers honestly, gently. "He has to be conscious for us to test for feeling and motor control in his legs," she explains.

Sarah finally turns to her.

"When will he wake up?" she asks, grasping to find some last vestige of strength within her.

The nurse takes a subtle breath, not out of frustration but more out of consideration. She moves a step closer to Sarah.

"I'm a mother too. It's tough," she confides, her heart breaking for Sarah. "To be honest, I can't say that we really know, definitively," she continues. "Sometimes it feels like it's all up to them."

She pauses a moment, reaching for Sarah's hand and looking into her eyes before continuing.

"I will tell you this, though—from what I've seen in this unit, I would bet that he can hear whatever you say to him. So talk to him from your heart."

With that she pats Sarah's hand and exits the room, leaving the mother alone with her son.

Sarah just stands there for a moment, her feet seemingly glued to the floor. Finally, she breaks their bond with the cold, tiled surface and forces herself forward, next to the bed.

Through watery eyes she looks at Joe's face; his eyelids closed, his lips swollen and dry.

"I'm sorry, Joey," is all she can think to say, her voice cracking over the words. She tries to continue, but is unable to formulate any of her other thoughts or emotions into verbal communication.

She silently reaches down and wraps her hands around his.

Without even being aware of it herself, she begins swaying back and forth the same way she always did when she would rock Joe to sleep as a baby.

Tears stream silently down her face as she helplessly watches her son numbly cling to life.

Sarah makes her way through the ICU waiting room on shaky legs, still gathering her emotions. The room is empty save the remnants of the group from the day before.

Brian, Coach Osborne, Trace, and Pastor Roman are all there. Each is a little better groomed today and wearing fresh clothes, but all have bags under their eyes—evidence of the previous sleepless night.

Pastor Roman rises as Sarah makes her way over to him.

"How is he?" the pastor asks.

"They say he's stable," Sarah responds, trying to force a small smile as she takes a seat next to him and he lowers back down into his.

"She said one at a time," Sarah quietly informs the group, referring to the directions the nurse had given her on her way in. "So whoever would like to see him next…" she finishes.

Brian looks around the room. "I'm sure Cindy would want to," he observes.

"She's in the bathroom," Trace announces. "I'll go," she quickly adds, rising and hurriedly heading down the hall before anyone can object or question.

Brian grits his teeth, biting his tongue as she disappears into the ICU. He stands and begins to anxiously pace the room in worry, unsure what to do.

Trace slowly enters Joe's ICU room, stopping next to the side of the bed as she takes in his condition.

"Oh, Joe," she breathes softly. The tears begin to flow; she tries to wipe them away.

She leans over and caresses his face.

"I don't know how to say this, baby," she begins, slowly. "And I don't know if you can hear me or not...thinking that you can't almost makes this easier..."

She pauses, nervously straightening the gown lying loosely around his neck.

"But when you were lying on that field," she continues, more emotion beginning to spill out as she revisits the image, "I felt like my heart had stopped. I was trying to comfort Cindy, I...I was feeling so guilty...but all I could think about were the times that we've been together. Every time that you held me, I felt safe."

She leans forward and kisses him on the cheek, then gently wipes the wetness of her tears from his face.

"How could you?" Cindy's quiet voice cuts through the room like a knife from the doorway behind her.

Trace's face loses its color as her mind races over the past minutes in a desperate attempt to calculate how long Cindy could have been there, how much she could have heard—all in the two seconds it takes her to reactively stand up and turn to face her friend.

"How could you?" Cindy demands again, tears of betrayal and grief spilling from her eyes.

"Cindy, I, I—" Trace tries to explain the unexplainable, realizing that however long she had been standing there, it had been long enough to learn too much.

"You're my best friend," Cindy continues, cutting her off. "You've been my best friend since college...you're my roommate, you're..."

"Cindy, I'm sorry." Trace tries again, trembling as she steps toward her. "I just—" she continues, before being cut off once more.

"You're sorry?" Cindy asks emphatically, her voice rising as the bitter anger of betrayal begins to boil inside her.

"You're having an affair with my boyfriend and you're fucking sorry?!" she shouts.

"What do you want me to say?" Trace pleads, beginning to cry in desperation.

"I don't want you to *say* anything, Trace, just get out," Cindy fires back, doubly pissed that her former friend is now trying to get sympathy from her after her grievous acts of deception.

"Cindy..." Trace tries one more time as she takes another nervous step toward her.

"Leave," Cindy commands, her stare and voice turning cold. "And have your stuff out of the apartment by the time I get there."

"Okay," Trace responds, looking away. "Okay. I'm sorry."

"LEAVE!" Cindy explodes.

Trace bursts into tears, covering her face as she rushes by Cindy and out the door.

With Trace gone, Cindy just stands there—unable to force her feet to carry her into the room as she tries to fit the broken pieces of her heart back together again.

She stares at Joe, her mind numb with pain and confusion.

For several minutes she holds her position as she fights with the thoughts swirling through her mind before finally deciding that maybe it was best she that hadn't forced him to have a conversation about their future life together.

It had been at the front of her mind and on the tip of her tongue repeatedly over the last month or so; but that perfect moment she had been waiting for just hadn't appeared. And until the last few minutes had transpired she had spent the last twenty-four hours continually berating herself for not having made that moment happen.

But now, now...

Finally, her voice finds its use once more.

"I don't know how I can leave you right now," she quietly confesses to Joe.

Then she abruptly turns and walks away.

Vising hours now long since over, Joe lies in his darkened room alone. It is silent save the rhythmic beep of his heart monitor and the steady hum of its companion life-monitoring machines.

Their sounds are momentarily overwhelmed by the *whoosh, whoosh,* of the red-tailed hawk's powerful wings as they create the necessary turbulence in the air to end its descent and bring it to a soft landing on the railing outside the window.

The hawk turns its majestic head toward Joe's room, peering in through the slanted vertical blinds.

It scans over Joe's body lying on the bed; its eyes search his face and torso before darting to the pointer and middle fingers of Joe's hand, which have just given a quick, small twitch.

"EEEE-AAAAAAAHHHHHHHHH!!!!" Joe gives voice to the rage caged within his chest.

Clad in his Rattlers uniform—minus the helmet—he wields an ancient samurai sword between curled, ram-like horns and into the hideous face of the monstrous demon before him.

The blood of his foe sprays into the red, dust-filled air, mixing with the creature's hissing scream as it crumples to the ground—vaporizing back into the red dirt from which it had sprung.

Another of his clan immediately steps forward, while a hundred more of his evil brothers slowly rise out of the ground behind him.

CHING! CHING! CHING!

Joe's muscles flash and his sword clashes with the demon's glowing red cleaver of a blade as its fiery eyes dance with hate.

Joe spins and thrusts, his sword finding the inside of the tormentor's belly. He refuses to give in though the mounting evidence suggests that this may be an impossible battle to win as three more demons take the place of the devil he had just vanquished into the dirt.

"Police have speculated that the attack was an initiation act for the infamous One Blood, inner-city gang," the news reporter's voice purrs with pleasure over the sounds of the battle.

Joe jerks his face up to his left to see the reporter's plastic facade on the jumbotron that hangs on nothing in the sky above the demon army.

The picture of James in uniform appears beside her; the back left side of his head is blown open and a spattering of crimson lies across that side of his face.

One of the demons deftly knifes its sword across Joe's shoulder, taking advantage of the vulnerability the distraction of the troubling images creates.

Joe slips to one knee in pain before rising back up with a vengeance.

His will to live pushing him on, he swings his sword with all his might, removing the demon's sneering head from its pointy shoulders.

"What are you doing now, QB?" Trace's giggling voice asks as a holograph of the hotel room they had shared births in the sky opposite the jumbotron. Joe sees a bewildered vision of himself snorting the cocaine off her inner thigh before looking to the floor beside him, where

Jennifer is in convulsions; the back left side of her head reveals the same damage as James'.

Joe's attention is forced back to the battleground by a new, searing pain across his thigh.

The demon next to him hisses through a ghastly grin as the claws of his bony fingers drip with the freshly drawn blood.

Joe's mind spins as the demons continue to surround him, his will faltering.

In a desperate, final burst of rage he forces his body forward, raising his sword over his head as his face contorts in a bloodthirsty scream.

He brings his blade down and across the two closest fiends, shattering their defending cleavers and ripping their bodies in two with a powerful slice.

He raises his sword again, advancing toward the next foe before suddenly freezing.

His eyes flash with a glimmer of hope as they catch a glimpse of James calmly walking between the rows of advancing destroyers.

The demon in front of Joe takes advantage of the opening created by the human fallacy and thrusts his sword deep into Joe's solar plexus.

Joe's face twists in confusion and pain as the demon's glowing blade slides back out of the grave wound it has inflicted upon his body and he crumples to the ground.

"Enough." James' calm, clear voice cuts through the air, instantly immobilizing the demons that surround his son.

The demon army parts like the red sea before the staff of Moses as James, wearing an ancient-looking white robe with a golden lace border, advances toward his fallen son from behind the throng of evil apparitions.

The hideous tormentors hiss at him, involuntarily backing away, powerless against the piercing gaze of his crystal-clear, compassionate eyes.

James kneels next to Joe as the demons emit their final objections before falling back into the ground below them.

The projected images in the sky turn their gazes toward the twosome, silently watching the events unfold.

"Dad," Joe breathes, his eyes filling with tears. "Dad, what happened? Am I dead?" he asks, painfully trying to sit up as his mind attempts to make sense of this place and his eyes of the oozing wound just above his belly.

"It's just a moment, son," James answers with a soft smile. He reaches out and takes Joe's arm, clasping his forearm with his hand, but leaving the lifting to his son.

"What do you mean?" Joe questions him, panting as he steadies himself against the strength of James' grasp. "Where are we?"

"It doesn't matter," James responds, turning his head and scanning the red dimension. "None of this is real," he says as the images fade from the sky with the wave of his hand. He turns back to Joe. "It will soon be time to wake up," he informs his troubled son with kind eyes.

"I don't want to wake up." Joe rejects James' words, wincing from the pain in his body and heart.

James reaches out and gently tilts his son's chin up toward him—Joe's bewildered eyes coming to meet James' serene gaze.

"I know." James acknowledges Joe's objection, his face full of understanding. "It's going to be okay," he assures Joe with a compassionate, knowing smile.

Joe's eyes fill with tears: tears of relief for the soothing connection with his father, tears of pain and confusion for the loss and torment of this place and his life, and tears of anger for the fear that this moment would end.

And then, as Joe had sensed, James' image begins to fade as his grip on Joe's arm lightens.

"Open your heart and don't be afraid," James advises him.

"Don't leave me," Joe begs, the tears starting to flow. "Don't leave me, Dad...please don't leave me again..."

James smiles at him.

"It's okay, son," he says, glancing over Joe's shoulder. "You're in really good hands."

Behind Joe, laying across a large, sandy, red boulder and looking on with compasionate eyes, is the curious man from the football stadium.

He again wears the Rattlers cap, along with the big foam finger. Joe's white, sideways number eight adorns his chest this time, as he has now added a Joe Gilmore football jersey to his attire.

Joe is so desperately focused on his father that he isn't even aware of the man's presence.

"None of this makes sense. You can't go!" he insists as James' figure fades further away.

"I love you, Joe," James tells him, looking back into Joe's eyes. "I always will," he finishes as he disappears.

"Nooooo!" Joe cries. "This isn't fair!" he adds, frantically searching the horizon for James but finding only red dirt as far as the eye can see.

Hope fading, Joe slumps back onto the ground—his hand sliding to the moist wound above his stomach.

He lays his head on the dirt, the pace of his breath increasing as tears run from the corners of his eyes and the red plasma continues to spread between his fingers.

The hawk, still on its perch outside the ICU room window, has its eyes locked on Joe's heart monitor, which is racing.

BEEEEEEEEEEEEEEEEEEP! it cries as the line on its screen goes into a nearly flat trajectory of very small, very fast up-and-down movements, signaling to any trained medical eye that Joe's heart is in ventricular fibrillation—a quivering organ, incapable of circulating blood through his body.

"KEE-AAAAAHHHH!" The hawk's shrill cry fills the air as it watches the medical staff come rushing into Joe's room.

The trained nurses and doctor only need a quick glance at the monitor to recognize the grave severity of Joe's condition.

"He's crashing!" one nurse yells, pulling out her medical shears, and immediately putting them to use in splitting his gown up the front while the second nurse begins loosening the brace around his chest.

The doctor rapidly slides the crash cart from the wall and starts readying the paddles of the AED machine with gel. He flips a switch and the machine begins building up its joules of energy.

"Charging," he informs the nurses in a loud voice.

Joe's chest exposed, the nurses step back.

The doctor comes forward and places the paddles at ten and four o'clock on each side of his chest. He glances at the AED machine—its illuminated red numbers reach 300.

"Clear!" he calls before pressing the button on the paddle that sends the electricity into Joe's chest.

Joe's torso tenses and arches slightly before flopping back to the bed.

The eyes in the room all look to the heart monitor.

BEEEEEEP, it responds as the EKG line returns from the high peak of the shock, back into the wavy, flat line.

"Prepare two hundred milligrams of lidocane!" the doctor barks to the nurses. "We're not losing him."

One of the nurses immediately complies, grabbing a needle and vial off the cart.

"Charging," the doctor informs them again as the AED whines, gathering joules once more.

The hawk holds its position, eyes still locked on Joe as the doctor places the pads back on his chest and his body rises and falls once more, to no avail.

Again the doctor charges the AED as the nurse fills the needle from the vial.

Again Joe's body rises and falls with no change on the monitor.

"Give him the lidocane," the doctor instructs, beads of sweat beginning to form above his brow as doubt starts creeping into his mind.

The nurse plunges the needle into Joe's IV and depresses it fully, knowing too well the dropping statistical chances that their efforts will yield the outcome they are trying to gain but pushing forward regardless.

"Charging to four hundred," the doctor informs the nurses, adjusting the setting on the AED.

"Come on, Joe!" he yells, placing the paddles back on his chest.

The hawk raises its head to the sky, releasing its cry once more as the doctor presses the button on the paddle.

"KEEEEEE-AAAAAAAAAAHHHH!!!" the hawk cries into the night air.

Joe's body tenses as the charge races through his chest.

The muscles tighten as his body raises up on the bed.

It holds there, everything straining as the electricity pulses through. Then it slowly releases its tension, falling back to the bed.

Everyone in the room holds their breath as their eyes race to find the heart monitor once more, its long *Beeeeep!* momentarily interrupted.

The EKG line peaks for a moment, holds, and then crashes back down flat.

The heads in the room all drop.

The head on the balcony doesn't. The hawk maintains its focus on Joe's eyes.

After a motionless moment that seems locked in eternity, one of Joe's eyelids finally flutters. Then both eyes pop open as the line on the monitor begins rising and falling in rhythm with its sound, announcing the return of life.

Beep, beep, beep.

The medical team breathes a much-needed sigh of relief.

The doctor smiles as Joe's eyes turn toward him.

"We've got a fighter," he observes.

Chapter 12

Once again Sarah is forgetting that traffic laws govern the roads she is tearing up as she steers through the city streets, while the early-morning sun rises outside her window.

This time it's hope and relief that push her right foot down as she flies through an intersection, the light turning red above her.

Thank you God! Thank you God! had been her persistent thought since receiving the call from the ICU nurse that caused her to literally scream with joy.

"Your son is awake," was all that Sarah remembered hearing. It was the only thing that mattered, as far as she was concerned.

Jumping out of bed, her eyes had met James'—in the photo of him hanging on the wall. Somewhere deep in her heart she just knew that he was watching over them, that he was sharing in her joy just now.

Sarah weaves her car around a slower traveler, anxious to look into Joe's eyes and to have him return the gaze; the thoughts of their recent fight, his reckless behavior, and her guilt for pressing him are no longer on her mind.

Trivial things of that nature just melted away when the bigger picture of a life-and-death situation came crashing into Sarah's world.

Only one thing mattered to this mother: her son was awake.

Whatever else there was to deal with could be handled. She had been given a second chance with her son, and she was desperately anxious to get started with it.

After finally arriving at the hospital, Sarah had ran into the kind nurse in the hallway, who informed her that Joe's surgeon was speaking with him at the moment.

Apparently, once Joe had fully regained consciousness, he had been quite insistent about seeing her immediately.

As Sarah eases herself into Joe's room she sees him lying in the bed, the tube gone from his nose. The tight brace around his torso has been replaced and is covered with a new, undamaged gown. Several wires still connect him to the monitoring machines in the room, though, and the IV is still flowing fluids and medicine into his veins. The catheter bag also still hangs off the side of the bed.

"I know you may not consider yourself to be very lucky, Joe," the kind and knowledgeable Dr. Woods acknowledges, having already explained to him what had happened on the field, which Joe had no memory of at present. "But in light of the trauma you've suffered, you are," she continues. "The damage to your brain could have been much more severe. At this point, I see no reason to think that you will not regain full use of your faculties. And though your spine has been damaged, it is not completely severed. The injury is also in the lower part of your spine, in vertebra T-12. Meaning, with treatment—"

"What about football?" Joe asks, cutting her off, still staring at the ceiling, as he has been since she tested for movement and feeling in his legs, with no result.

As far as he was concerned, the rest was irrelevant. He didn't care about his condition and he sure as hell wasn't feeling lucky to be alive, regardless of how excited the ICU staff was about it.

Sarah quietly takes a step forward, making eye contact with the surgeon.

The observant doctor recognizes the family resemblance and concern of a mother immediately.

She gives Sarah an understanding nod as she gently continues. "So with treatment, it is possible that you could regain some use of your legs again," she informs Joe, finishing her sentence.

"What about football?" Joe demands again, bringing his troubled eyes to her.

He sees Sarah, who now stands next to the surgeon.

Sarah tries to give him a supportive look, but Joe fixes his eyes back on the doctor, awaiting the answer he already knows is coming but is still fighting against accepting.

"I'm sorry, Joe," Dr. Woods says, genuinely feeling for him. Knowing from experience that honesty, however painful, is what is called for in circumstances like this she adds, "Your sports career is over."

"Can you just..." Joe's voice trails off. His hand tries to wave her and the news away as his eyes avert the view of the two women once more.

"Of course," Dr. Woods answers, turning for the door.

She reaches out and gives Sarah's arm a light squeeze as she passes by, then closes the door behind her as she leaves the room.

Joe stares blankly at the wall to the right side of his bed, though his neck—still constrained by the protective collar—can only slightly turn in that direction.

His mind races with past images of the life he has lost and with questions and confusion over the one he has inherited from an event he can't recall.

Sarah eases over to Joe's left side, most of her excitement having turned to heaviness for the loss now evident on her son's face.

She reaches for his arm, runs her hand down it, and grasps his.

"What am I supposed to do now?" Joe's empty voice asks, his spirit numbed by the unwelcomed reality he has awoken to.

Sarah takes a moment to gather her strength before she responds.

"First, you're going to hurt," Sarah answers softly, compassionately, and honestly.

Her eyes moisten but she won't allow them to spill the breaking of her heart for her son—a fight no mother is very good at when watching one of her children in pain.

"You're going to grieve," she continues.

Joe still refuses to look in her direction, tears beginning to cascade down his darkened face.

"And then, you're going to fight," Sarah adds, squeezing his hand as the barricade in one of her eyes cracks, and a tear streaks down her cheek.

"Everything I've worked for is gone," Joe replies, his brows furrowing in confusion and inner pain.

Sarah doesn't really know what to say, so she just squeezes his hand a little tighter.

"Why did this happen to me?" Joe asks, suddenly turning toward her. "Am I being punished?" he questions.

"What?" Sarah replies, shocked by the nature of the query. "No, no, Joey," she stammers, "That's not, it's…it doesn't work that way."

It had been the main question on his mind since his exit from the planet of red dirt.

The presence of his father had been soothing, but the way he had left him to die alone, the insurmountable challenge of his tormentors—it all seemed so cruel.

Punishment, he thought, was the only explanation that fit. *Abandonment,* at the very least.

Hell, he'd felt abandoned by God ever since he had lost James the first time. Now he was sure He was punishing him, although for what he wasn't exactly sure.

"How do you know?" Joe pleads with Sarah, certain his assessment has to be right. "How do you know it doesn't work that way?"

"I don't know," she tries again. "But it…it just doesn't work that way."

"But how do you know?!" Joe demands as his undercurrent of anger over the punishment that he feels far outweighs his crimes begins to gain leverage over his confusion.

"Joe," Sarah tries, shaking her head. "You can't go there. There's no help there."

"I'm already there!" Joe shouts. "Look at me. Look at me!" he continues, indicating his legs. "This is hell. It's hell with no answers. It's hell trapped in a broken body. And I want to know why," he growls, with fire in his eyes.

"Uh," Sarah breathes, her brows now the ones furrowed in angst. "I..." but she has no answers for this, no words to calm the storm inside her son.

Joe's eyes turn to the ceiling; his mind traveling beyond it.

"What about you?!" he barks defiantly. "You got any answers for me?" he continues, his anger at his mother's God now boiling over.

"First my DAD, now my LEGS, MY CAREER...WHAT ELSE DO YOU WANT TO TAKE FROM ME??!!" he demands from the silent ceiling.

"ANSWER ME, GODDAMN IT!!!" he explodes.

"JOSEPH!" Sarah cries. "Dear God, have mercy on his soul," she immediately prays, fearful of the defiant challenge Joe is spraying toward the Almighty.

"NO MERCY!" Joe yells, turning his anger on her now. "No mercy," he says again from between clenched teeth as he stares in her direction. "I've had His judgment, and I don't need His fucking pity."

The venom pouring from her son, as he jerks his arm and hand from her grasp, stuns Sarah.

She takes a step back, her face blank. She blinks her eyes, feeling like she has just received a stunning body blow.

Joe whips the sheets that cover his damaged body aside.

"I can walk," he declares, rejecting the reality of his condition.

"Joe..." Sarah tries, panic rising in her chest.

"I can walk," he repeats, ripping off the wires to the EKG and grabbing the railing on the bed.

He painfully pulls his torso upright, determined to prove the surgeon, his body, and a cruel God all wrong.

"Joe. Stop it!" Sarah demands, frantically reaching to grab him.

"DON'T TOUCH ME!!" he snaps, his eyes shooting daggers at her as he jerks his arm away once more.

Sarah steps back again, starting to panic as Joe grabs his legs with his right arm and, while turning his torso in her direction, lifts them up and slides them off the side of the bed—leaving his bare feet hanging just inches above the floor.

The pain that knifes through his body causes him to gasp.

"Uuuhh-phhh," he breathes though a grimacing face, refusing to accept what his body is signaling.

"Joey, please," Sarah pleads, tears racing from her eyes as she reaches for him once again.

Joe knocks her arms away with a swat of his hand, his athletic upper body strength still too much of a match for his mother.

"Please!" she begs again, her eyes wide with terror.

"I can walk," Joe coldly declares once more, staring her in the eye.

He pushes himself up and onto his feet.

Despite Joe's defiance, the harsh truth of his crippled state is unavoidable. His apathetic legs immediately fold under the weight of his body and he instantly crashes to the floor, taking the metal bedside tray he clutches for with him.

Everything hits the hard, cold floor with a heavy thud and a loud crash, including Joe's IV pole—the strong tape still holding the tubing in his arm. The catheter tube strains to stay connected to both his body and the crooked bag hanging from the bed.

"AAAAAHHHHHH!!!" Joe screams, reaching for his back, the unbearable pain shooting like lightning bolts in all directions from his damaged spine.

Sarah falls to her knees beside him, the nightmare of her son's all-consuming pain racking her body with emotion.

The door to the ICU room is swung open by the nurse who has heard the crash and scream.

"I need help in here!" she yells to the rest of the staff over her shoulder as she charges forward.

Sarah instinctively reaches for Joe, who lies crumpled on his right side, facing her. He continues to quietly insist through quivering lips as his tears drip to the floor, "I can walk. I can walk..."

"Please ma'am," the nurse requests to Sarah, dropping to the floor as well, "I need room."

Sarah slides backward on her knees as the nurse fills her space.

"Don't move, Joe," the ICU nurse instructs. She immediately grabs his head, supporting and realigning his spine. "Just lie as still as you can," she adds as her fellow nurses come rushing into the room.

Although Joe's face doesn't register any sign that he's received her request, his mind blank and in another place now, his body does lie still as the mumbled mantra becomes a quiet murmur. "I can walk…I can walk…"

Sarah, on her hands and knees in the corner she has been forced into—both literally and figuratively—helplessly watches as the medical personnel work to get her son turned over onto his back and stabilized.

Crouched on the floor, she keeps trying to catch his gaze through the bodies of the nurses, aching to let him know—*I'm here! I'm here! I'm here and I'm never leaving…*

But Joe's eyes don't see her. The feel of hands on his body and voices in his ears all seem a million miles away as his mind fights to escape from the pain of this moment.

Chapter 13

The chilly wind slides around the beautiful auburn feathers of the red-tailed hawk as the majestic bird sails on the cold currents of the air.

It swings back and forth across the sky, checking the ground far below it from time to time.

The top of a white van goes in and out of the hawk's view, disappearing now and again under the canopies of mixed evergreen and barren trees that dot rolling winter hills traversed by a two-lane highway.

The mountainous countryside is a mixture of beauty and ugliness; the frozen ground having sucked the fringes of life from many of the trees.

Inside the van a Mexican driver in his early forties, Raul Martinez, turns off the main road and onto a beautiful, long driveway covered by a tunnel of overhanging trees that intertwine above the passing vehicle.

Brian sits in the seat next to the driver, looking out at nature's serene, comforting display.

Behind them, Joe, oblivious to this beauty, stares off into nothing.

He rides in a wheelchair that's locked into place in the Park Memorial Hospital transport van.

After weeks of fitful recovery at the hospital, necessary to ensure his body had fully stabilized, Joe is now free from all the wires. However a brace around his torso, although a smaller version than the original, still remains—along with the catheter bag that hangs on the side of his wheelchair.

His burning anger is buried, more than gone, at this point. His fight had slipped further and further away as the reality of his situation had forced itself more and more to the forefront of his damaged psyche, during his weeks of resentful recovery at the hospital.

The van emerges from the tunnel and arrives at an inviting, stone-colored-brick and redwood two-story structure, which sprawls across a manicured lawn in front of a paved circular drive.

A hand-painted sign hangs from the roof over a quaint, wood-post porch at the entrance.

Agape Rehab, it reads, in soft blue letters.

Large oak trees that have held their positions as the centuries have passed stand scattered across the lawn.

A particularly beautiful one holds its post in the center of the green grass surrounded by the circular drive.

Away from the main building, farther out into the lawn, another tree provides cover over an inviting sitting area.

A man sits on one of the padded chairs there, holding the hand of a quadriplegic woman who is strapped into her motorized wheelchair.

Both of them are wearing wool caps with earflaps and thick coats. They are enjoying the view across the landscape with rosy cheeks and hearty laughs, despite the cold temperature.

The van pulls to a stop in front of the entrance to the facility, where a smiling African-American orderly stands at the door, holding a clipboard. He wears comfy scrubs, which match the blue color on the lettering of the center's sign, over body-warming thermal undergarments.

The orderly, Gary Masterson, steps off the porch toward the van as its front doors open.

Brian hops out and steps to the side doors of the van, swinging them open as well, while Gary continues toward him.

The driver, Raul, makes his way around the front, papers for Gary in his hand.

"Hey, Raul," Gary waves to his friend as he arrives next to Brian.

"Hey, Gary," Raul responds across the white hood of the van.

Brian steps back, waiting for Raul to operate the chair lift. He turns to Gary, who extends his free hand.

"Hi, I'm Gary. I'm an orderly here at Agape Rehab. I'll be helping you guys get settled in," he informs Brian in a friendly tone.

"Hey, I'm Brian," Brian responds, taking his hand. "Just here to help Joe."

"Great," Gary replies with a smile.

They both turn to Joe, who is sitting at the edge of the door, absently waiting for the platform that is rising up to the van's floor level—Raul operating the controls.

"Hi," Gary offers, still with the big smile. "You must be Joe."

"Yeah," is all Joe offers back. He resents Gary's cheerfulness as much as the cold air on his face.

The platform now at his level, Joe rolls himself out onto it and pulls the brake levers over the wheels, locking the wheelchair in place.

Brian, true to his helpful nature, heads around to the back of the van to grab Joe's bags as the platform brings his buddy to the ground.

As the descending metal chair lift reaches the ground, Raul hands the transfer papers he holds to Gary and steps behind Joe to help roll his chair off the lift and onto the ground.

Resisting any offers of assistance, Joe releases the brakes and rolls himself off. He stops a few feet past Gary and resets the levers over the wheels.

"It's fucking cold," he complains, putting his hands between his legs in his lap.

"Yeah, winter has come," Gary acknowledges to Joe, maintaining his friendly and caring demeanor as he flips through the transfer papers.

Joe looks away, trapped in his resentment of this place and hating the loss of control he feels over the direction of his own life.

Brian arrives back at the group, sliding Joe's bags over his shoulders and positioning himself behind Joe's wheelchair.

"You guys can head inside while I finish up here, if you like," Gary offers, taking into consideration Joe's objections to the frigid temperature.

"Okay, sure," Brian agrees. "You ready?" he asks Joe.

Joe offers no response as he stares off into space at nothing.

Brian reaches down next to the catheter bag, releases the brakes, and starts pushing Joe up the walk.

"I got it," Joe snaps, grabbing the wheels.

"Okay," the faithful Brian patiently responds.

Although Brian had spent the initial twenty-four hours after Joe's accident tormenting himself over his blundering involvement in Joe's injury on the football field, he wasn't here for him now out of guilt. He had put that aside after his own tearful private moments with the unconscious Joe, after observing the blubbering Trace rush through the ICU waiting room and then walking a shattered Cindy to her car several minutes later.

He was here because of his own personal code about how he lived his life.

A long-time student of the teachings of Islam, Brian particularly strove to live out one of the hadiths, or sayings, of the prophet Muhammad.

The specific hadith he gravitated toward came from An-Nawawi's collection of the prophet's teachings, which refers to one's treatment of others. "None of you [truly] believes until he wishes for his brother what he wishes for himself," the English translation of the passage read; a sentiment similar to the Golden Rule that was so dear to the hearts of followers in many of the world's various religions.

Brian simply knew that, were he in Joe's shoes, he would hope that a true friend would be there for him—despite any resistance he might outwardly put up against the gesture.

So, in accordance with his faith, Brian steadfastly walks behind Joe toward the entrance to the center, carrying his bags over his shoulder and disregarding his sour mood. Joe was his brother and he would be there for him, just as he had been, as often as circumstances would allow, during Joe's time at the hospital.

Above the two the hawk, having perched itself atop the highest branch in the big tree in the circle drive, carefully peruses the scene as they disappear into the rehab center, while Gary wraps up the paperwork with Raul.

At the front desk inside the warm building, Joe finishes signing the last of the admitting documents. He shoves the clipboard holding the papers across the desk with a sigh and a sour face.

The friendly front desk clerk takes it from him and offers a bright smile in return.

"Welcome, to Agape," she says. "We're glad to have you here, Joe."

Joe just looks away.

"Thank you," Brian politely replies in Joe's stead.

"Alright," Gary begins as he rejoins them, "Let's get you settled into your room. If you'll just follow me," he adds, leading the way.

Joe reluctantly grabs his wheels and starts after him, Brian riding shotgun.

"You know, Agape has an interesting history," Gary announces. He then proceeds to elaborate on its main points, beginning with the tale of a mysterious basket that had been left one day on the building's front steps, which was then a ranch and home to the kind-hearted LeBlanc family.

The five-hundred-acre ranch, nestled into the mountains of Colorado, contained a number of buildings for lodging and had originally been a reservation for exotic and endangered animals that responded well to the climate. It had also been a fishing resort of sorts—a large lake bordered a big portion of the majestic property.

The surprising contents of the enigmatic basket on the doorstep, however, had sent the ranch in a new direction.

The strange gift had contained only two things: a note that simply read *"Agape Rehab,"* and a bond for one million dollars.

Chrissy and George LeBlanc, the property's gentle owners, were initially very confused. The ranch was in no financial trouble and the two were very happy providing for the animals who lived there and the tourists who came to visit and stay in the lodges.

However, the following day their newest cowboy, Johnny Thomas, had fallen from a bucking horse while breaking him in.

The fall had severed his spine, paralyzing him from the waist down.

While Johnny was recovering in the hospital, Chrissy had had a dream.

In the dream, she saw the ranch filled with injured patients being cared for by a friendly and compassionate staff. She saw herself standing on the front porch, greeting another soul arriving at the facility. She turned around to what was then just a large house and saw a hand-painted sign hanging over the front porch. *Agape Rehab*, it read in light blue text.

She had awoken the next morning inspired and, with tears streaming down her face, she shared the dream with her husband, George.

George immediately knew what to do with the funds from the basket and he rapidly went to work transforming the ranch into the Agape Rehab facility it was today.

Of course Joe heard none of this as they traveled through the center. He didn't notice the beauty of the great room, with its large windows looking out over the spacious property and adjoining lake. And he barely saw the other partially or fully paralyzed patients gathered in front of the room's massive stone fireplace, some playing checkers or chess, others laughing at a *Cheers* rerun on TV.

His mind had pretty much lost its ability to stay in the present moment. And without the hope of football to bring it back into focus—which he had used after the passing of James—he had begun to spend most of his time in silence, staring off into space while trying to process everything he had lost amid scattered thoughts that fought to help him find a way out of his current condition. This had slowly become his dominant state more and more.

During his time in the ICU he had resisted all attempts at real communication. When Sarah, desperately trying to reach him, had brought Pastor Roman in for a visit, he had immediately told him to "get the hell out" of his room.

He had even rejected Sarah a few days later, asking her to leave because he "needed some space."

And he had refused to let her accompany him today, intending to travel alone.

But the faithful Brian had showed up at the last minute, ignoring Joe's objections and jumping in the van.

The trio has reached an exterior door at the end of one of the hallways. Gary opens it and the cold air pulls Joe's attention back to the present—for the moment at least.

"You'll be staying in the lodge," Gary informs Joe, leading the way back out into the elements.

Outside the big house a long, paved walkway leads toward another sprawling building.

The exterior of this one looks somewhat like an old barn. Its metal siding is stained and streaked with rust here and there. Wooden doors and a big covered porch, with weathered slats and posts running the length of the L-shaped building, gives the place a rugged, rustic feel.

The three cross the walk and come up onto the porch with Brian starting to worry about Joe's arms tiring out and Gary seemingly oblivious, although he actually isn't.

Compassion was in abundance here at Agape, but sympathy, which reinforced the status of victimhood the patients often let themselves fall into, was something that wasn't offered by the staff here. However painful or cruel it initially seemed, the best therapy for the damaged souls had proven to be a helpful hand in assisting the patients to again realize their own strength and gain confidence to live new lives.

So Gary continues forward, never slowing his pace, until the three arrive at one of the doors along the porch. He swings it open and steps inside.

Joe follows Brian into a nice sitting area complete with a comfy-looking couch and chairs, a fireplace, and a small fridge on the opposite side of the room. A tiled floor leads to the back of the room, where closed, large, barn-size doors hang; a hallway leads off to the right.

"This is the sitting area," Gary comments as he leads them through it and turns down the hall.

The group enters a nice-size bedroom with separate setups for two occupants. Both sides of the room have a bed and chest of drawers. There are slatted floor-to-ceiling windows along two adjacent walls and another fireplace in one corner. Two high-backed, cushioned chairs sit in a small open area in front of the currently flameless fireplace. There is also an open door to an adjoining bathroom.

The nearest half of the room, with the bathroom door along its wall, appears occupied. A couple of books lie on their side on the dresser, and the nightstand is adorned with a statuette of a sitting Buddha wrapped with prayer beads and a burnt incense stick in a tray in front of it.

"Home sweet home," Gary announces with a wave. "That's your side of the room," he informs Joe, indicating the unoccupied area along the windows. "Your roommate's out right now," he continues. "So tell you what—why don't you go ahead and unpack and get settled in? I'll be back to check on you in a little while. Just hit that red button next to your bed if you need anything."

Joe rolls into the room without responding.

Again Brian covers for him.

"Thanks, Gary," he says, stepping toward Joe's side of the room and dropping a bag on the bed.

"My pleasure," Gary replies with a smile, turning and leaving the two alone.

Joe rolls over to a window that has open blinds. He parks in front of it and stares outside.

Brian drops the second bag on the floor and unzips it. He starts opening drawers and placing Joe's clothes inside.

"Stop," Joe tells him, over his shoulder.

"Not gonna happen, brother," Brian replies. "I told you already, you can refuse everyone else's help if you want to, but you're going to take mine."

Joe takes a frustrated breath, then finally offers a quiet "Thanks."

"You're welcome," Brian responds, pulling Joe's toiletry bag out of the duffel and disappearing into the bathroom.

Joe turns back to the window. Outside the glass, a good stone's throw from the building, is a large, picturesque body of water—an inlet from the massive lake.

The inlet's glassy surface reflects a lone, majestic tree standing next to a wooden dock that juts out into the water. Under the tree is an old, slightly-weathered red picnic table.

It's the kind of setting that recalls fishing with a grandfather as a child, or other adventures of youth. Simply put, it has an aesthetic ambiance that emanates safety and security.

Of course, this isn't Joe's current take on the beautiful image: the dock looks rickety and dangerous to him, and the water looks cold. The tree hasn't even registered in his view, much less the old picnic table or even the reeds that line the near side of the inlet and sway serenely in the breeze.

Joe's blank stare toward the window remains as Brian places the last item in place. It's something he got from Sarah when he went to check on her the day before and assure her that he would be here with Joe, despite how they both knew Joe would feel about it.

The item he places on top of the dresser is a small picture frame. In it is an image of a younger Joe and James in the stands at a football game. Both of them beam as Joe holds up an autographed football.

The unpacking complete, Brian steps over to Joe. He is about to say something when Joe's roommate rolls through the door behind him.

"Howdy," they both hear as they turn to face the door—Brian a little faster than Joe.

Into the room rolls Johnny Thomas, full of energy and wearing a warm smile and a cowboy hat. He has a relaxed air and a country drawl.

Johnny makes a beeline for Joe.

"Hi, I'm Johnny," he says, extending his hand. "You must be my new roommate, Joe."

"Yeah," Joe responds, absently going through the motions.

Johnny turns to Brian, reaching to shake his hand as well.

"Johnny Thomas," he says with a firm grip and a smile.

"Brian Taylor," Brian responds. "I'm Joe's brother," he adds, trying to add a little levity after Joe's listless reception of Johnny.

Johnny grins back.

"I can see the family resemblance," he plays along with a wink before turning back to Joe. "So what'cha in for?" he asks, getting right to the point.

Couth had never been Johnny's strong point. Not that he was rude by any account—he just wasn't one to beat around the bush. "Scares up too many critters hiding in that bush," was Johnny's thoughts on the matter.

Joe, of course, is a little caught off guard by Johnny's question, not to mention confused.

"What?" he replies.

"What's your injury?" Johnny clarifies.

"Uhm...uh..." Joe stammers, not really wanting to answer.

"What are *you* in for, Johnny?" Brian interjects, coming to the rescue once again.

"Ah, mine's a T-12 sever," Johnny responds, slapping his legs. "These don't have no more use than tits on a bull now." He grins at the two of them, continuing, "See, I was breakin' in this beautiful, spirited horse we called Big Red. On account of he was, well, big and red. Anywho, he threw me off and then stepped on my back. Not on purpose, mind you. It was just one of those things."

The boys are a little shocked by Johnny's casual retelling of the life-changing event—a little shocked, but despite themselves, or perhaps a little more accurately despite *Joe's* self, they were somehow also slightly more at ease.

The cowboy had a way of infusing his interactions with others with so much affinity that people just couldn't help but like him, although Joe was still trying not to, and trying hard.

Johnny turns to Joe.

"How 'bout you?" he tries again.

"I don't want to talk about it," Joe responds, still refusing to give in to Johnny's warmth.

"Totally understand," Johnny replies, spinning his wheelchair away from Joe and heading for one of the high-backed chairs in front of the fireplace. "I felt the same way myself," he admits, stopping next to the chair and flipping his brakes on.

In one motion Johnny slips up onto the arm of his wheelchair and then down into the chair next to it, as easily and naturally as Brian would have done it, despite his limited mobility or age—he is at least in his late forties by now.

"You and me are some of the lucky ones here, though," Johnny says to Joe. He glances at Brian. "No offense, 'walker'," he adds with a wink.

Joe pounces on Johnny's statement to him. "How the hell am I lucky?! What do you think you're saying to me? You don't even know me, man."

Johnny looks back to Joe.

"I'm sorry, brother," he says, sincerely realizing how the statement could be construed as offensive. "Didn't mean no harm."

Joe turns his sour eyes away from him, looking back through the window and outside.

Brian gives Johnny an apologetic look.

Johnny smiles softly at him in return. He's not offended. In fact, he totally understands Joe's bitterness and resentment, having been through it all himself when he was a younger man.

Joe sits in his wheelchair by the empty front desk. Brian stands across from him; night is falling through the windows behind his back.

Joe's mood isn't quite as sour now, at the end of the day.

After the little blow-up earlier, Johnny had rolled out the big barn doors of the sitting area and retrieved a lap full of wood. He arranged the logs in the fireplace and then started them burning by rapidly twisting a narrow stick against one of the smaller branches until it sparked. Brian had watched him, fascinated by the cowboy's resourcefulness.

As the fire burned, an ember had popped loudly in front of Johnny while he leaned over the grate.

He had nearly jumped out of his wheelchair before roaring with infectious laughter that caused Joe to join Brian in looking his way.

Johnny had then leaned back in his chair with a big grin across his face.

"You know what that reminds me of?" he asked the boys.

Brian shrugged in response—he had no idea.

"When I shot my older brother in the head with my pellet gun," the cowboy told them with a laugh.

He had then proceeded to recount the episode.

He, his brother, and a close pal had been playing with their new guns down by a creek, not far from the house his father was building for the family.

As Johnny had been looking out over the water, his brother, after checking to make sure that his chamber was empty, had pumped up his gun with air, placed it at the back of young Johnny's head, and pulled the trigger.

It was only a puff of empty air that parted Johnny's hair, but he had nearly soiled his britches, certain that he was "hit and a gonner for sure." His older brother and his friend had died laughing.

"But that ain't even the funny part, or the thing that scared me most," Johnny had informed the boys as Brian laughed and Joe fought to keep a grin from stretching across his face.

Biding his time, Johnny had quietly pumped up his own gun and waited for the perfect moment to strike his revenge. And when that moment came, he had slipped the barrel of his gun right up against the back of his unsuspecting brother's head and squeezed the trigger.

His eyes had just about come out of his sockets when he saw a pellet bounce off the back of his brother's skull.

Apparently Johnny hadn't been aware of the one crucial part of the joke—making sure the chamber was empty.

Johnny had screamed louder than his brother, "downright certain, I was about to be deader than a doornail this time."

The second his eyeballs had come back into his head, and before his brother could even check to make sure the pellet hadn't broken the skin, Johnny had dropped his gun and "tore ass," for the house and the protection of his dad.

His father, Len, and his lanky brother Roy were outside working on the structure. They had already put down their hammers and were looking toward the creek, having heard Johnny coming before they saw him.

"I'm sorry! I'm sorry! I'm sorry!" Johnny screamed as he topped the hill as fast as his little legs would carry him—continuing the mantra he had been yelling since he had dropped the gun, and would keep yelling until he reached the safety of the house.

It was the one and only time he had outrun his brother in his whole life. And he was sure his speed had saved him too—the terror-fueled adrenaline had helped him stay out of arm's reach of his charging older brother the full quarter mile from the creek to the house.

Johnny was darn near sweating from how hard he was laughing by the end of the story.

Brian was wiping tears from his eyes and holding his sides, and even Joe had lost the battle with his grin.

The cowboy had won again.

"Was your brother okay?" Joe had been unable to stop himself from asking when the laughter had finally subsided.

"Hell yeah! You'd have better luck cracking a green walnut than that coot's hard melon!" Johnny had responded, the laughter returning as Brian reached for his side once more.

"You got one damn funny roommate," Brian tells Joe, chuckling a little at the memory of the story.

"Yeah, I guess so," Joe agrees, one corner of his mouth crawling up his face into a half-grin.

Brian takes a peek at his phone.

"Well, I guess it's about that time, kid," he observes. "I'll see you later this week," he assures Joe.

"Hey, how you getting back?" Joe asks, the thought hitting him for the first time.

"Melissa's picking me up," Brian responds, referring to his wife. "I texted her while you were making love to the window," he quips.

Joe grins, shaking his head. Only a true friend knows how to bring you out of your gloom with the perfect insult at just the right moment.

Brian laughs.

"Alright, brother," Brian says between chuckles while reaching for Joe's hand and doing their shake.

"Alright," Joe responds.

"Anything I can do for ya before I hit it?" he questions.

"Wow, that's too much information about you and Mel, bro," Joe fires back, although not with the level of enthusiasm he and Brian traditionally displayed in their playful battles of juvenile wit.

"Hohoho," Brian laughs, glad to see that Joe is at least trying now. "And he's back, ladies and gentlemen."

"No seriously, though, B.," Joe says, squelching back his smile. "I do need one favor."

"Name it," Brian responds.

"Just keep everyone away for a while, alright?" Joe requests.

Despite the moment of levity, he still wasn't feeling equipped to confront even himself, much less anyone else—Brian excluded, of course, as Joe had no choice in that matter.

"You got it," Brian responds, totally understanding and actually agreeing with Joe's request. "Take care of yourself," he tells his friend, turning for the door.

Joe gives him a nod of his head, and watches him exit.

The door closes and Joe just sits there, still staring at it, the empty feeling slowly returning, with loneliness leading the way.

Behind Joe a janitor wearing gray slacks and a matching button-up shirt and cap swishes a wet mop back and forth across the floor.

He seems to be very focused on doing his job thoroughly; his eyes trace the floor, making sure he gets every square of the tile. He wears an old Walkman tape player and headphones that he quietly hums along to.

His mopping is bringing him closer and closer to Joe.

Joe doesn't see or hear him, though, that far-off look having returned to his eyes and his mind wandering once again.

Eventually the janitor ends up right next to Joe and clangs his mop against the large wheel on the side of his chair, in one of his swishes across the floor.

The bump pulls Joe out of his trance of despair. He looks in the janitor's direction but only makes eye contact with the flat bill of the guy's hat.

"Excuse me," the janitor says to Joe, still looking down at the ground as he stands there, holding the mop and waiting for Joe to move so that he can continue.

Joe shakes his head, breathes a frustrated breath, and rolls off toward his room.

The janitor slowly looks up in Joe's receding direction, revealing himself to actually be the curious man who was at the stadium for Joe's last two games—as well as somehow behind him while Joe fought for his life against the demon army on the red planet.

The man, returning to the bobbing of his head to the beat of his Walkman, goes back to his mopping.

The movements begin to make their way from his head down to his hips as he begins swaying with a little more feeling, a little more funk.

His head starts swimming back and forth to the beat as he gives up on the mopping altogether, the song taking him over.

He grabs the mop and spins around it as lyrics begin to ring from his throat.

"I been so dooooowwwn baby," he croons, the blues song pumping through his ears and now feeling so good in his bones, *"Eeeeeva' since that dark day!"*

His feet slide out to the right and then back as he grabs his mop-handle mic.

"I SAAAAAIIII-YA-I-YA-I-YA-IIIED I've beeeeen so dooooowwwn baby! EEEEEVVVAA' since that da-e-arkened day! There is NOTHIN' left for me but the bluuueees! BAAAAAAABBY, how blue can a man geee-ee-ye-ee-yeeeet…"

Chapter 14

Joe lies in his bed, in the heaviness of his dark room. Johnny is on the other side of the room, relaxing peacefully in his.

Joe rolls onto his side, frustrated that he's unable to get comfortable with the brace around his torso. He struggles with his legs under the sheet, still not used to the fact that they won't turn without assistance. It's maddening to him how even the simplest of things has become such a process of moving and adjusting to accomplish it. He used to dance across the football field with ease, displaying the strength, poise and grace of a *danseur noble* while commanding the orchestration of the organized chaos of a play with effortless precision, ten devoted behemoths under his exact command; but now even his mind felt crippled by a lack of control over the most minor processes he had always taken for granted.

With a frustrated breath, he reaches down and pulls his legs into place, fighting with the sheets to finish the task.

Finally in place, he lays his head back on the pillow. His eyes land on Johnny.

Even in the dark, Joe can still see him offer him his big smile from across the room.

"Night," Johnny says to him.

Joe exhales again and goes through the process of rolling onto his other side, dragging his legs behind his torso.

His back now to Johnny, he punches his pillow in frustration before plopping his head down onto it.

His eyes drift up the dresser in front of him and land on the picture of him and his dad at the game.

It's the first time he's noticed it in the room, having been staring out the window when Brian put it up there. He exhales once more.

"The first night's the toughest," Johnny offers in a soft voice. "It's a battle at first, but you will make it," he encourages. "Just keep breathin', brother."

Joe subtly shakes his head.

Jesus, doesn't this guy ever stop? he thinks.

After a moment his focus shifts back to the picture. He stares at it, his mind drifting back to the day it was taken.

James and the young Joe from the picture rushed for the edge of the stands of a football stadium, to the section where the tunnel leading to the locker room ran underneath it.

Sarah was bringing up the rear, a little more cautious than her charging boys.

It was the first pro football game that Joe had ever been to, and they had just finished watching his favorite quarterback throw three touchdowns to help his team defeat their division rivals.

Joe carried his own football in one hand, a silver marker in the other.

His determination to grab a place along the railing had one purpose—he *would* get an autograph from Troy Johnson.

Joe darted across a stairway, between rows of seats, and down another row by stepping on the arm of a chair and hopping over it. He continued speeding toward the edge and the tunnel.

"Be careful!" Sarah nervously called from a few rows above.

James jogged after him, grinning at his son's resoluteness to gain his football hero's mark.

Joe reached the pack of fans already hanging over the railing just as Troy was wrapping up his post-game interview with a television reporter at the edge of the field below them.

Joe saw him turn away from the reporter and toward the tunnel. He quickly dropped to his knees and crawled through the legs of the screaming fans.

Behind him James was laughing, Sarah worrying.

Joe realized he was through the crowd when the top of his head found the concrete wall at the edge of the stands. Luckily, a kind man heard the *thud* next to his legs and looked down.

"Are you alright, buddy?" he asked Joe over the noise around them as he bent down to him.

"Is he here?" was Joe's only reply, his eyes wide with anticipation.

"Who?" the man questioned.

"Mr. Johnson! Is Mr. Johnson here?" Joe asked as the man helped him to his feet.

The man gave the excited boy a big smile as he pointed over the railing to Joe's right.

Troy was there, alright. He was reaching up toward the fans who hung over the railing and signing the paraphernalia that they offered.

Joe's heart nearly jumped out of his chest.

The little guy dove against the railing so hard, with his arms extended and holding the ball and marker, that he probably would have flipped right over the edge had the man not had sons of his own who had primed his instincts to be ready for impulsive jumps. Children, he knew, sometimes tended to forget about the limits of bodies.

The man caught Joe's legs and held them down, keeping the lower half of his body on the safe side of the metal rail.

It was probably a good thing that Sarah still hadn't been able to locate Joe through the mass of the crowd, or she may have fainted on the spot.

And then there he was, Troy Johnson, smiling up at Joe; he gave the proper response to the elated "Mr. Johnsoooooon!" that was being directed at him from a young boy with a face lit up like a Christmas tree.

"Please sign my ball, sir," Joe requested as Troy reached up for it.

"My pleasure, buddy," Troy replied, taking the ball and the marker. "What position do you play?" Troy asked him as he wrote on the ball.

"I'm a quarterback, like you!" Joe answered. "But I don't know how to read defenses yet," he confessed.

"Well, that's alright," Troy said with a chuckle as he finished making the pigskin an instant family heirloom. "That will come," he assured Joe, handing the ball and marker back to him. "You just keep practicing. Show me how you hold that ball."

Joe slipped the marker in his pocket and held the ball up next to his chin, both hands on it in an upside down V, just like James had taught him.

"Very nice," Troy said, genuinely impressed.

"Thanks!" Joe beamed, "My dad taught me."

"Well you just keep listening to your dad then," Troy responded, with a smile. "Stay in school," he called as he turned toward the tunnel.

"I will!" Joe yelled after him.

Joe looked down at the ball in his hands as the crowd began to slowly dissipate, still excited over the encounter with the football icon.

#8, TROY JOHNSON, the silver handwriting read.

Finally Sarah caught sight of Joe, who was doing a perfect impression of Tigger—minus the tail—as he bounced up and down with the ball over his head.

"He signed it! He signed it!" Joe shouted as his parents made their final weaves through the crowd, arriving next to him at last.

"Wow! Let me see!" James exclaimed, excited for his son.

"Let's get a picture, let's get a picture," Sarah called, pulling her camera from her purse as James examined the autograph.

"That's awesome, buddy," James told Joe, handing the ball back to him and tousling his hair.

He slipped behind and Joe and the two faced Sarah.

"Okay," she said, focusing the camera on her boys, "On three. One, two, three..."

Joe stares up at the picture with a somber face; the excitement, joy, and carefree spirit of his youth have been dissuaded by the seemingly cruel realties of adulthood.

He closes his eyes tight, trying to block out the memory while he waits for sleep to take him on a momentary repieve from this place.

The blurry burnt-orange image slowly orients through the black bars of Joe's football helmet facemask. It's the defensive line of the Coyotes, standing ready in the dust-filled air of the red planet.

Joe steps toward the butt of the crouched-over Big Salt, licking his hands in his pre-snap routine—the roar of a stadium crowd in his ears as his mind tries to make sense of this place once again.

Joe glances into the stands at the boisterous fans. They wave signs that read MVP = JOE, JOELICIOUS, JOE IS GOD, as they jump up and down in the stands in worship of their idol on the field.

Joe turns his eyes back to the defense and the Coyotes' middle linebacker, whose face is turned to the side as he spits out directions to his team. His head slowly turns back to face Joe, red fire burning in his eyes.

Joe freezes in place as the linebacker's helmet splits open at two points. Ram-like horns grow up out of his head, and his face transforms into the hideous visage of one of his demonic tormentors.

Joe steps back from the line, panicking and instinctively reaching for a sword that isn't there.

He glances to his right, desperate for help, when his eyes catch sight of the faithful Brian calmly staring back at him.

Brian gives him a confident nod that says *You're the man*, as raucous laughter starts coming from above him.

Joe looks to the sky over Brian's shoulder—the jumbotron has appeared once more.

On the screen is the plastic blonde reporter; the back left side of her head is blown open.

Despite her injury she points at Joe, the demon army behind her. They laugh uproariously at him, right along with the newscaster.

Joe looks down at himself to find his useless legs hanging over the seat of his wheelchair. His football uniform has now been replaced by a flimsy hospital gown, and the catheter tube snakes from underneath it to a bag hanging from the side of the chair.

Joe quickly looks up. The Coyotes' transformed linebacker poses imminent danger in Joe's helpless state. But the demon is gone, as are his imposing comrades.

In their stead stands a younger Joe, dressed with the age and the clothes from the picture on Joe's dresser. He holds the autographed football in his hand.

Everything goes silent save the sound of Joe's own ragged breathing.

His younger self leans toward him; his eyes flash as they twinkle with light.

"It's time to wake up," he says, and fires the ball at Joe.

Joe's eyes pop open with a start to find the dark ceiling of his room above him. He is covered in beads of panicked sweat.

He glances over at Johnny, who is snoring.

He looks back to the ceiling, taking a couple of breaths to try and slow his racing heart.

He glances at the clock on his nightstand. 2:03 a.m. the glowing face mockingly stares back at him.

"Shit," Joe whispers to himself amid a forceful exhale.

He grabs the pillow from behind his head and buries his face in it, trying to escape the harrowing and confusing images from his dream as well as the reality of his waking nightmare.

Chapter 15

Sarah sits in an easy chair blankly staring into the empty space in front of her as steam slowly rises past her troubled face from the rim of her morning mug of coffee.

Pastor Roman is on the couch, cradling his own cup in his hands. His weathered Bible lies next to him.

Gone are the pretty red bows that had decorated the hand-carved wooden mantle above the old red-brick fireplace—the Christmas tree in the corner is long since taken down.

The wind quietly howls across the top of the chimney's chute; the cold of a January winter has replaced the cheer of December holidays in the Gilmore home.

"I just feel so unsure," Sarah explains to Pastor Roman, continuing their conversation.

It had been another fitful day and restless night for Sarah, as most had been since Joe had separated himself from her.

Her stomach felt continually knotted and her heart like it was in a vise. There was no doubt that it was due in part to Joe's physical condition, but what had begun to worry her more was the condition of his soul.

She had been unable to find peace or strength to understand his suffering on her own, and so, as she usually did in life's more trying times, she had placed a call to her pastor, requesting his guidance.

"When James passed, I...I never questioned God," she explains to her spiritual leader. "But now..." she adds before her voice trails off as her mind tries once again to find the words to make sense of her struggle.

"I understand," Pastor Roman replies caringly.

"Joe was looking for help," Sarah asserts, turning to the pastor, trying to convince herself as much as the man on her couch.

"I mean, in his own way he was...I could sense it, I saw it," she insists. "He was searching for answers. He was ready to...How can this be help?" she questions.

“Well,” Pastor Roman begins, before stopping himself, realizing that Sarah had more confusions she needed to voice.

“But now…” Sarah continues, looking into the dark liquid in her cup as she loses her train of thought once more.

“I mean, he was literally cursing God,” she tells the pastor. “And he’s completely separated himself from me.”

Pastor Roman’s brows furrow as the biblical passages regarding the consequences of such action, as well as the scriptural advice to mothers of such sons, begins pouring into his mind.

“I just don’t know what to do,” Sarah finishes, glancing up at the fireplace as the sound of a cold gust of wind pulls her eyes there.

Pastor Roman takes his time placing his cup on the worn coffee table in front of him.

He leans forward, elbows on his knees, hands clasped in front of him; his pensive face staring straight ahead.

He knows the teachings of the church thoroughly. He has spent years dissecting the Scriptures in search of God’s will. But he is unsure of how to share them with Sarah at this moment.

He reaches for his Bible beside him, turning to the safety of the Word. He opens it slowly, flipping the worn pages to Psalm twenty-seven.

“If I may?” he softly says to Sarah, before continuing.

"Please," Sarah responds.

His eyes fall on verse ten. "When my father and my mother forsake me, then will the Lord take me up," he reads.

He raises his head and looks searchingly at Sarah, who is thoroughly confused by the verse and its use in this context.

"I don't understand," she responds, "Are you telling me to forsake my son, pastor?" She is obviously not in agreement with that course of action.

Pastor Roman flips to another passage, in Matthew; chapter nineteen, verse twenty-nine.

"And everyone that hath forsaken houses, or brethren, or sisters, or father, or mother, or wife, or children, or lands, for my name's sake, shall receive an hundred fold, and shall inherit eternal life," he quotes.

"What's your point?" Sarah asks, her face starting to flush with the rising anger she is trying to squelch.

"You said it yourself, Sarah," he says, trying to balance kindness with firmness in his role as the leader of the flock he feels his Father has entrusted to him. "He is cursing God, Sarah," he continues. "The way is not always easy. Sometimes our family and friends can force us to choose between them and the Lord."

Sarah is dumbfounded.

She feels betrayed by the words of the man she has trusted for years; the man who comforted her through such incredible pain only a year ago. She had found strength through his teachings, a stronger connection to her faith that had carried her through. But now...now she just wants him and his interpretations of God's Word out of her house—only she is too afraid to tell this mouthpiece of the Almighty that he has to be wrong.

She closes her eyes, trying to focus, as Pastor Roman flips to yet another verse.

"I didn't want to bring this up," he tells her, stopping at the book of Mark, chapter three. "But are you aware of our Savior's words concerning blasphemy?" he asks.

"Yes," Sarah replies, a bit assertively. "Well...maybe not specifically," she nervously confesses.

Pastor Roman's eyes scroll down to verses twenty-eight and twenty-nine.

"Christ said," he begins, looking to the red-lettered text, "Verily I say unto you, All sins shall be forgiven unto the sons of men, and blasphemies wherewith soever they shall blaspheme: But he that shall blaspheme against the Holy Ghost hath never forgiveness, but is in danger of eternal damnation."

He slowly turns his head back to Sarah.

She quickly averts her eyes from his, allowing them to fall back on the fireplace. A tear runs down her cheek as her hands, cradling the stained coffee cup, begin to tremble.

Johnny sits in his wheelchair next to his freshly made bed. He has a cup of hot coffee in one hand, the *Tibetan Book of the Dead* open in the other.

He reads silently, part of his daily morning routine. "A little philosophy and a little coffee—no better way to start the day," he always happily informed anyone around the center who cared to listen, which was pretty much everyone.

The buzz of Joe's vibrating mobile phone on his nightstand grabs Johnny's focus; he glances over.

Joe, awake but yet to force himself to rise from his bed, picks up the phone and looks at the screen.

COACH, the illuminated face reads.

Joe silences the phone and places it back on the nightstand.

"Good morning, Johnny." The friendly voice of the slender, upbeat physical therapist T. J. Birdman calls from the doorway as he steps into the room.

"Morning, T. J." Johnny replies with a nod, a grin, and a tip of his ever-present cowboy hat.

T. J. passes by him, headed for Joe, as Johnny goes back to his book. He knows what's coming—from both sides of the coin.

"Hi, I'm T. J. Birdman," T. J. announces to Joe, arriving at the foot of his bed with a smile. "You must be Joe Gilmore."

Joe just turns his head toward the window and away from T. J.'s greeting, wanting to be left alone.

T. J. is unfazed by Joe's snub of a response; he's seen it many times before. "I'm here to stretch your legs," he informs the dejected patient.

"Not interested," Joe replies, still staring out the window.

"I can understand that, Joe," T. J. acknowledges, still maintaining his friendly tone. "But we need to stretch those muscles out or your legs are going to start stiffening up on you."

"When are you going to take this catheter out?" Joe asks.

"You were in the hospital for a while, buddy," T. J. reminds him. "First thing we have to focus on is rehabbing those muscles," he explains. "We'll stretch out your legs, and you'll have to spend some time sitting without that brace, help build those core muscles up again—"

"When are you going to take this catheter out?" Joe repeats, cutting him off and finally looking in his direction.

"Possibly in a couple of weeks we'll be far enough along to remove it and start retraining your bladder," T. J. informs him, holding onto his easygoing demeanor.

Mental strength was one of his many endowed traits; it made him a perfect physical therapist for Agape. And it had served him well in dealing with some of the more recalcitrant patients that ended up at the center.

"You'll have to keep one of those urinal jugs close, though," he calmly advises Joe. "It'll take some time."

"I want to piss like a normal person," Joe tells him.

"Then let's start stretching those muscles," T. J. replies with a gentle smile.

Joe just looks back to the window.

"No?" T. J. questions.

Still no response from Joe.

"Alright, Joe, I'll give you today." T. J. concedes for the moment only. Experience had taught him well that at times it took repeated, persistent attempts to win over a patient—and that that must be accomplished before any real progress could be made on the body.

T. J. turns and exits the room.

Johnny glances up from his book, giving him a wink as he passes, acknowledging a job well done.

The day of lying in bed having past, and the evening light now slowly fading, Joe sits in front of his window, staring out at the lake inlet.

His phone, still lying on the nightstand, buzzes, announcing another call.

Joe glances over at it.

MOM, it reads over a picture of Sarah laughing.

Joe stares at it until it stops buzzing, knowing he should pick it up, but not able to force himself to do it.

The phone silent once again, he turns his head back to the window.

Behind him Johnny comes rolling into the room, a bowl in his lap.

"Missed a good dinner," he announces.

"Wasn't hungry," Joe replies, his eyes still looking outside, his mind in a million other random places.

Johnny rolls over next to him.

"What'cha lookin' at, partner?" he asks, tipping up the front of his cowboy hat with his finger and peering out the window next to Joe.

A man sits in a folding chair at the edge of the lake, between the dock and the tree. He wears a fishing vest over a bulky coat, along with a winter hat; he swings his fishing pole forward, casting the line into the water.

"Well, that's interesting," Johnny says, reaching into his bowl and popping one of the chocolate-covered peanut butter balls it holds into his mouth.

Joe glances at him.

Johnny raises the bowl toward him. "Peanut butter ball?" he asks, his mouth full.

"I'll pass," Joe replies, turning away and starting to roll toward the sitting room.

"Suit yourself," Johnny responds, looking back out the window at the man. "They're amazin' though."

Joe sits in his wheelchair between the couch and chairs in the sitting room. The TV is on in front of him. Night having fallen, he watches the end of the Championship Bowl.

The Bears are already celebrating along their sideline. Victory over the opposing Wolves team is basically assured at this point.

The Bears lead the game thirty-two to ten as the clock counts down its final minute.

Joe clicks the TV off, having seen enough.

The dark of the room descends on him, matching the foul mood that stemmed from watching others enjoy the spoils he had spent a lifetime of preparation to have for himself.

He just sits in the darkness—his eyes going to that faraway place once again.

Chapter 16

Joe steadily rolls toward the tree-covered sitting area and padded chairs on the lawn in front of the rehab center's main building. Brian ambles beside him. The subtle warmth of the noon sun is above them.

"So how's it been going?" Brian asks.

"Tiring, confusing…don't really want to talk about it," Joe replies, arriving next to the chairs.

"Alright," Brian responds, getting his drift and taking a seat in one of the chairs.

Joe doesn't have any resentment toward his buddy, he just doesn't feel like rehashing the events of his first week adjusting to life at the center. After all—even if he didn't know how to totally shake it yet—he did know that he was getting a little tired of feeling sorry for himself.

He still hadn't accepted his life as it was or opened himself up to the continual outreach from Johnny, who treated him like a lifelong friend, but he had at least finally started working with the persistent T.J. on rehabbing his legs.

Lying in his bed all day and staring at the ceiling was something that the fighter inside of him could take for only so long.

"I told the team how you felt about visitors right now," Brian informs Joe. "They said they would respect that. But Big Salt said he's coming next week, whether you like it or not."

"Not yet," Joe insists quietly.

"You've seen the size of that guy, right?" Brian asks, his eyebrows arching up to match the corners of his mouth.

Joe cracks the smallest of grins.

Behind the guys, off to the side of the main building, stands the jovial man, last known to be moonlighting as a janitor. Today he wears a dark green jumpsuit and matching cap. He is intently at work raking the last of the fallen leaves from the trees into a pile.

The boys continue their conversation unaware.

"Have you heard from Cindy?" Brian questions, not having been able to reach her himself since the incident at the hospital.

"It's over," Joe admits remorsefully.

"I'm sorry, bro," Brian tells him.

"Aw, hell, man," Joe continues, "It's been over for a while...way before Trace anyway..."

Joe knew that he and Cindy definitely loved each other, but he was being honest with Brian. They hadn't ever really been *in* love, not from his point of view. It was more a relationship of convenience, really.

They had met at a party a few years ago. Cindy had just done a modeling campaign for a French makeup line and she was on the cover of a handful of top magazines. They related to each other. Both were celebrities on the outside, but neither obsessed with that position.

Cindy had come from a broken home and was really drawn to the comfort and stability of Joe's tight, supportive family.

Joe was originally attracted by Cindy's outer beauty, but it was her smile and kindness that really got to him.

In the end it was just...comfortable for them to be together.

"Have you checked on her?" Joe asks Brian, still concerned for her.

"I keep trying," his buddy answers. "I'll get her," he assures Joe.

The man has finished raking up his leaves into a monstrous-size pile behind the oblivious twosome. He casually walks away, carrying his rake as though he is proud of his accomplishment, and disappears behind the building.

"You know, you should talk to your mom," Brian tells Joe, putting on the role of big brother once again.

"Jeez, do you ever stop?" Joe asks, with a breathy chuckle, looking at Brian.

Brian just shakes his head no, smiling at him. He chuckles too.

Behind them, the man comes running from around the back of the building toward the big pile of leaves like he is being chased by a swarm of bees. When he comes within a couple of yards of the pile, he leaps into the air and belly flops onto it, disappearing into the mound.

The guys glance back in that direction at the sound of the crunching leaves. Seeing only the big pile, they shrug it off and turn back to face the field and the tall grass, which moves gently in the breeze.

Brian reaches over and squeezes Joe's shoulder.

"Just keep hanging in there, kid," Brian encourages his brother.

In the middle of the pile, the man rolls onto his back, spreading his arms and legs and moving them up and down, creating a "leaf angel" figure while grinning from ear to ear with the unbridled joy of a child.

Joe lies in his bed, breathing, as T. J. stretches out his legs.

Johnny sits in one of the easy chairs, coffee and book of inspiration in hand, while he happily—but very subtly—observes the progress being made.

T. J. places one hand on the back of Joe's right thigh and the other on the front of his shin and bends Joe's knee, continuing their session.

He leans his chest into the bottom of Joe's foot and folds the leg in farther, toward Joe's waist.

Joe strains in response; sweat beads on his forehead. It still hurts, but he's starting to get somewhat used to it.

The first time was the worst. He felt like his leg was literally tearing away from his hip.

It was really odd; he didn't necessarily feel the movement of his legs, the stretching of the muscles in them, but every once in a while he would feel the pain. It would come on all at once, like a lightning bolt from the bottom of his foot straight up through his spine, and then radiate through his head like a thousand needles pricking him all at once.

T. J. was still teaching him how to breathe through it.

"That's good," T. J. says to Joe, recognizing from the grimace on his face that this was one of those lightning bolt times. "Focus on your breath. In through the nose, focus on pulling the pain there. Good. Now, out through the mouth. Release it," he instructs.

Joe hits each step of the sequence right along with him.

In his second week of this treatment now, he was learning how to go with the flow and has been surprised how the process brought focus. It wasn't football by any stretch of the imagination, but it was something; something that at least pulled his scattered mind toward a single point. And if for no other reason, he enjoyed the process for at least that benefit.

"Alright, Joe," T. J. says, placing the more-limbered leg back down. "That's it for today, buddy. Nice work."

"Thanks, T. J.," Joe replies.

"Make sure you spend some more time without the brace this evening, okay?" T. J. reminds him.

"Yeah," Joe responds. "It's getting easier."

"Excellent!" T. J. exclaims, truly excited for Joe. "Alright, gentlemen," T. J. says to both of the guys; he gives a wave to Joe and a nod to Johnny as he walks toward the door. "My work here is done. I'll see you at dinner."

At Agape, the staff all ate with the patients and everyone ate at the same time—if it was at all logistically possible and as long as the patient was willing to join in. It was one of the many ways they helped to build a sense of family and support among both those giving and those receiving care.

"Alrighty, then," Johnny calls to the exiting T. J. over his shoulder, his nose still seemingly in his book.

Joe responds with a sort of goodbye half-wave.

With T. J. through the door, Joe drops his head back on the pillow. His hands come to his head, lightly fingering it as his eyes dance across the ceiling in thought.

After a minute or two, he reaches over and grabs his phone off the nightstand. He pulls up his Favorites page. His mom is listed at the top.

His thumb hovers over the phone as he debates whether or not to press the screen and connect himself with his mother. He nervously sucks his upper lip in and out of his teeth, the action making a squeaking sound at one point, as he mulls over the decision in his mind.

Johnny looks up in his direction.

"You alright, buddy?" he asks.

"Yeah," Joe responds, quickly tossing the phone down on the bed—as though he'd been caught holding a cookie that he had snuck before dinner.

"Okie dokie then," Johnny says, turning back to his book, a smile in his eyes.

"I'm gonna get cleaned up," Joe announces, sitting up and starting to slide toward his wheelchair at the side of his bed.

"Sounds good," Johnny replies. "Not much use in a muddy mule," he observes off-handedly, his eyes still on the pages.

"O-kay," Joe replies under his breath as he slides into his wheelchair, disconnects the catheter bag from the rail, and places it on the side of his chair.

Everything free and clear, he then rolls toward the bathroom, still not sure how he is supposed to respond to Johnny's joke, or if he was joking in the first place.

An image of a dirty mule slipping in the mud did make him smile though, on the inside at least.

Cindy, tightly wrapped in a thick, ankle-length coat, with a scarf around her neck, is braving the freezing elements.

She hurries from the front door of a two-story brown building, adjacent to Park Memorial Hospital, toward her white Mercedes S400 Hybrid sedan.

She hops into the warming interior, with its ash-gray leather and burnt-walnut wood trim, having remotely started the luxury vehicle on her way over.

She takes a deep breath and backs out of her space, exiting the parking lot in thought.

Although she had been worrying about Joe constantly since leaving him at the hospital, she kept telling herself that she had done the right thing. In her condition, she knew she definitely needed to focus more on herself and moving forward, but it was hard.

She felt very alone. She missed having Joe with her—even if it was often only physically, his mind off in other zones.

Her own father, a Wall Street tycoon, was too busy with his third wife and dismantling the new company he had just acquired to be any support to her, especially emotionally. She had never had much of a relationship with him anyway. And her mother was living in Europe again, with a new boyfriend, again.

She missed the stability of Joe, and especially of Sarah. But even without the infidelity, she, like Joe, had been unsure of their future together.

Regardless, she did feel like she should probably let him know what was happening with her. She just didn't know how, or if he would even want to know, with all he was dealing with.

Maybe it was a blessing she found out about Trace when she did. It was obvious, in her mind at least, that Joe didn't love her the way she was looking for. And the last thing she wanted was for him to stay with her out of guilt or because he felt sorry for her.

I just have to focus on me for now, she decides, pulling through the gates to her apartment's garage while trying to push all of her conflicting thoughts and worries out of her mind.

Joe comes rolling into his darkening room, the sun setting outside the windows. He flips on the light and heads toward his bed. Johnny is nowhere to be seen.

As he rounds the corner of the bed, he spots a couple of chocolate-covered peanut butter balls sitting in a bowl on the nightstand. Next to it is a handwritten note: *They're amazing – Johnny.*

Joe's face softens a little, the thoughtful and persistent cowboy continuing to weasel his way past the protective barriers Joe had set up as his tough exterior.

He picks up one of the balls, considers it, then pops the whole thing in his mouth.

It only takes a couple of chews for Joe's face to turn sour.

"Holy crap," he mumbles, grabbing the bowl and spitting the remains of the chocolate ball back into it. "Wow, that is sweet. How does he eat that crap?" he wonders out loud. "I gotta get some water." He continues the solitary conversation as he turns back to the hall and the cafeteria.

Chapter 17

Joe's eyes pop open to find his room flooded with sunlight.

"Mornin', sleeping beauty," Johnny calls from his post in one of the easy chairs in the room, the usual coffee and book in hand.

"Morning," Joe replies quickly, as he hurriedly begins making his way toward the side of the bed and his wheelchair.

"Where's the fire?" Johnny questions, with a grin.

"I gotta piss," Joe informs him, sliding down into his wheelchair.

"You just got that catheter out yesterday, bud. You might wanna hang on to the ol' nightstand toilet for a while," Johnny suggests, referring to the urinal bottle that T. J. had left on Joe's nightstand the previous day.

"I don't like peeing in something that close to my hand," Joe replies, wheeling around the edge of the bed.

His real reason was that he just wanted to do something that had some semblance of normality. And although it might seem minor, relieving himself in a toilet was significant to him, even if the only way he could do so now was while sitting down.

Johnny understood the implications, but he also knew that with most, a gradient approach to recovery seemed to work out best. However, he was certainly not one to interfere with someone who was reaching beyond their apparent present limitations.

"Well alrighty, then," he responds to Joe with a supportive smile—despite the fact that Joe had cut the corner around his bed a little too close in his rush to the bathroom, and was presently struggling to free himself.

A couple of yanks later, Joe is free of the bedspread and wheeling for the bathroom.

A lowered sink, a raised toilet, and an open-access shower with a metal-framed, plastic chair sitting in it adorn the sandy-colored, tile bathroom. Both the shower and the toilet have accompanying metal handrails along the wall, and an emergency call button hangs from a cord protruding from the wall beside the toilet.

Joe hurries into the room, flinging the door closed behind him. He rolls over to the toilet, flips the brakes on the wheelchair, and begins to try and maneuver himself off of it and onto the toilet.

Despite his athletic upper body strength, he can't quite figure out how to make the transfer.

Finally, in frustration, his bladder about to burst, he places one hand on the rail and one on the arm of his chair and tries to hop over.

He doesn't quite complete the full transfer of his lower body, so the bottom of his thigh ends up bouncing off the side of the toilet, causing him to crash to the floor.

"Shit!" he exclaims.

Johnny, having heard the fall from the bedroom, quickly places his coffee and his book on the small side table between the chairs, expertly slides into his waiting wheelchair, and then heads toward the bathroom.

"Hey, Joe, you alright?" he calls, arriving outside the bathroom door.

"Go away!" he hears Joe yell back to him.

On the floor, Joe is in a panic. There is a wet spot in the crotch of his boxer shorts.

The bathroom door cracks open, a concerned Johnny beginning to roll in.

"You need my help?" Johnny asks as he makes it partially into the room.

Joe frantically grabs one of the towels off of the rack above him and covers his wet shorts.

"I SAID STAY OUT! GET OUT!" he yells at Johnny.

Johnny quickly backs out of the doorway.

"Shoot," he says to himself in a hushed voice as he closes the door in front of him. "Sorry, man," he calls, his face a mixture of compassion and concern.

Joe is mumbling to himself, slumped on the hard floor. "I pissed myself, I fucking pissed myself."

"Hey, it's happened to all of us once or twice, partner," Johnny calls, trying to console his embarrassed roommate.

"GO AWAY!!" Joe's voice explodes through the door.

Johnny slowly backs away from the door. He is saddened by—but totally understands—Joe's embarrassment.

Joe angrily drags himself over to the shower. He reaches up and turns the handle and the water begins to rain down on the chair and the tile.

He pulls his shirt off over his head and tosses it to the side, fighting back tears of frustration.

He begins trying to pull off his wet underwear but can't get them down, the dead weight of his legs impeding the attempt and pinning his wet shorts against the floor.

He pulls at them harder as he begins to break down. Frantically, he makes one last effort, shoving at the stubborn shorts with as much might as he can muster in the compromised position.

Still unable to get the boxer shorts beyond his thighs, he collapses on the floor.

His body shakes as he sobs over all that he has lost: his career, his lifestyle, his status, independence, and mobility. Everything he worked so hard to create is gone, and the weight of that harsh reality is crushing.

As the last remnants of dignity wash from his face, he looks up at the yellow handle of the emergency pull cord.

Realizing he doesn't even have the strength to call for help, his gaze falls to the base of the toilet as he goes limp on the floor, giving in to the darkness of his mind.

"I can't do this," he mumbles, the fight running away from his empty eyes.

Johnny holds a small laundry basket in his lap. He places the last of the fresh clothes it had held into his dresser.

Behind him, the breakfast tray he had brought back to the room for Joe lies untouched on the nightstand next to Joe's bed.

Joe sits at his window, his back to Johnny, blankly staring off into the space outside.

There is a light knock at the open door.

Johnny looks over to see an anxious Sarah Gilmore standing there.

"Howdy, ma'am," Johnny says, placing the basket on the floor next to his dresser.

"Hi," Sarah nervously responds as Johnny rolls toward her, removing his cowboy hat and extending his hand with a smile.

"I'm Johnny Thomas."

"Sarah Gilmore," Sarah replies, shaking his hand and appreciating the warm embrace of his kind eyes.

Joe glances over his shoulder at the two before taking a deep breath and turning back to the window.

"Really nice to meet you," Johnny tells Sarah.

"Likewise," Sarah replies, returning the smile, albeit with less enthusiasm than Johnny.

They both turn to Joe, who still resists their presence.

"Well," Johnny offers, breaking the silence as he replaces his hat. "Why don't you come on in? I was just heading out," he lies, knowing the two need a moment alone.

"Thank you," Sarah says, in response to the invitation.

"Absolutely," Johnny replies as he rolls in reverse to the laundry basket. He picks it up and wheels past Sarah, tipping his hat to her as he exits.

With Johnny gone, Sarah takes another tentative step in Joe's direction. She stops at the foot of Johnny's bed, unsure exactly how to proceed, having shown up uninvited.

"I just...I wanted to see you," she begins, softly. "I know you said that you didn't want me to come, but..." her voice trails off.

Joe doesn't respond—his back still turned to her.

"I just..." Sarah tries again. "I just had to see you, check on you."

"Don't you understand?" Joe finally responds, dropping his head.

"Understand what, honey?" Sarah asks, her heart in her throat.

"I don't want you to see me like this," Joe quietly admits.

Sarah takes another step toward him, her heart breaking. She stops herself, fighting against the weight of her emotions. She takes a seat on the edge of his bed, only a few feet from him now. Her eyes travel from the back of his head down to her lap.

"When you were born," she slowly begins, "I swore to myself that I would never let anything happen to you." She pauses, taking a breath to hold back the pain that tries to squeeze out through her voice and eyes. "I think every parent makes that promise to themself," she continues. "An impossible promise that rips your heart out each time you break it..."

She stops again, wipes away a tear that has escaped her resistance and trickles down her cheek.

"I don't know how to help you, Joey," she admits. "But I do know this," she adds, looking up at him, "You're the strongest person I know. Don't let this break you."

Joe is touched, but doesn't really know how to respond—not that Sarah was necessarily looking for a response. He still can't bring himself to turn and face her, the embarrassment of this morning's event still too recent.

Sarah stands. She starts for the doorway, pauses in it before exiting.

"I'm here, Joey," she tells him, finding her strength once more. "Whenever you're ready, I'm always here."

And with that, Sarah exits.

Joe looks back out the window. A tear leaks over the edge of his lower eyelid and rolls down his troubled face. He just sits there, still not knowing how to move forward or what would really be the point.

Chapter 18

A thick, early morning fog hangs over the placid lake inlet.

The backs of two figures are barely visible in the white mist as they sit at the end of the dock—the one on the left quite a bit larger than the one on the right.

The laughter of a small boy drifts up the weathered planks toward the shore, followed by another with quite a bit more bass in it; the level of affinity in the laughter indicates a close bond between the two.

Joe sits on the dry land just at the edge of the dock, watching the dream unfold before him from his view in his wheelchair.

A soft breeze parts the fog a little, revealing the figures to be James and a younger Joe—back when each day was still filled with a lot more magic and light.

Young Joe casts a fishing line out into the fog. However, when he does, he whips it a little hard in the back swing, causing it to come right over his head. The hook snatches his ball cap and takes it with the fishing lure into the cold water.

James sort of holds his breath for a second, unsure of exactly how Joe will respond; it was one of his favorite caps, after all.

"Oh wow," the little guy offers after taking a moment to register what just happened. "That was aaawwe-some!" he exclaims.

"You have the most unique casting motion I've ever seen," James declares.

The two crack up again.

James reaches over and puts his arm around young Joe, pulling him close. Young Joe lays his head against James' shoulder. The two of them look out over the lake and the beauty of its surroundings, fully taking in the serenity.

Joe rolls a little closer to them, the warmth of their embrace pulling him in.

James turns his head and looks back at him, smiling.

"Such a beautiful moment," he tells him. "Don't miss it, son."

Joe is frozen at the edge of the dock by the clarity, compassion, and love in James' reassuring eyes.

He doesn't move, even as James turns his head back around and the images dissolve into the mist in front of him.

He just stares out at the empty dock, not sure what it all means.

He would normally be losing it, his father having just disappeared in his moment of need once more, but this time is different. He's not sure how or why, but it's different.

There was something so reassuring in his father's face, his voice. Something so certain.

He turns his gaze upward as the sound of the red-tailed hawk flying over him pulls his attention toward the sky, the sun cutting through as the fog quickly dissipates.

He looks back down at the end of the dock as the hawk flies out of sight.

His younger self is there once more, staring back at him.

The carefree boy's eyes flash as they twinkle with light, just before he winks at Joe and then does a backflip into the water, plunging through the surface with a big splash.

Joe slowly opens his eyes from the confusing yet somehow comforting dream.

Lying in his bed, he turns his head to his dresser and the picture of him and James, contemplating this latest encounter with his deceased father and his younger self.

Johnny is already awake on his side of the room and sitting up in his bed. He takes a sip of his coffee.

Joe looks over in his direction.

"You alright, cowboy?" Johnny questions, glancing his way.

"Yeah," Joe responds, looking away. "Just a dream," he adds, his eyes finding the clock on his nightstand next to Johnny.

It reads 5:10 a.m.

"This place is full of 'em," Johnny acknowledges with a grin.

T. J. pushes Joe, lost in thought, through a hallway in the center. He's taking him to one of the rehab rooms to work on showing Joe how to use his upper body strength to help him more easily make the transfer from his wheelchair into other chairs and onto toilets and such.

T. J.'s mobile phone buzzes as they pass an adjoining hallway. He stops a few paces past it, just outside a door with his nameplate on it, and checks his phone.

"Hey, Joe, it's my wife," T. J. informs him. "We're expecting our second little one so if you don't mind, I'm going to step into my office here and give her a quick call. Reception's not so good on my mobile..."

"Sure," Joe absently responds, still distracted by the thoughts swirling through his head.

"Thanks. I'll be right back," T. J. tells him, stepping into his office and closing the door.

Joe sits in the still hallway, alone.

A Jamaican woman comes wheeling around the corner and past Joe, mumbling to herself.

"From de top, to de bottom," she says, as she passes by him. "From de bottom, to de top."

She stops a few paces past him. Joe notices her for the first time.

She turns her dreadlocked head and her chair back to face Joe and slowly rolls alongside him again, this time a bit more face to face.

"From de top, to de bottom. From de bottom, to de top," she repeats her line with dancing eyes.

Joe looks at her cautiously, not sure what she's referring to or even what she's saying, exactly.

She laughs as her eyes grow wider and then flash as they twinkle with light, just like the younger version of himself in his recent dream—not to mention the nightmare on the red planet.

Despite Joe's resistance, it gets his attention.

"How did you do that?" he asks.

"'Ave you found de ansa'?" the Jamaican woman questions.

"Come on, how did you do that?" Joe insists.

"Soul magic," she informs him, her eyes sparkling again. "'Ave you found it, den?" she questions once more.

"Found what?" Joe replies, a little frustrated by the elusive question.

"De ansa' to de question you been ansa'rin' wid everyone else's ansa'," the Jamaican woman tells him.

Joe just stares at her. He has no idea what she is talking about and is beginning to wonder about her sanity.

She leans toward him, grinning. "You ree-ly don't know, do you?" she questions.

"Know what?!" Joe fires back, starting to lose his patience with this crazy patient.

"It's de same question dat everyone been askin' since foreva', mon," she continues, dramatically spreading her arms to indicate the expansiveness of it. "It's de question who's ansa' bring freeee-dom, and end all sufferin'," she adds.

"Well, isn't that helpful," Joe responds sarcastically.

She looks him directly in the eye, "De question is, *Who am I*?" she informs him. "And de ansa' can even be found in hell, mon," she finishes, laughing.

"You're crazy, aren't you?" Joe asks her. "The voices in your head tell you to say that?"

"No mon. It's de voices in *ya* head be talkin'." She laughs harder. "Sometime to rememba' who you are, you first 'ave to know who you are not," she proclaims.

Joe doesn't respond. He just stares at her, resenting her "magic" and laughter.

Her chortling subsides. She looks at him compassionately. "Don't worry, mon," she assures him. "Dat's what you here to find out."

Joe looks away, shaking his head and wishing he could escape this conversation.

"Sorry about that," T. J. calls, stepping out of his office and turning to pull the door closed in front of Joe, along the wall opposite the Jamaican woman. "False alarm," he adds with a smile.

Joe looks away from him and turns back to the Jamaican woman—who is no longer there.

Joe spins around, looking down the hallway behind him, but no one is there either. He pushes his wheels forward to the adjoining hallway they had passed. He looks both ways only to find it empty as well.

"You lose something?" T. J. asks from behind him.

"Only my mind," Joe responds, totally confused.

Joe and Johnny sit in their wheelchairs at a long wooden table, under the exposed wood-slat roof of Agape Rehab's dining hall. Other patients and staff are scattered around them, both at their table and at others in the room.

The rustic mess hall has large windows along the walls, which share the serene view of the lake and the mountains that surround it with the diners. Cherry red, round wooden posts support the roof over the painted concrete floor. A large stone fireplace roars in one corner, warming those convening for dinner.

Chef Robert Speir happily prepares dessert for everyone, in an open kitchen behind a half-wall built from fallen tree limbs.

Joe pauses from picking at his dinner for a moment.

"Hey, Johnny," he says, looking across the table at his roommate. "Does this place have a mental ward?" he asks.

"Nothin' like that around here," Johnny replies with a chuckle. "Why do you ask?"

"Just wondering," Joe replies, going back to his food.

Johnny takes the last bite of his delicious brisket and pushes his plate away. He looks over at Joe.

"Hey," he says, "You know what Robert is making for dessert tonight?"

"No," Joe replies.

"Chocolate-covered peanut butter balls," Johnny says, rubbing his hands together in anticipation, a big smile spread across his face.

Joe chuckles, shaking his head as he looks back down to his plate, forking another bite of the smoked brisket.

The barn-type doors are open to the sitting room by Joe and Johnny's bedroom.

Johnny sits on the deck outside the screen doors that had been covered by the usually closed barn doors. He looks out across the lake inlet at the setting sun.

Joe grabs his thick coat and rolls out onto the deck. Johnny wears only a flannel shirt to shield him from the cold.

Joe parks his wheelchair next to Johnny's and looks toward the water as well.

"Beautiful, ain't she?" Johnny says.

Joe looks at the glassy surface, the reeds swaying in the breeze. He takes it in for the first time, really, despite having spent so many of his days sitting in front of his window in the bedroom.

"Hey, Joe," Johnny continues, since Joe's actions seem to be his answer. "That picture on your dresser. Is that of you and your pop?" he asks.

Joe hesitates, not sure he wants to answer. Finally, he does.

"Yeah," he responds softly.

"Looks like you two have a pretty special relationship," Johnny observes.

Again Joe pauses before he responds.

"We did," he replies, the cowboy's genuineness somehow making him feel safe enough to continue. "He died a little over a year ago," he adds, surprised himself that he is revealing this to Johnny.

"Aw, hell, man," Johnny responds compassionately. "I'm sorry, brother."

"Me too," Joe admits. His eyes find the dock stretching out into the water as he continues. "I got that football autographed by Troy Johnson at the first game my dad ever took me to," he informs Johnny. "Knew right then and there what I was going to do."

He looks over at the peaceful tree and the table.

"Sure was pissed when I lost that ball," he adds.

"I bet," Johnny acknowledges, understanding the significance of the memories tied to the football.

The two just sit there for a moment in the silence of the cold night air.

"Hey, Johnny," Joe says, breaking the quiet. "Since we're getting all personal and everything..." he grins sheepishly.

"Shoot," Johnny replies, smiling at him. "This cowboy is as open as the ponderosa."

"Not sure what that means," Joe chuckles. "Anyway, you ever...you have weird dreams or see strange things around here?" Joe asks.

"As much as I can," Johnny responds, his smile growing. "One of the lucky breaks of slowing down," he adds.

"What the hell does that mean?" Joe questions, a little frustrated at having opened up some to Johnny and now feeling like he was just being toyed with. "And why does everyone around here speak in freaking riddles?" he adds.

"Oh, it's not a riddle, partner," Johnny assures him. "I'll tell you what I mean. You see, the way I see it," he begins, "life as it usually is for most folks is just too busy. Every day is filled with so many distractions that we just miss it."

"Miss what?" Joe questions, still not completely following.

"Life," Johnny responds, leaning back in his chair and tipping his hat up a little. "Everybody is so busy doin' this and tryin' to get that so they can be happy, but hardly anybody is. For me, being in this chair limited my options so much that I had a lot of time to just sit and observe life. And you know what I found out?" he asks, turning to Joe.

Joe shrugs—no idea.

"That I had lived most of my life without livin', almost like sleepwalkin'," Johnny explains. "I'd been tryin' to be what I thought everyone else wanted me to for so long that when I finally stopped and just looked in the mirror I said, 'Who is that cowboy lookin' back at me in there?' I don't know if that makes any sense or not," he admits, "but it's how I figured it in my cluttered ol' mind, anyway."

"Makes more sense than anything I've heard in a while" Joe admits quietly, fully understanding the cowboy's previous plight.

"Good," Johnny responds with a smile. "I tell you what, you take a step back and really observe and listen to life." He pauses for effect, leaning toward Joe and grinning. "You just might be able to find out some of her secrets."

"Well, why don't you just tell me?" Joe asks with a chuckle.

"I would if I could, partner," Johnny responds, leaning back in his chair again. "But then you'd just know my version," he adds. "Truth be told, it ain't the hearin' of it that changes a person—you have to experience it for yourself."

Joe takes a frustrated breath.

"Don't worry, cowboy," Johnny acknowledges Joe's understandable frustration. "You'll have your moment when you find grace," he assures him. "And then *wham*, it'll be like you're wakin' up for the very first time."

Joe looks down at the deck, the conversation with Johnny having brought even more questions into his mind.

But he did have to admit that, although he didn't fully understand the whole of what the cowboy was talking about, the chat had definitely made an impression on him.

"Well heck," Johnny says, interrupting Joe's thoughts. "It's colder than a witch's titty out here," he announces, shuddering. "Let's go back inside."

Joe backs out of the way, turning toward the doors as he chuckles at his odd but affable roommate.

Johnny winks at him with a grin as he passes by, leading the way back inside.

Chapter 19

HERE LIES DETECTIVE JAMES GILMORE

DEDICATED SERVANT,

TRUSTED HUSBAND, FATHER

AND FRIEND

Sarah kneels before her husband's cold gray headstone.

She carefully places the flowers she holds into the concrete vase attached to the base of the stone before sitting back on her heels and shoving her hands deep into the pockets of her long, wool-lined coat.

Her breath fogs in the cold air in front of her mouth as she stares at the headstone, not sure how to begin.

After James' burial, she had initially come to visit him nearly every week. But as the weeks turned into months and she began to find the strength to carry on, those visits became more and more only on special family dates, which were the most difficult to get through without him.

Her last visit had been at Christmas, when she sobbed to the memory of her husband the details of the fight she and Joe had had and his subsequent injury; all as Joe laid in a coma in the ICU.

And now here she was once more, looking for strength at the resting place of the man who was her rock for the better part of her life.

"He needs you so much, James," she tells her deceased partner, finally finding the words. "Sometimes I feel like he's still a little boy."

She looks down at her lap, continuing softly, "I need you."

A tear rolls down her cheek. She quickly removes her gloved hand from her pocket and wipes the liquid away in the frigid air.

She looks back up toward the gravestone. "I used to feel so strong with you to lean on, but now, now I just feel torn, pulled in so many directions..." she admits.

She just sits there for a moment, her tears having dried up; her grief has been replaced by the numb confusion caused by her pastor's instructions, her conflicting instincts, and her son's distance.

She sniffs, her nose beginning to run in the freezing temperature of the winter day.

Sarah rises and steps next to the headstone, not sure what else to say and feeling even more alone all of the sudden.

"I love you," she softly tells the memory of her husband as she leans against the headstone. "I miss you," she adds quietly.

She pulls her hand from her pocket again, kisses her fingers, then touches them tenderly to the headstone before turning and heading back toward her car.

Brian sits in a little hometown diner across from the stunning and vibrant Raquel de los Rios—Rachel to her friends.

Brian is pulling cash from his wallet; the two have just finished a satisfying but greasy home-style dinner.

"So what do you think, Rachel?" Brian asks, putting his wallet back in his pocket.

"For my brother, of course," she replies with a strong Spanish accent.

Brian and Rachel had met in college and she, like so many others, had just immediately felt safe with Brian. Like someone would with an attentive and caring big brother.

Most men couldn't get past how physically attractive she was—in a very natural way. But Brian saw the true Rachel. He knew that when she walked into a room, everyone actually was drawn to her because of her inner joy and love of people. These qualities just happened to be covered by an exterior beauty as well. Even as a child, Rachel had a way of just lighting up a room.

She had appreciated that Brian didn't treat her like an object, as most men did. She respected his kind heart, and he hers. The two had become very close friends.

"That's great." Brian smiles, happy to have her agreement. "I really appreciate it," he tells her as the waitress, Toni Diane, walks up.

"That all for you, sweetheart?" she asks Brian.

"Yes ma'am," Brian replies, handing her the check and the cash.

"Be right back with your change, then," Toni tells him, taking the check and turning from the table.

"Come on, Toni," Brian calls. "You know better than that. Keep the change."

Toni stops, turning back to him. "Hey, a girl can't just assume these things. But that's why I love ya." She winks at him before adding, "Nice to meet you, Raquel."

"It was a pleasure to meet you as well," Rachel replies with a smile.

"What a wonderful place," Rachel continues to Brian. "The hospitality reminds me of my childhood," she adds, referring to the shops in Spain she grew up frequenting, and the care and appreciation the shop owners all commonly showed for their customers. There was an overall sense of community to it—an art unfortunately sometimes lost in many parts of the modern, big cities of the world.

"Yeah," Brian responds. "One of the reasons we love this place. Melissa and I eat here all the time."

"How is she?" Rachel asks.

"Fantastic," Brian tells her, his face lighting up. "She's at home with the boys."

"I bet they are growing like a, a...what is it you say?" Rachel asks, her English very good for the most part but still sometimes a bit broken or searching, despite her intelligence.

"A weed?" Brian asks.

"Yes!" Rachel replies, laughing. "A weed!"

"Well, yes, they are," Brian assures her, laughing as well. "Speaking of which," he adds, checking his watch as the laughter dies down, "I best be getting back to say good night, before they're asleep."

"Oh, yes," Rachel tells him, rising. "You must do that."

Brian stands as well.

The two of them take their coats off the back of their seats and slip them on as they head for the door.

"Hey, I almost forgot to ask," Brian says as they walk. "What's the latest with Thomas?"

"Ugh," Rachel responds with a grin. "I'm beginning to think it's impossible to find a guy who is real enough to be honest," she tells him.

"Yeah, I know what you mean," Brian replies with an exaggerated feminine flare.

Rachel playfully slaps him on the arm.

"Why can't there be more like you, B.?" she asks, really loving this guy.

"I think that's why Melissa snatched me up so quick," Brian jokingly responds with a smile and a laugh.

Rachel laughs too. "Be sure to give my love to her," she tells Brian as the two of them exit through the door.

The powerful beams of the light banks penetrate through the red dust in the air, to illuminate the white lines of the football field on the red planet.

Joe and his team break their huddle. Crimson dust rises from his feet as he steps toward the line of scrimmage.

Opposite his offensive line, on defense, is the demon army. The news reporter, wearing a Coyotes jersey and her ever-present slick, plastic smile fills the defensive middle linebacker position.

Joe licks his hands and looks down the line to his left. He sees the fans screaming in the stands beyond his teammates. They wave their usual signs: MVP JOE, MY TEAM - RATTLERS, EVERYONE'S QB – JOE GILMORE, and JOE IS GOD.

Joe eases in behind Big Salt, glancing down the line to his right at Brian.

Brian gives him the slow nod that says, "You're the man."

Beyond Brian one person stands in the stadium seats, alone.

It's James Gilmore in his ancient white robe. He raises a cardboard sign. It reads BREATHE IN THE MOMENT SON.

Joe shifts his gaze back to where the defense was; as the dust clears it reveals, this time, only the curious, jovial man. He wears Joe's jersey instead of a Coyotes one.

The man grins. He leans in toward Joe.

"It's time to wake up," he says as his eyes flash, twinkling with light.

Joe wakes up in his bed. He looks around.

"Mornin'," Johnny calls, sitting in his wheelchair next to his own bed.

"Morning," Joe responds, looking toward his nightstand and his clock.

Its face reads 5:02 a.m.

"Don't you ever sleep?" Joe asks jokingly as he rolls toward his wheelchair.

"It's a dirty habit I'm trying to break," Johnny responds. "This darn body keeps objecting, though," he adds with a smile.

Joe glances at the plastic urinal jug on his nightstand, pauses, and then slides into his chair.

"You sure you don't want the jug?" Johnny questions.

"Gotta wean off that thing sometime," Joe tells him as he starts for the bathroom.

"It's a worthy quest," Johnny acknowledges as Joe rolls past him.

Joe rolls into the bathroom, closing the door behind him.

Johnny waits, his ears trained in that direction.

Silence...

And then finally the sound of the toilet flushing.

"Yeehaw," Johnny says quietly to himself. "Finally broke that buck."

A moment later the shower turns on.

The last of the incense stick on Johnny's nightstand emits a small, steady stream of calming white smoke.

Johnny sits on his bed, his eyes closed. His hands are clasped together in his lap. The Buddhist prayer beads that usually adorn the figurine on his nightstand are wrapped in a figure eight around the middle finger of each of his hands.

Johnny bows his head forward and then sits up, opening his eyes, now finished with his meditation.

He removes the beads and places them back around the Buddha statuette as Joe rolls out of the bathroom from his shower.

Joe glances at Johnny as he rolls to his side of the room.

"Hey, Johnny, what's the deal with your statue?" he asks, having been curious about it for a while now, but having no clue as to its significance.

"You mean the Buddha?" Johnny responds.

"Yeah, if that's who that is," Joe answers, taking out a long-sleeve shirt from one of the drawers in his dresser and pulling it over the fresh T-shirt he's already wearing.

"Ah, he was just this guy that was able to find some answers to handlin' all the sufferin' in life," Johnny responds. "He said we all have the truth within' us," he adds. "Made it his life's purpose to help people realize that. I just keep him there to remind me to try and do the same."

"Hmm," Joe responds thoughtfully, never having met a Buddhist before, especially a cowboy one.

Something outside the open blinds of the window catches Joe's eyes. He turns his head in that direction.

The red-tailed hawk dives down toward the water of the lake inlet. It spreads its wings just above the wet surface and glides across the top of it.

Johnny sees it too from his position across the room.

"You know, the Native Americans said that the hawk was a messenger," he informs Joe. "He flies up to the Great Spirit, Wakan Tanka in the tongue of the Lakota, and brings the message down to us Earth Walkers on the Good Red Road."

Joe turns his head back to him. "You're weird, Johnny," he says with a grin, surprised but not entirely shocked by the cowboy's insight into yet another area of life.

Johnny smiles back.

"Aw, it's just a reminder to be aware, look at things from a larger perspective, see the magic of life and all," he replies with a chuckle, sliding into his wheelchair.

"Truth reflects everywhere, partner," he continues. "Try to keep my eye on as much of it as I can."

"Hmm," is Joe's response again as he turns back to the hawk.

"Well," Johnny calls, "I'm gonna head down to the TV room. You wanna come?"

"Lots of truth down there?" Joe asks, still looking out the window.

"Not usually," Johnny replies with a smile.

Joe turns his head to him, smiling back.

Johnny has grown on him despite Joe's initial, stubborn resistance.

"I think I'll pass," Joe tells him.

"Suit yourself," Johnny replies, grabbing his cowboy hat from the bedpost and plopping it on his head before exiting the room with a tip of it in Joe's direction.

Joe turns back to the scenery outside. He takes a deep breath.

His eyes follow the hawk as it circles back over the pond again. He just sits there for a few minutes, relaxing, as his eyes become heavy.

"Keee-aaaah," the hawk's shrill cry breaks the silence.

Joe's eyes pop open. Much to his surprise, he finds himself now sitting next to the picnic table, the hawk skimming across the surface of the water in front of him.

The curious man stands next to the water. He wears a fishing vest over his bulging coat and a fishing hat on his head.

Joe watches him in silence, still a little shaken from finding himself in this new location.

The man's fishing rod clicks as he reels in his line. Once he has it all the way in, he leans the pole up against his folding chair and picks up a half-eaten sandwich lying on the seat. He takes a bite and looks back out at the water as the hawk arches back up into the sky.

Joe looks him over; something about him seems familiar, but he can't quite place him—the recent dream not presently in his mind.

"You catch anything?" Joe asks, trying to get him to look in his direction.

The man turns to him, smiling and holding up his sandwich.

"So far only the PB and J," the man admits. "I was just waiting for a friend anyway," he adds.

Joe nods politely, certain he knows this guy but still not sure from where.

"You fish?" the man asks.

"Not since I was a kid," Joe responds.

His curiosity finally gets to him.

"Hey, do I know you from somewhere?" he asks.

"Sometimes," the man responds.

"Sometimes? What's that supposed to mean?" Joe asks, not appreciating what he figures is a joke.

"Sometimes you are aware of me and sometimes you're not," the man replies matter-of-factly as he reaches inside his bulging vest and pulls out a small football.

"Hey, you want to play catch?" he questions with a big smile.

"Is everyone around here crazy?!" Joe demands.

The man shrugs as he pulls off his fishing vest and then his coat, revealing Joe's Rattlers football jersey over his frame.

"Aw shit," Joe frustratedly sighs. "You're not some obsessed fan or something are you?" he demands.

"I'm the biggest fan you've ever had," the man informs him, grinning from ear to ear while pulling off his hat and tossing it onto the chair.

A competitive fire fills his eyes as the smile slides from his lips. He steps forward, moving the ball from hand to hand as he licks his fingers, emulating Joe's pre-snap football routine with precision.

"Buffalo nineteen!" he shouts, crouching down behind the imaginary line. "Buffalo nineteen! Set, hut!"

He sprints back from an imaginary line, plants his feet, and fires the small football to Joe.

Joe catches the ball in front of his face out of self-defense. He brings it down toward his lap.

He's about to tell this crazy person off when his eyes catch the silver writing on the weathered ball.

He looks down at the oblong pigskin, rotating it in his hands.

It reads *#8, TROY JOHNSON.*

Joe's body is immediately covered with goose bumps.

"Where did you get this?" Joe questions, still staring at the youth football.

"Where you left it," the man replies, pulling Joe's jersey over his head and tossing it onto the chair.

"This is my ball," Joe informs him, looking in his direction accusingly.

"I know," the man responds, now kicking off his boots and unbuckling his pants.

"What the hell are you doing?" Joe questions, the man's actions distracting him from the mysterious return of his football for a moment.

"I'm going for a swim," the man tells him as he pulls down his pants, leaving him buck naked in front of Joe.

"Jesus, man!" Joe exclaims. "You can't just take off all your clothes."

"Why not?" the man questions innocently.

"Because..." Joe stammers. "Because you just can't."

"That's not a good reason," the man informs him.

He grins at Joe and then turns and runs into the freezing water.

"Oooohhh, that's cold!" the man exclaims, once again grinning from ear to ear as he bounces up and down in the chest-deep water.

Joe watches in shock for a moment before his mind returns to the treasure that rests in his hands.

He looks back down at the ball.

Knock. Knock. Knock.

Joe opens his eyes, surprised to find himself sitting in front of the window in his room and empty-handed once again.

He turns toward the sound to find T. J. standing in the doorway of his room, holding a small football.

"Someone left this at the front desk for you," T. J. tells him before tossing him the ball.

Joe catches it, quickly turning it over in his hands.

And there it is: *#8, TROY JOHNSON*.

Joe's body feels the chill of remembrance once more. He quickly looks out toward the lake. No one is there. He looks back to T. J.

"Who left this?" he questions.

"I don't know, there was just a note that said it was for you, from a friend," T. J. answers. "You want me to get rid of it?" he asks.

"No," Joe answers, looking back down at the ball.

"You alright?" T. J. asks him.

"Yeah," Joe answers, absently.

"You sure?" T. J. questions again.

"Yeah, I'm sure," Joe replies, looking back at him and forcing a smile.

"Okay," T. J. says. "I'll see you at dinner, then?"

"Yeah. Yeah, sure." Joe answers.

"Alright," T. J. replies as he exits the room.

Joe turns and looks at the picture of him and his dad on his dresser, then back down at the ball.

For a moment, he considers the most recent of the odd events that seem to have become his life, before rolling over next to his bed, bending down, and placing the football under it. He sits back up as Johnny rolls into the room.

"I think I'm going crazy," Joe informs Johnny.

"Good," Johnny responds brightly.

Chapter 20

Joe sits outside the front of the rehab center in the afternoon of a slightly warmer day, a harbinger of the coming spring.

A few other patients are scattered about, also enjoying the break in the weather.

Joe has his mobile phone pressed to his ear.

"Well I just...I just wanted to call," he says into the device.

Sarah sits at her dining room table wearing an apron, a steaming pot on the stove behind her. The phone cord stretches from the wall to the receiver against her ear.

"Well, I'm glad to hear your voice," Sarah responds, her face very lit up while she tries to play it a bit conservative.

"Yeah," Joe responds, looking down at his lap. "Yeah, yours too," he admits, a bit surprised at the comfort it brings him.

There's a moment or two of silence in which Sarah's mouth opens a number of times, but she manages to hold her words back, trying to wait for Joe to lead the call.

Finally he speaks again.

"So how are you, Mom? You doing okay?" he asks.

"Yes, Joey, I'm fine," Sarah responds with a smile in her voice, her heart touched. Her son is thinking of her well-being, even with what he is going through. That's pretty special to her.

"Good. Good," Joe replies, nodding his head as he looks around the grounds of the center.

A gardener is planting some early flowers around the tree in the center of the circular drive.

"So," Joe begins, looking away from the worker, his attention still on the call. But then he whips his head back to the gardener, realizing it's the man from the lake.

"Yes?" Sarah questions from the other end of the line.

"Hey!" Joe calls to the man.

"Yes?" Sarah's voice comes through the phone again.

"Oh, sorry Mom, not you," Joe tells her. "Hey, listen," he quickly adds, "Can I call you back?"

Sarah is a little disappointed and confused, but she does a good job covering it.

"Of course, that's fine," she replies with a wave of her hand to reassure him, as though he was there in the room with her. "Thanks for the call, sweetheart."

Sarah starts to hang up the phone, but then quickly brings it back to her ear, trying to catch him.

"Joey, can I come visit you?" she asks, hoping he's still there. But the dial tone is the only response she gets.

Sarah rises, straightening her apron as she hangs the phone back on the wall.

"That's okay," she audibly tells herself with a smile, her heart feeling a bit lighter as she returns to her hot stove. "At least he called. It's a start."

Joe wheels across the paved driveway toward the man who, wearing his green jumpsuit and hat again, works over his spade in the ground.

"Hey," Joe calls again, as he crosses to him.

The man looks up at Joe.

"Heeeey," he offers a big smile to Joe.

"What are you doing?" Joe questions.

"Planting flowers," the man responds as though confused by the question with a seemingly obvious answer.

"No, what are you doing?" Joe demands. "Why are you messing with me?"

"I didn't know I was," the man tells him honestly.

"Come on," Joe insists. "You know what you're doing. You can't keep stalking me like this, I'll call the cops."

The man starts chuckling. He looks up at Joe, emulating the face of Heath Ledger as the Joker.

"Why, so, serious?" he asks Joe as his eyes flash, twinkling with light.

Again, this grabs Joe's attention and momentarily distracts him from his intention to be rid of the odd character.

"Who are you?" Joe asks.

"Just a friend," the man replies in an offhanded way.

"Well I got enough friends," Joe informs him, his original intent returning. "So beat it," he orders the man.

"As you wish," the man calmly responds.

And then he vanishes into thin air, the spade and plant he had in his hands dropping to the ground.

Joe stares at the spot for a moment, trying to figure out what in the hell just happened.

He spins his chair around, scanning the rest of the grounds, but only his fellow patients are there—the man is nowhere to be seen.

"What the hell is going on around here?!" he shouts to no one in particular.

The patients all look at him.

"It's okay," Joe quickly recovers, raising his hand to reassure them. "I was on the phone, just...it was a call...all good, all good."

The patients find his behavior a bit odd, but lots of odd things seem almost normal at Agape, so they just go back to their own business.

Joe slowly backs his chair to the edge of the porch, where he can get a better view of the whole area in front of the main building. He's determined to see this guy again, even if he has to wait all night.

The sun has gone to warm another part of the world, this spot of the earth having spun away from it for the day.

Joe still sits huddled in his chair, fighting the cold without his coat; everyone else had gone inside a while ago.

T. J. opens the front door of the center and spots Joe.

"Hey Joe," he calls. "It's freezing out here. Come on in for dinner, man."

Joe wants to resist but the combined forces of the cold, his hunger, and the utter lack of justifiable reasons that he can offer in protest win out.

"Okay," he calls back to T. J., flipping his wheelchair breaks off and turning toward him. He gives one last glance over his shoulder before he disappears into the building, the dark lawn still lying empty behind him.

The early morning fog blankets the surface of the lake inlet.

Young Joe sits on the end of the dock, holding a fishing pole. James sits next to him. The two laugh and joke with each other.

Young Joe casts his line out into the water again. The red-and-white bobber splashes through the surface before rising to take its place on the gentle waves rippling across the water.

Young Joe and James quiet down, enjoying the stillness and serenity of the moment together.

Young Joe looks from his bobber to James.

James is now in his police uniform.

James looks back to young Joe, who has now become Joe of present day.

Joe sits on the edge of the dock, his legs hanging down into the water. He looks from his father to the useless limbs.

"I can't use them," he tells his dad.

"I know," James responds compassionately as Joe looks back over to him. "Just keep fighting, son," James encourages Joe. "It'll come."

James looks back out at the water.

"Such a beautiful moment," he reflects.

Joe opens his eyes and sees the ceiling in his room once again. He turns his head to his clock, the bright sun coming through the blinds. The clock reads 8:00 a.m.

"Well at least I slept in this time," he mumbles to himself.

"What's that, partner?" Johnny asks from the other side of the room.

"Just more weird dreams," Joe responds, looking toward Johnny.

Johnny sits in his wheelchair in front of his dresser. He wears a nice, colorful snap-button shirt and pressed jeans. He holds a small mirror in his left hand and combs his moustache with his right.

"Yeah," he responds to Joe, "This place is full of 'em." He suddenly pauses his primping as he turns to Joe. "Can I offer you a piece of advice?" he questions.

"Why not," Joe responds.

"Go with it," Johnny says. He then turns back around and resumes primping, figuring that was clear enough.

"Uhm...go with what, exactly?" Joe questions.

"The crazy," Johnny tells him, totally serious, as he puts the finishing touches on his 'stache.

"Solid advice," Joe retorts sarcastically as Johnny puts down the comb and reaches for his cowboy hat.

"What are you all spruced up for?" Joe questions.

"I gotta date," Johnny informs him with a wink. "The lovely Miss Megan Reece. Room 215," he tells Joe. "We're meetin' in the mess hall for breakfast."

"Have a good time, then," Joe offers to the beaming cowboy.

"Thanks," Johnny replies, tipping his hat to him as he exits the room. "See ya when I see ya," he calls from the hall.

Joe looks back up to the ceiling, grinning a little as he shakes his head.

"That crazy must be contagious," he says to himself with a chuckle.

A few patients are still scattered about at the tables, finishing up their breakfasts.

Johnny sits in his wheelchair in front of the fireplace, happily entertaining a plump little red-haired paraplegic gal, Miss Megan Reece, who laughs at the story he is relaying with emphatic gestures of his hands and arms.

Joe sits at a table watching as he finishes up his own breakfast. He smiles at the pair.

Johnny definitely knows how to tell a story, he thinks, really having grown fond of the guy.

The front doors of the cafeteria swing open, catching Joe's attention.

Brian comes through the door. He looks around and spots Joe. He gives Joe a nod of his chin and starts his way.

"Hey B.," Joe says as Brian arrives.

"Hey," Brian replies, grabbing a seat. "Just thought I'd stop by."

"Cool," Joe acknowledges. "You want some breakfast?" he asks. "I'm sure chef Robert would be happy to whip something up for you."

"No, no, I'm good," Brian assures him, glancing around.

"So what's up?" Joe questions.

"Oh, nothing," Brian shrugs. "Like I said, just thought I'd stop by."

"Bullshit," Joe calls him on his somewhat nervous behavior, always able to read his friend. Brian definitely had something on his mind.

"What's up?" Joe asks again.

Brian takes an anxious breath.

"Okay," he begins, "You're going to think I'm crazy, but just hear me out on this alright?"

"I'm listening," Joe responds. "But I ain't making no promises," he adds with a grin.

Brian is still hesitant to reveal what's got him so jittery.

"Just say it already. Jesus, what are you, a chick?" Joe jabs at him.

"Alright, alright," Brian gives in, finally getting to it. "Here's the deal—I'm practical right? So I was thinking, you know, when you get out of here, you're gonna need something to do. And we had talked before about managing our money and maybe opening a few restaurants together—"

"What, you need money?" Joe questions, cutting him off.

"No, I don't want any money!" Brian responds, incredulous. "I don't need...Look, you promised your dad you would go back and finish college at some point, right?"

"What the hell does that have to do with anything?" Joe demands.

"You did, right?" Brian insists.

"Yeah, of course. But—" Joe tries again before being cut off by Brian this time.

"Okay. Well what better time than now?" Brian questions.

"Are you screwing with me?" Joe asks, pointing at him with an accusing finger.

"No," Brian replies flatly. "With a business degree, you could manage the restaurants when you get out of here."

"Get…Maaan, you gotta be crazy," Joe replies, pushing back against his chair and shaking his head in disbelief.

"I brought you a tutor," Brian admits suddenly.

Joe just stares at him like he has to be out of his mind.

"You remember how I told you that I was having trouble with my studies, toward the end of college?" Brian asks.

Joe still just sits there, not answering, not believing what Brian is spilling to him.

"Well, this gal was spectacular," Brian continues. "She helped it all make sense to me, man. She's a really close friend now. You'll love her," he adds, trying to reassure his friend, who he can see is totally opposed to the idea—as he was afraid he would be.

Joe hasn't moved. This is so out of left field that he doesn't even have a response.

"So what do you think?" Brian presses.

"Dude," Joe finally responds, looking away and shaking his head, then looking back to Brian. "You did *not* bring me a tutor."

The two of them start talking over each other, each trying to make his point.

"How could you possibly think I would want a tutor?"

"It will give you something to focus your attention on outside of this place."

"If you had any idea what I was dealing with in this place..."

"Hey, dickhead!"

Joe stops, the shout from Brian bringing silence to the whole cafeteria.

"Just meet her, okay?" Brian pleads in the sudden stillness of the room.

"Hey, Brian," Johnny calls from behind the guys, as he and Megan have paused in their rolling toward the door.

Brian turns back to him.

"Hey, Johnny," he replies.

"This is my friend Megan," Johnny informs him, grinning from ear to ear.

"Hi," Megan offers to Brian.

"Nice to meet you," Brian tells her, his attention still on Joe.

"This is Megan, Joe," the love-struck Johnny now informs Joe. "The one I mentioned this morning."

"Yeah, yeah," Joe says, fighting back a laugh at Johnny's boyish behavior. "Yeah, we know each other. We've met."

"Hey, Joe," Megan says to Joe.

"Hi, Megan," Joe nods in return.

Everyone just sits there for a minute, awkwardly.

"Well, I guess I better be getting to my rehab with T. J.," Megan announces.

"Right, right," Johnny agrees. "Okay fellers, we'll see ya'll later," he calls to Joe and Brian.

"Alright," Joe responds.

Johnny and Megan resume their exit as Brian turns back to face Joe.

"So what do you say?" Brian questions

"You're an asshole," Joe tells him, seemingly giving in but still not happy about it. "Let me at least finish my breakfast and then I'll meet her. And then you *and she* can leave," he adds.

"Fine," Brian says.

At least the door is cracked, Brian thinks, somewhat relieved and figuring he can work on trying to push it all the way open after the introduction.

Brian walks into the great room of the main building, Joe rolling beside him while still admonishing him about the ridiculousness and impracticability of this idea.

"I'm telling you I have no freaking interest in this crap," Joe insists.

"I know, I know," Brian says, stopping.

Jazz music coming from a PBS special playing on the small TV finally reaches Joe's ears, pulling his attention away from Brian.

He turns his eyes toward the sound, but they never make it there.

In the center of the room, in front of the majestic stone fireplace, is the captivating Rachel.

She is dancing around Megan's chair. The girl wears a broad smile across her beaming face, as Rachel laughs with her.

A few of the other patients are there too. They clap or tap their chairs to the beat of the music. Johnny has his hat off and thumps it to the rhythm as he swings his head. All eyes are on Rachel as her vibrant energy fills the room.

Joe is mesmerized, completely forgetting about the conversation with Brian for the moment.

The music ends and Rachel curtsies to Megan, who nods in return. Everyone claps.

Rachel blushes. That wasn't what she had been doing it for, she had just gotten caught up in her love of music and the beautiful souls she had seen in the eyes of those around her.

"Hey, Rach," Brian calls.

"Excuse me," Rachel says to Megan, Johnny, and the others as she makes her way over to Brian and Joe, her eyes still dancing from the fun.

"Whew, I just love jazz," Rachel tells them in her thick Spanish accent as she arrives. "Don't you?" she asks the boys.

Joe just stares at her. *THIS is the tutor?!* is all that is running through his head. He finally forces out a verbal response to her question.

"Well, yeah, of course," Joe says, nodding his head.

Brian gives him a surprised look, knowing full well that Joe was not by any stretch of the imagination a connoisseur of soulful sounds.

"Well, I mean..." Joe stammers, embarrassed by the fact that he had just blurted out a lie to her. "I've never really listened to it before, actually, but yeah, it sounded great," he admits, obviously nervous.

"I know what you mean," Rachel agrees.

Brian is getting a kick out of this. His intentions really were just as he had stated them to Joe. But it was very apparent that Joe was smitten by Rachel's presence and beauty. Brian is enjoying seeing him nervous around a woman, for the first time since, well, ever.

"You okay, bro?" Brian smirks.

"What? Yeah," Joe responds, trying to recover. "I'm sorry," Joe says to Rachel. "I'm just a little caught off guard," he admits. "You're not at all what I was expecting."

"Oh, well I'm sorry to disappoint," Rachel replies, smiling.

"Oh, no, no. There's no disappointment, believe me," Joe's mouth runs away from him again.

Brian laughs out loud at this one.

"You know you're not helping," Joe tells him, with an accusing look.

He turns back to Rachel.

Her presence has just overwhelmed him. He'd met hundreds of beautiful women, especially since he signed his contract and became the face of the Rattlers football team. But *they* were usually the nervous ones.

He wasn't quite sure why he was so tongue-tied over this gal, or why his heart was racing so hard he was sure its thumping could probably be seen through his shirt. There was just something about her, the magic of life in her eyes. The way she looked at him was so clear and present.

"Can we just try this again?" Joe asks, fighting off the thoughts in his mind, as well as the flush of heat rising in his cheeks.

"Of course," Rachel replies, flattered by Joe's response to her but remaining focused on her purpose here.

She is to be his tutor, and she would never allow that role to cross over into anything else. She knows that it could completely cloud his progress if she did. Regardless of whether or not she wanted to reciprocate the flow, it was something she simply did not do.

"Hi," Joe says to her, extending his hand and hoping it won't shake. "I'm Joe Gilmore."

"Pleased to meet you," Rachel replies, taking his surprisingly steady hand in hers. "I'm Raquel de los Rios, but you can call me Rachel, if you like."

"Nice to meet you, Raquel," Joe says, respecting the Latin heritage of her given name.

Brian can barely contain himself. He had played this scene out in his mind over and over, but never had he imagined this.

The door wasn't just cracked—it had been blown off its hinges.

He just hoped that Joe would be able to keep his mind on his studies instead of the beautiful Latina woman who would be helping him with them. But, knowing Rachel, he knew for sure that she would be doing her best to ensure that he did.

Chapter 21

Midmorning beams of sunlight stream through the large windows of the cafeteria, where a somewhat trepidatious Joe sits at one of the tables next to the confident and relaxed Rachel.

Brian had already arranged courses with Joe's former college and had dropped off his books later in the week, following the initial meeting with Rachel. At that time, and much to Brian's surprise, he had had to talk Joe into the whole idea all over again.

After pressing past Joe's initial excuses—he didn't have time, didn't see the point, and he just plain didn't want to—Brian had finally gotten to the root of the issue.

Apparently, despite his immediate, overwhelming response to Rachel, Joe was embarrassed to be around her; this was both because of his physical condition and also because of his feelings of ineptitude as a student.

Brian had explained to his buddy that he totally understood the slow-student quandary, especially when the tutor was a beautiful woman. He had felt the same way himself when he first met Rachel. And luckily, having been there, he was able to reassure Joe that she had such a unique way of explaining things and teaching someone *how* to learn, as opposed to *what* to learn, that he promised he would not be feeling that way any longer after even just one session.

The physical consideration had been a bit tougher to negotiate. Instead of tackling it head on, Brian had chosen to come at it from the side.

The clever and caring big brother to both Joe and Rachel was very aware of her feelings about mixing romance and tutoring. He explained this in detail, even telling Joe of examples of guys he knew in college that she had refused to work with, no matter how much they offered to pay or promised to change, once it had become obvious that their real intentions never had anything at all to do with learning.

With this laid as a foundation, he was able to convince Joe that Rachel would only be looking at him as a student, so there was no reason to worry about what she thought about him physically.

"Besides, she doesn't judge people that way," he had assured Joe.

This actually made sense to Joe. He had seen how Rachel interacted with Johnny, Megan, and the rest of the paraplegics and quadriplegics in the great room. And even if he had only caught the last moments of the interaction, Johnny's continual recounting of the dance between Megan and Rachel was enough to drive home the positive impression she had made on all of them. That good feeling would have been impossible to achieve if she had not seen and treated them as regular people instead of cripples.

Even though Joe also knew that he saw no judgment or pity in those beautiful eyes when she looked at him, in the end the promise he had made to his father became his overriding, deciding factor.

He couldn't get past the desire to keep his word to James now that Brian had rekindled it. Nor could he really continue to argue with Brian's logic that there was no better time or place to do so, regardless of how much he had tried to fight with both himself and his buddy about it.

So although it made his stomach flip-flop in many different directions at once, for all the various reasons, he had finally agreed to the tutoring—and to keep his attention on his books instead of his tutor.

The college textbooks that Brian had delivered are stacked on the table in front of Joe.

The initial hellos and Rachel's explanation of her focus on teaching Joe some simple but very valuable tools that would help him learn for himself having been handled, Rachel reaches into her backpack and pulls out a large dictionary, plopping it down next to the other books.

"You're not going to make me use that, are you?" Joe questions, only partially joking.

"Have you ever come to the end of a page that you were reading and found you couldn't remember anything you read?" Rachel replies with a question of her own.

"That pretty much sums up college for me, yeah," Joe admits.

Rachel smiles understandingly. Just because she had a policy on focusing on tutoring didn't mean that she became some heartless, driving disciplinarian—which was probably along the lines of what Joe had initially envisioned. No, Rachel did her best to remain herself; she was calm, kind, and caring, despite the particular hat she might be wearing at any given moment.

"You read past words that you didn't fully understand," she explains the phenomenon of blankness to Joe. "If you just keep going and going, after a while it piles up and you don't even have interest in the subject anymore," she continues. "Many people start studying a course without even knowing what the title of it means." She pulls out one of the prerequisite course books in Joe's pile. "For instance, what is the meaning of the word 'mathematics'?" she asks, reading the title of the *Business Mathematics* course aloud.

"Uhm...like numbers and stuff," Joe offers, grinning sheepishly.

Rachel smiles back, her easy manner continuing to make him feel more comfortable.

"It comes from ancient Greek," she tells him, "and it actually means, 'fond of learning'."

"Math?" Joe questions, shocked that a subject that had often been his torment had such a different origin than he could have imagined.

"Yes," Rachel assures him.

"Hmm," Joe replies, his interest ever so slightly piqued. "So the secret to learning is a really big dictionary, huh?" he asks, playing the class clown once again.

"I know it seems pretty simple, but it really is the most basic step in learning," Rachel tells him, sidestepping the invitation to enter into the arena of banter and instead gently pushing home the point. "I should say, the most basic step besides of course actually *wanting* to learn a subject," she adds with a smile.

The tutoring time over, Joe rolls next to Rachel through the rose garden paths, which are beginning to bloom in the early spring air, as he escorts her back to the front of the center and her car.

"So have you always loved jazz?" Joe asks, making conversation.

"Yes," Rachel responds, her eyes lighting up with the thought of it. "All kinds of music, actually," she admits. "I grew up with it in Spain. My family would gather for *cenas*, dinner or supper I think you say."

"Yeah," Joe assures her she is correct in her translation.

"Well, my father and my uncles all played instruments and the whole family would sing and dance together," Rachel tells him. "It was just always part of us."

"That sounds pretty cool," Joe admits, genuinely intrigued by the tradition.

"Do you have a big family?" Rachel asks him as they round the side of the main building, heading toward the front lawn.

"Not really," Joe tells her. "It's just me and my mom now; my father died a little more than a year ago."

He's kind of surprised himself, about how easily the statement spills from his mouth. But there was something about this gal that just felt safe and open, so out it had come, without him really paying much attention to it.

"Oh my God, I'm so sorry," Rachel replies compassionately. She can't imagine losing one of her family members. "That must have been really hard on you and your mom," she observes.

"Yeah, it was," Joe admits, his mind drifting to his last conversation with his mother, realizing he forgot to call her back, and promising himself to do so that evening.

The two arrive at the circular driveway and Rachel's little red Volkswagen Beetle that's parked there.

"Well, it was a good start," Rachel says, referring to the study time.

"Yeah," Joe chuckles, "I guess it was," Joe admits. He's amazed at his actual interest in the material despite the initial frustration and embarrassment of having to stop and look up words in the dictionary so often.

"Okay, Joe," Rachel says, "I will see you later this week, then."

"Definitely." Joe responds, "Thanks, Raquel."

"It was my pleasure," Rachel replies, opening her car door. She sits down and starts up the engine, then gives him a little wave before closing the door.

Joe waves back as she pulls the car out along the drive, heading back out the tree-lined tunnel.

She might just turn out to be a pretty cool friend, Joe thinks to himself while trying to ignore the way his palms had begun to leak liquid as the two had chatted on their way to her car.

Sarah sits on the edge of her bed. A small cardboard box filled with some of James' police memorabilia is next to her. A few pieces, already nostalgically reviewed, are scattered across the embroidered comforter.

She softly sets a news clipping aside and reaches into the box, lifting out James' Bible.

She pulls the red ribbon bookmark, and the inspired book opens to the page the ribbon lies across.

Her eyes find the Book of Psalms, chapter 118. Yellow highlighting pulls her gaze to verse eight and the words of David that James had marked at some point.

It is better to trust in the Lord than to put confidence in man. the scripture reads.

Sarah's eyes flick to James' handwritten notes in blue ink next to the passage.

To the left of the highlighted verse he had written, *The kingdom of Heaven is within*, and to the right, *Trust in the Lord within*.

A tear of relief comes to Sarah's eyes as she contemplates this.

She turns her face from the words in her lap up to the picture of James in uniform. She smiles at him.

He still cared and still knew how to inspire her to follow the instinct of her heart, which could never be wrong.

"*The plans of a man are sealed within his heart*," the verse from Job comes to her mind.

The ring of her doorbell interrupts her simultaneously comforting and confirming moment with her husband and her feeling of being at peace with her God and His guidance.

She quickly places the Bible on the bed and hurries downstairs to the door, making sure to wipe her face clean of the tears her eyes had released along the way.

She swings the front door open to reveal an emotional Cindy.

"Sarah," Cindy chokes out between sobs, "I need to talk to you."

"Well, come in, sweetheart" Sarah responds, immediately taking Cindy into her arms and ushering the troubled girl inside.

Joe sits in his wheelchair by the window in his room, lost in thought.

His phone buzzing on the nightstand grabs his attention, and he rolls over and picks it up.

LARRY PATTERSON, the screen reads.

Joe considers answering for a moment and then changes his mind, unable to confront the teammate he knows he betrayed. He hits End instead and places the phone back on the nightstand with an audible exhale.

Johnny, sitting in one of the chairs and reading a new book, notices Joe's angst and closes the pages.

"What's on your mind, cowboy?" he asks.

"Ah," Joe begins, glancing down at his lap, "I've just been thinking about my life."

"Yeah?" Johnny replies. "What'cha think about it?" he questions.

"I think I may have made quite a mess of it," Joe admits, both to himself and Johnny.

"Don't be so hard on yourself, partner. We all make mistakes," Johnny offers.

"Yeah, but I've just really gone over the edge with everything," Joe tells him.

"How d'ya mean?" Johnny asks.

"Aw, just taking advantage of...of the position I guess," Joe replies, considering it. "Coach always talks about being accountable," he continues, turning his gaze to the window. "I wasn't," he recognizes sadly. "Not to my team, not to my girlfriend. Not even to myself, really."

He pauses; Johnny continues listening.

"I wasn't always like that, you know," Joe tells him. "I had this fight with my mom and—"

But before Joe can finish his thought, in through the door, bubbling with excitement, bursts Dr. Raj Deepak, an Indian doctor with stark black hair, thick glasses, and a goatee.

"Excuse please," Dr. Deepak interrupts. "We are Joseph Gilmore, yes?" he asks, stopping just long enough for his flowing white coat to catch up with him as he stares at Joe, eyes bounding with energy.

"Uh, yeah," Joe replies. "I am," he clarifies.

"Okay, good," Dr. Deepak responds. "We go to the brain test today," he announces as he resumes his beeline across the room to Joe.

Joe glances at Johnny who shrugs, raising his eyebrows along with his shoulders.

"Uhm, okay," Joe nervously replies.

"Excellent!" Dr. Deepak exclaims, jumping behind Joe's chair and pushing him out of the room and past Johnny, who grins at him in wonder over his effervescent energy.

Dr. Deepak hurriedly pushes Joe into a stark white room, closing the door behind them.

It's an average-size medical examination room with cabinets along one wall. A large computerized machine sits in one corner. The side facing the far wall has several screens, a keypad, and a place for printouts. The other side has a bundle of colored wires coming out of it.

Dr. Deepak positions Joe next to the wires as he excitedly explains. "This is most sophisticated machine that has been made for testing brain and neurological systems," he tells Joe as he slides a cloth skull cap of sorts onto the anxious patient's head and begins attaching electrodes to the connectors spread across its surface. "It is new addition to Agape. You are ready for most important test today?" he questions.

"Not really," Joe admits.

"Ah! Forgive me. I'm so excited I almost forgot the testing materials!" the doctor exclaims as he connects the last wire.

He quickly grabs a small, circular white table from next to the wall and places it in front of Joe. He then reaches into his left pocket and takes out a Hansen's key lime–flavored soda, opens it, and places it on the table. He reaches into his other pocket, pulls out the same brand's root beer flavor, and opens it as well.

The liquid spews all over him, the table, and Joe.

"Jesus, man!" Joe exclaims.

"Sorry, so sorry," Dr. Deepak immediately apologizes, shaking his head.

The doctor sets the root beer down on the table. He hurries over to the cabinets and pulls a towel out of a drawer, then dries himself off.

He grabs another towel, returns to the table and Joe, and starts attempting to pat him dry as well.

"I got it," Joe snaps, grabbing the towel from him.

"Oh, okay," Dr. Deepak responds, apparently unaware of the inappropriateness of his actions. He continues his busyness though, and uses the first towel to dry off the table.

Joe does the best he can to get himself dry, then sets the second towel on the table.

Dr. Deepak grabs both of the soiled towels.

"We are okay? Ready for brain test?" he queries.

"I guess so," Joe answers, frustrated and confused. "Except that I have no idea what I am supposed to do," he adds.

"Oh, correct," Dr. Deepak acknowledges, realizing he has completely forgotten to explain the process in his excitement over what he envisions the coming results will be. "I will go around, put machine on correct setting. Then I call to you, then you point to your choice," he explains with a smile, indicating the cans of soda.

"And this is some important test?" Joe questions, definitely not buying it.

"*Most* important," Dr. Deepak corrects him, giddily disappearing behind the machine.

Joe's takes a frustrated breath. *This is ridiculous*, he thinks as the doctor types instructions into the machine, readying it for the procedure.

"You are ready?" Dr. Deepak calls.

"Yeah," Joe replies, shaking his head at the absurdity of the test and the doctor.

"Okay, choose," Dr. Deepak excitedly directs.

Joe just sits there.

Dr. Deepak pokes his head around the corner of the machine.

"We must choose or there is nothing to test," he urges Joe.

"Okay," Joe resentfully responds.

Dr. Deepak ducks back behind the machine and Joe reluctantly raises his hand and points at the root beer can.

"You have chosen, yes?" Dr. Deepak asks over the whirring of the machine.

"Yeah," Joe informs him, calling back.

Joe leans forward, picks up the root beer, and takes a swig before placing it back on the table.

The machine buzzes as it prints out the results.

Dr. Deepak practically bounces back around the machine to Joe.

"Here are the results!" he announces, holding up the printout. "This is so exciting. My little heart, it goes boom, boom."

Joe just looks at him. *The crazy is definitely contagious*, he concludes. This is the only explanation he can come to at the sight of the giddy doctor in front of him, who seems barely able to keep himself attached to the ground.

Dr. Deepak picks up the key lime soda and places it back in his pocket. He grabs the root beer and takes a quick swig before starting to set it down on top of the cabinets.

"Dude!" Joe exclaims, his frustration with the bumbling doctor increasing, "I was drinking that."

"Yes I was, thank you," Dr. Deepak replies, bringing the can back and handing it to Joe.

The oblivious doctor begins spreading the printout across the table. Joe looks at the can and then sets it down on the ground, again shaking his head at the crazy doctor's antics.

Dr. Deepak—completely unaware of or totally ignoring Joe's protest—excitedly begins pointing out different wavy lines on the graph paper as he explains the results of the test.

"This line is brain sending signal to muscle in right shoulder to contract and raise arm," he tells Joe. "This line is brain sending signal to muscles in back of right arm to contract and straighten arm," he continues, intently deciphering the graph despite Joe's obvious disinterest.

"This line is brain sending signal to top of forearm to contract and raise hand," he points out. "And these lines is brain sending signal to muscles in hand to contract in such a way to cause all fingers to curl in except one."

He proudly looks up at Joe, smiling.

"Great. So my brain works to move my arm. This is exciting," Joe offers sarcastically. "Very revealing. Can you take these off now?" he asks, referring to the electrodes that still hang from his head.

"Oh. Yes, of course," Dr. Deepak replies.

He begins to disconnect the electrodes from the cap as he passionately continues.

"We have record of everything that occurred to cause that event. Everything except one," he says, pausing for Joe's response.

Getting none, he leans expectantly forward, next to his face.

"What?" Joe finally asks, to the doctor's great pleasure and Joe's ever building frustration.

"The choice!" Dr. Deepak beams as he removes the cap from Joe's head.

"What choice?" Joe fires back while tousling his own hair from its flattened state.

"Your choice—between key lime and root beer," Dr. Deepak answers, his enthusiasm undeterred. "This is the most sophisticated machine man can make for testing body, brain, and neurological systems, and it works brilliantly," he continues, pulling off the final electrodes and setting them aside. "It can record everything that happens in the body, but it cannot capture us!" he explains, coming back around to face Joe and giggling like a little kid as he points to the paper once again.

"There is no record of where the choice was made," he explains. "Only the carrying out of the choice," he laughs. "Just like Mr. Oz in the movie. We can see everything he is doing, only this time, when we pull back the curtain, there is no one there. Ha, ha—ha!" his laughter finally spills out in full force, his joy taking over.

Joe just watches him, still not totally following, but his curiosity growing despite his resistance.

Dr. Deepak throws his head back and howls with glee as he removes his glasses and wipes at his eyes.

When his gaze comes back down and meets Joe's questioning eyes, Joe sees that he is the doctor no more.

The curious man now stands across from Joe, still chuckling.

"You are not your choices or the result of them," he explains—without the Indian accent. "You are the one who chooses," he smiles.

Joe just stares at him, stunned. He is beginning to worry about his own sanity and whether or not he has also been infected with the crazy that seems to be running rampant in the center.

"Am I imagining you?" he asks the man sincerely.

"No more than you are imagining all of this," the man replies, indicating the room with a wave of his arm.

Joe looks around the room and takes a deep breath, convinced he definitely is coming down with the mental virus. His eyes land on the computer printout.

"What's it mean?" he questions.

"Whatever you want it to mean," the man replies.

"Look," Joe barks, whipping his head back up to the man. "I'm trying to go with the crazy here. Just answer the question," he demands. "What's the point of the damn test?"

The man looks at him with understanding eyes.

"What the machine—and actually life itself—experiences, expresses, and records physically is the carrying out of the choice," he explains. "It's like a copier. Whatever is put on the glass is what comes out the side. If you don't like the results, it does no good to beat yourself up about it; just make different choices and you'll get different printouts," he adds.

"That's it?" Joe questions, realizing the analogy's relation to his life, but thinking this is much too simple an answer to be true.

"Yeah," the man answers. "That and a little elbow grease sometimes to wipe the previous image that was being copied off the glass, but yeah, it's definitely where the process starts—no question."

"Fine," Joe replies, still refusing to give in. "Can I leave now?" he asks.

"Anytime you like," the man smiles.

Joe unlocks his wheels and heads for the door.

The man slips the glasses back on, along with the accent.

"Excellent. We will talk later, yes?" he calls.

Joe pauses, now holding the door open with his hand. He looks back at the man, who is grinning at him expectantly.

"Just keep your clothes on from here out," Joe tells him.

"I will if you will," the man answers, his smile growing.

Joe shakes his head. *This guy's relentless*, he thinks as he exits the room, leaving the man alone.

"I will if you will," the man says to himself with a chuckle, the accent gone again. "That's a good one."

He walks over to the table and begins straightening up the room. He picks up the root beer, takes a swig.

"Good choice," he acknowledges before downing the rest of the drink and then belching loudly.

Joe sits in the hallway pondering the absurdity, but unable to ignore the simplicity of the message that the events of the testing room had revealed.

T. J. comes walking down the hall toward him and sees Joe lost in thought.

"Hey, Joe," he says, "I've been looking all over for you."

"Oh, yeah," Joe replies, pulling himself from his thoughts. "I was in for a test," he explains, his thumb indicating the door he just exited.

"A test?" T. J. asks, confused. "Where?"

"In the..." Joe begins, looking behind him and finding only a solid wall.

Joe slowly looks back at T. J., considering.

Just as T. J. is about to question Joe once more, Joe suddenly punches the physical therapist in the leg.

"Ow!" T. J. exclaims.

"Sorry," Joe quickly apologizes.

"What are you doing?" T. J. asks, rubbing the now-tender spot.

"I was just checking to see if you were real," Joe explains, choking back a laugh.

"What?" T. J. asks him, grinning at the confusing explanation to the unexpected action.

"Sorry," Joe says again, laughing out loud now. "Sorry, man. You can hit me back if you want to."

T. J. starts chuckling too, still not sure about Joe's behavior or logic, but happy to see the guy finally laughing—regardless of the sacrifice his slightly bruised leg had apparently had to give to get it.

Chapter 22

Joe sits at one of the tables in the cafeteria. His business management book is open in front of him. He has a notepad as well, and a few notes he has made on the material fill in the top of its page.

His eyes are on the book, but he keeps glancing up across from him, with each glance beginning to last a little longer than the previous one.

Rachel sits across from Joe, reading her own book. At this point in her tutoring, she has Joe doing more and more of the studying on his own while she simply supervises.

She becomes aware of Joe gazing at her. Without looking up, she reaches toward the middle of the table and slides the dictionary closer to Joe.

Joe is embarrassed that she caught him staring at her; he hadn't even realized that he was doing it.

He quickly grabs the dictionary and looks up one of the words he passed over earlier on the page.

Rachel fights back the smile that threatens to creep across her face despite her policy of being nothing more than a tutor to Joe.

Regardless of the facts that he is her student and that he is confined to a wheelchair due to his paralysis, she has found her thoughts drifting to him more and more between her visits to the center.

There was something about the rawness of Joe's vulnerability and transparent honesty that had begun to burrow its way into her heart during the chats that accompanied their customary treks through the rose garden to her car. And she appreciated the way he had really dedicated himself to his courses and to getting his degree in a renewed effort to keep his promise to his father.

He also had begun speaking with his mother more regularly again, and even invited her to visit him at the center recently. It was obvious to Rachel how much the man cared for his mother and how important family was to him, deep down. Often, the image she saw in her rearview mirror of him watching her drive away was the vision that kept coming back to her during their days apart.

*There is something about his eyes...*her mind flashes with the thought as she watches Joe studying again. She quickly shuts down that train of thought, however, in a renewed effort to focus on her job as she hurriedly shifts her eyes back to her book.

Across from her, Joe continues his reading—completely unaware of the effect he has had on his lovely and kind tutor.

Joe and Brian sit in the great room of the main building. Joe is in his wheelchair beside the couch, and Brian is sitting in one of the cushioned, cloth-covered chairs.

The TV is on in front of them. Joe's face is turned toward it, but his mind is lost in thought.

He's thinking of Rachel again, of her laugh. He feels so comfortable with her, like he can really be himself—or perhaps even better than himself.

Brian notices that Joe is staring off into space. He stealthily reaches over and picks up one of the small pillows that lie on the couch. He slowly cocks his arm and fires the pillow at Joe, bouncing it directly off the side of his head.

Joe, snapped back to reality by the blow, looks at Brian, who is dying laughing.

"Welcome back," Brian says between guffaws.

Joe quickly reaches into the chair next to him and grabs the ammunition of a pillow himself.

"So that's how it's going to be," he declares. He fires the pillow at Brian and laughs as it strikes him dead in the face.

The room quickly becomes filled with a flurry of flying pillows, laughter, and insults.

Johnny comes rolling around the corner and immediately sees the two in battle.

"Yeeeehaaaaw!" he cries, flinging his hat into the air and joining in the friendly war of soft bombs, bullets, and jovial banter that has broken out.

The room quickly becomes strewn with pillows, couch cushions, and overturned chairs as the three compadres lose themselves fully in the joy of the game.

Everyone pauses for a breather and Joe, bent over laughing, spots two pillows on the floor next to his chair. He covertly slides his arms forward and latches onto one of them with each hand, then quickly jerks back up, readying to fire them both across the room at Brian and Johnny.

"Die, suckers!" he cries before freezing with his arms cocked as the two duck down.

Behind them stands Gary, who stares at Joe.

"Okay, okay," the chagrined Joe offers, dropping the pillows. "We'll clean up."

Gary laughs as Johnny and Brian raise up and turn sheepishly in his direction.

"It's okay, fellas," he tells them good-heartedly. "Just make sure it's all back where it was when you're done."

With that he turns and walks out.

Joe quickly reaches back down for the dropped pillows—already being pelted by Johnny and Brian before he can retrieve them.

The battle is back on.

Joe sits inside, next to the main building's front door, as Brian comes jogging back toward him with his hooded jacket in his hand. Night has fallen outside the windows.

"It was under one of the cushions on the couch," he informs Joe, laughing.

"I bet Johnny buried it there," Joe replies with a grin.

Brian reaches him and begins pulling on the jacket.

"So how's the studying going?" he questions Joe as he readies to leave.

"Good, man," Joe replies. He is surprised at how much more he is enjoying learning now than he did back in college.

Brian gives him a look.

"I'm not hitting on her, man," Joe says, knowing what he's thinking. "I don't think of her like that. I mean, I think of her like that, but…it's just…she's different. I respect her."

Brian grabs his chest and starts stumbling around à la Fred Sanford.

"It's the big one, it's the big one, Junior," Brian jokes.

"Maaan," Joe says, shaking his head with a grin. "I can respect someone."

"Yeah, just not usually someone with a skirt and a pretty smile," Brian points out, grinning back at him.

"Hey," Joe replies, his arms stretched out from his sides in a gesture of innocence, "can't somebody change?"

"I hope so, brother," Brian responds, smiling and extending his hand.

"Alright, then," Joe says as they do their handshake.

"Alright, kid," Brian replies.

The shake and obligatory flipping each other off over, Brian grabs the handle of the door.

"Until I see ya," he tells his buddy, stepping through the doorway. "Keep changing, playa, just don't call no audibles in your studies," he calls as the door closes behind him.

Joe just sits there for a moment grinning at his friend's jab before his thoughts turn to what he has just admitted to Brian in regards to his feelings about Rachel.

He ponders this in the silence of the hall for a minute or two.

Then another thought hits him.

Slowly, Joe looks down the hall to his right, and then his left.

The coast is clear—no janitor tonight.

Joe and Rachel sit at a table in the cafeteria again.

Joe is reading a definition in the dictionary and making notes on his page.

Rachel has been reading her book, but she catches herself peeking over it more and more as she watches Joe work.

She has continued to be impressed by Joe over the past weeks. He was really applying himself to his studies, and it seemed that he now had a very firm grasp of the concept behind her tutoring methods.

Almost all of her time was now spent simply supervising Joe while he worked through the material on his own.

And at this point, she was convinced he understood her teaching methods. He now knew *how* to learn and could apply that lesson to any subject. In fact, she hadn't even caught him sneaking glances at her in quite a while.

I guess he's got it, she thinks to herself, both happy and, at the same time, a little bit anxious about what that observation inevitably means.

"Okay, time's up," she hears Joe say.

"Oh," Rachel replies, popping back into the present from her thoughts and confirming Joe's announcement with the hands on her wristwatch.

Joe places his books and notepad on the corner of the table—their usual resting spot while he escorts Rachel to her car.

He's in a good mood, his confidence soaring due to his new ability to grasp the concepts in the material he's studying.

He was starting to believe that he could actually get his degree. It was amazing how making progress toward a goal that he had once thought impossible was boosting his morale.

"You ready?" he asks, already rolling back from the table, his eyes smiling at her.

"Yes," Rachel replies, placing her book back in her bag and rising.

Joe rolls to the door and opens it for her, as he always does; Sarah's training about how to be a gentleman had been ingrained in him early on, and she would have been proud to see how it had now become a part of him.

Rachel passes through the door and, as Joe rolls out after her, he asks, "Hey, did I tell you about the pillow fight I had with Brian and Johnny?"

Rachel comes walking around the edge of the main building. Joe is continuing to relate his story with excitement, while Rachel seems oddly distracted.

"So Brian and I are pelting each other with these pillows," Joe tells her. "I mean, we are at war—like when we were kids or something."

He chuckles in anticipation of the next event in the story.

"And out of nowhere I hear this 'Yeeeee-hawwww,' and *wham* I get smacked upside the head with a couch cushion," he laughs.

Rachel laughs too, but not as heartily as she normally does.

Joe is so into his story he isn't even aware that Rachel is a bit off.

"A couch cushion!" he continues, still cracking up. "I don't even know how Johnny could pick one of those things up, much less hurl it across the room. That cowboy is crazy."

"He seems like a good roommate," Rachel acknowledges with a smile that covers her nerves.

Joe pops his wheelchair into a wheelie in his exuberance as they reach the circular drive. He starts to wheel over toward Rachel's car, but she has stopped.

"So, Joe…" she says from her position behind him.

Joe spins around to face her, still balancing on his back wheels. "Yeah?" he responds.

"It seems as though you are really getting your studies under control, correct?" she questions him.

"Yeah, I'm feeling good about it," he admits whole-heartedly as he brings the front wheels back down again.

"That's wonderful," Rachel acknowledges.

"Yeah," Joe responds with a grin. "Who knew the jock could learn business?"

"So I guess we're done, then," Rachel announces suddenly.

The wind goes right out of Joe's happy sails. He is absolutely stunned and barely able to choke out a response. "Oh. Yeah, okay," he says, feeling like he has just been kicked in the gut.

"Okay," Rachel tells him, her nerves even more on edge now.

Joe tries to process this unexpected turn of events as Rachel nervously fidgets, neither knowing exactly what to say next.

Finally Rachel tries.

"Feel free to give me a call if you need help with anything else," she tells Joe.

Joe just sort of blankly stares at her for a moment before an "Okay" slides out of his mouth.

Rachel starts to walk past him toward her car. Joe slowly spins his wheelchair to maintain contact.

"Okay, bye," Rachel says with an odd little wave as she increases her pace.

Joe doesn't even get his arm up to wave back before Rachel spins back around to face him again.

"Keep me updated, you know," she tells him, her head tilting to the side. "Maybe we can have a cup of coffee or something...down the road sometime...or something."

She waits for his response, which feels like an eternity in coming.

"Okay," Joe replies...again.

It wasn't his fault, really; he simply couldn't decipher what was happening.

Thirty seconds ago his life was magic, and now one of the absolute brightest spots in it was leaving; hell, it felt more like she was abandoning him.

And despite his gentlemanly behavior of late and assurances to Brian that he was keeping this whole thing professional, he could barely hear Rachel right now over the sound of his heart thumping in his chest and his own voice screaming in his head *DON'T LET HER LEAVE!!*

But all he can manage to add, along with an awkward head bob, is "Yeah, that'd be great...sometime."

Rachel just stands there, her head nodding in awkward agreement as well.

"Okay-bye-Joe," she spits out the sentence so fast it's almost one syllable, before abruptly spinning and heading toward her car again.

She had to move quickly, actually. If she had stood there one moment longer, she might have fainted. Or she might have run screaming to her car and tearing up the driveway. Or her Latin passions might have overcome her and forced her forward, pressing her lips to his. And then again, she might have just fainted.

A casual walk toward the car, to be followed by a casual wave, and then a calm drive off the property definitely seemed to be the best of all options at the moment. However, she was failing spectacularly at the first part of that plan just now, with all her sudden stops and starts.

Joe's heart felt like it would jump clear out of his chest and stop her itself if he didn't do something or say something to halt the seeming inevitability of what was occurring.

Her hand was on the door...she was opening it...she was about to sit down in the seat...and, finally, he got the courage.

"Hey Raquel?" he calls, his palms as sweaty as a schoolboy with his first crush.

"Yes?" Rachel replies, reversing her sitting motion and coming back to her feet so fast she nearly falls over.

"Uhm," Joe begins, "uhm..."

He swallows, his momentary courage waning as fast as it had come.

"Be careful," is all he can finally choke out.

"Oh," Rachel replies, her face and heart dropping together in an odd combination of total disappointment and slight relief. "I will," she tells him.

"Okay," Joe replies, his expression looking like he is trying to recover from a direct punch to the face—one he had just delivered himself.

He slowly spins away from her and starts rolling back around the Agape building toward his books. The thoughts that fuel his fears bury the hope that, a moment ago, had been in his throat. And now he feels like it's creeping sheepishly out the bottom of his motionless feet.

How could I even think that she would be interested in someone like me!? She's a beautiful and amazing woman, inside and out, and I'm a freaking cripple, he pounds away at himself as he wheels away.

Rachel is still standing between her open door and the inside of her car, watching him roll away.

She feels like her heart is going to explode or she is going to throw up—maybe both at the same time.

"*¿Qué estás haciendo, estúpida?*" she mumbles to herself, truly beginning to question her own sanity.

Totally unaware of her actions, she starts bouncing up and down a little, the emotions inside of her running rampant in all directions.

As Joe gets close to rounding the corner of the building, Rachel bounces free of her door and breaks out in a full sprint toward him.

Joe doesn't even hear her coming across the grass until she passes him in a flash, stops on a dime, and turns back to face him.

"Hey, Joe," she says, not waiting to catch her breath—she has to get her idea out now, or she may never have the courage again. "Do you ever get to leave this place?" she asks between gasps.

Joe's total confusion at this point is clearly evident on his pensive face as he stares back at her.

"I mean, just for a few hours or something," Rachel quickly adds.

"Uhm," Joe responds, trying to gather his thoughts, still with no clue why she is asking this. "I mean, I've heard of day passes and stuff. I guess I could probably get one," he adds with a shrug of his shoulders.

"Okay, well...see," Rachel begins, looking down at her feet. She begins to pace in a circle around him—while totally unconscious of it.

She has only one focus at this point, she *has* to get this out or she will explode.

"Well...I'm, singing-at-a-jazz-club this weekend," she continues, breaking into rapid-fire speech, the words pouring out of her mouth. "It's-no-big-deal-really, but-I-mean...well, it kind of is...maybe...anyway, it...it's kind-of-like my-debut..."

Joe's head now feels like *it's* spinning as he tries to follow both her movements around him and her scattered flow of words.

Rachel accents the word "debut" with jazz hands, immediately wishing she could die and stop this runaway locomotive being fueled by her emotions—her inner dork on full display.

But she's already gone too far; she can't stop now.

"Anyway...I-would-really-like-it-if-you-came-with-me," she ends—the statement she was trying to get to coming out with a speed that matches the pounding of her racing heart as she stops in front of him.

This is the absolute last thing that Joe was expecting to hear. He's still not totally sure she even just said it.

"Really?" he asks, his brows deeply furrowed.

"*Sí*, yes!" Rachel replies, anxious for his response and frustrated by his lack of enthusiasm toward the emotional risk she has just exposed herself to for him.

"But I thought you said we were through?" Joe questions. Even though he was beginning to follow her line of thinking a little, the hope still hadn't managed to crawl back up through his feet, or, if it had, he certainly couldn't feel it yet.

"No," Rachel responds, turning away, frustration overcoming her anxiousness now. "That's not what I meant..."

She steps to a nearby tree, feeling safer facing the stable trunk instead of Joe.

"I just didn't want to mix things up while I was your tutor," she explains before quietly adding, "but I just thought that now that we are done with that..."

Again she feels that contradicting mixture of relief and her heart breaking into a million pieces at his lack of acceptance of her offer.

She kicks the tree in frustration.

"Oh." Joe says behind her. "Oh, I'm sorry, I thought that...nevermind..." he adds, searching, stalling—the question he really wants to ask immediately beginning to terrorize him, now that he has fully realized his precious Raquel has just asked him out.

He feels like his stomach is going to empty its contents as he watches Rachel's beautiful dark hair falling across her vulnerable shoulders.

"But do you really want to be seen with a guy in a wheelchair?" the question whose answer, he knows, will bring a horrifying end to the hope that is fighting its way back up into his chest, finally comes out through his emotional voice.

And there it is, Rachel thinks. The same question that had been sending her heart in both directions simultaneously since she had first begun noticing his soulful eyes watching her was finally out in the open.

It isn't the thought of others seeing her with Joe in his condition that is causing her trepidation; after all, she made almost none of her decisions based on how others would feel about them. It was probably more the unknown of what it meant to be with someone who was a paraplegic, the limitations her rational side kept telling her it would place on their relationship, regardless of how her heart felt about it.

She leans her forehead against the strong tree, feeling devoid of strength at this moment.

"No," the honest answer to his question quietly slips through her lips.

Joe instantly feels like he is back on the red planet, the demon having just withdrawn the blade that it had sinisterly run through his exposed gut.

This was the answer he had known would come, no matter how many times he had secretly hoped against it.

The courage he had summoned to finally ask immediately fled from him—hope having led the charge away from his heart the moment before.

Rachel turns to face him. Her eyes are wet with emotion.

She slowly ambles over to him and stops next to his chair.

She reaches down and touches his face tenderly, turning his downcast eyes up to meet hers.

"I'm sure that I want to be seen with you." She smiles softly as she finishes her answer to Joe's question, her heart winning out over her reason.

And as quickly as the feeling of hope had gone, it comes rushing back in the heat Joe feels in the touch of her hand upon his face and her words upon his heart.

He reaches up and grabs her hand, vulnerably squeezing it to his face.

Rachel leans down and kisses him on the cheek. She presses her face against his before standing back up, each releasing the other's hand.

"Okay," she says to him, smiling as she wipes away a tear that had escaped down her flushed cheek. "I will pick you up at seven on Saturday, then," she informs him.

"I think I can fit that into my schedule," Joe says, smiling back at her, his entire body relaxing from the release of the tension that had been gripping it.

Rachel laughs. "You better, *señor*," she warns him, backing away.

She stops and looks him lovingly in the eyes.

"Bye, Joe," she says before she turns for her car.

"Bye, Raquel," Joe calls after her.

Raquel. Wow, do I love the way that white boy says my name, she thinks, giggling to herself.

"Drive careful," Joe calls again as she opens her door.

"You already said that," Rachel replies, smiling back at him as she sits down and closes the door. She gives him a little wave as she starts the car and is finally able to calmly exit the driveway.

Joe just sits and watches her go, his face glowing, his breath finally finding the bottom of his lungs once again.

Johnny rolls out the front door of the center. He sees Rachel's red Beetle making the turn around the circular drive before spotting Joe and rolling his way.

Joe still has the same puppy-dog look on his face when Johnny reaches him. He stares after Rachel's car as it disappears under the tunnel of trees.

"I've never been around a woman like her, Johnny," Joe informs his roommate thoughtfully.

Johnny considers this as he turns to look after the disappearing car as well.

"Maybe that's it," he offers. "Then again, maybe you've just never been this way around any woman you've known," he adds off-handedly.

Joe hadn't thought of that.

"'Course," Johnny continues as Joe was beginning to consider his observation, "more than likely it's a bit of a combination of both."

Satisfied that he has assessed the situation as succinctly as any good cowboy could, Johnny gives Joe a pat on the shoulder and heads off, leaving his roommate to ponder.

Whichever it was, Joe knew one thing for sure—his life had just changed, and Brian was going to be the first call he made to tell someone about it.

Chapter 23

Joe sits in his wheelchair next to his bed, holding his mobile phone to his ear.

He listens intently for a moment before responding.

"I know, I know, I have no right to ask," he agrees with the objections of the person he has called. "It's just that...I'm trying to fix something here. It's important...please," he begs.

He waits as they consider his request, his stomach flip-flopping all the while.

"Thank you," he acknowledges their agreement gratefully. Strangely though, his face doesn't lose its pensive look even though he seems to have gotten the answer he was asking for. "So I'll see you then. Okay, bye."

Joe pulls the phone away from his ear. He exhales, hoping to blow out some of the butterflies in his stomach. He looks at his recent call log and redials one of the numbers.

"What am I doing?" he mumbles to himself as he brings the phone back to his ear.

"Hey," he says as the person on the other end picks up. "She said yes," he informs them. "Thing is, I didn't exactly tell her you'd be here."

He pulls the phone away from his head, the person yelling at him in response to the news.

"I know, I know," he admits, putting the phone back to his ear, the tirade apparently over. "I just didn't think she'd come..."

Another explosion.

"Wait, wait," he begs. "I'm sorry. Look, you know how delicate this is...please don't back out. It's pointless if you're not here."

He waits.

"I need to do this. Please," he pleads.

He waits again.

"Thank you," he exhales, finally getting the response he wants. But, again, his face still fails to relax.

He pulls the phone from his ear, presses End, and places it on his nightstand.

His hands come to his head, trying to rub away his anxiousness.

"This is either the best or the worst idea you've ever had," he tells himself.

He grabs the wheels of his chair and starts for the door, suddenly needing some fresh air.

The bathroom door opens as he rolls past it. Johnny sits in the doorway.

Joe stops.

"Hey, can I have the sitting room this evening?" he asks Johnny.

"Sure," Johnny replies. "What's up?"

"Follow me outside so I can puke and I'll fill you in," Joe tells him, grabbing his wheels once again and heading down the hall.

"Okie dokie," Johnny replies with a grin as he takes up the rear.

Joe sits in his wheelchair, nervously thumbing the armrest under his hand. Trace sits opposite him on the couch, fidgeting, neither of them talking.

Trace straightens her skirt, again.

Joe checks his watch and then the open front door of the lodge, again.

The silence hangs in the air.

Joe pushes himself farther back in his chair. Trace flips her hair.

"Thanks again for coming," Joe tells her, trying to fill the awkward, empty air. "I'm sorry about all this."

"I still can't believe I let you talk me into it," Trace replies.

"I know it's crazy," Joe admits. "But everything around here's crazy. I had to do something. It's my fault—"

A knock at the open door interrupts him.

"Joe?" a familiar voice calls.

Joe and Trace's heads whip to the door simultaneously. Cindy stands in the frame, the screen door halfway open in her hand.

"Hey," Joe responds.

Trace anxiously bolts up from her seat.

"Oh my God!" Cindy exclaims. "What the hell is she doing here?!"

The screen door bangs closed as Cindy spins away from the lodge, totally pissed and feeling betrayed. Immediately she begins to lecture herself about how she should have known better than to trust him.

Trace sighs. Her eyes filling with tears as the reality of the damage her previous affair with Joe has caused to her relationship with her former best friend crashes down on her once again.

"Just wait," Joe tells her, his focus on Cindy as he rolls for the door. "I'll be right back."

Joe exits the lodge and spots Cindy heading toward the main building. He pushes his wheels after her.

"Cindy!" he calls "Cindy, wait!"

Cindy keeps stomping away, furious.

"How could you do this to me, Joe?!" she demands. "Was I not humiliated enough the first time for you?!"

"That's the last thing I want, I swear," Joe assures her, still trying to chase her down. "Cindy, please," he calls.

Cindy takes a few more steps and then stops, still fuming.

As Joe finally catches up to her, she turns her body back to face him but refuses to give him her gaze.

"I'm sorry," Joe apologizes sincerely. "Cindy, I'm sorry. I just didn't know what else to do."

She still won't look at him, the reminder of the embarrassment and pain of the discovery at the hospital having caused her thoughts and emotions to scatter once again.

"Look, I...I..." Joe tries, searching for the right words but finding none. "Just...just come back in there with me for two minutes. Please." He figures if he can at least get the two of them in the same room he will have some sort of shot at trying to mend the relationship he feels he destroyed.

"No!" Cindy shouts in response to his request, finally turning her burning eyes to him. "Why should I, Joe? What do you think—that I owe you?" she demands, fighting back tears of anger and hurt now.

"Not a thing," Joe answers truthfully, quietly. He feels the damage he has done to her, the hurt he has caused. "And I can't give you one good reason to trust me," he adds, regretting the pain he has inflicted. "You're right to be upset. You're right to hate me."

"I don't hate you, you arrogant jerk," Cindy insists. "I hate what you did, what you're doing now."

"I'm just...I'm trying to fix something that is screwed up because of me," he tries to explain.

He looks up at her, wanting to take her hurt away.

Cindy looks away again, not wanting to face the man she feels has betrayed her once more.

Joe reaches his hand out toward her.

"Just come back in there with me and let me say this," he pleads. "Then you can do whatever you want."

Cindy looks back at him. She just stands there, staring at him for a moment in silence before responding.

"I'm pregnant," she says matter-of-factly, finally dropping the bomb she's been carrying for seven and half months now.

"What?" Joe responds, nearly choking on the word.

Cindy raises her sweatshirt to reveal a plump belly.

"You're going to be a daddy, you prick," she tells the stunned father.

Joe has no words or thoughts to respond to the news that has just dazed him. Silence and a confused face are all he can offer her.

Cindy shakes her head at him, disapproving of his lackluster response. "Figures," she mumbles, and then resumes her exit.

Joe just sits and watches her go, still trying to process the reality that has just changed his entire world.

Trace stands in the open doorway of the lodge behind him, in shock, her hand over her mouth.

Rachel shuts the hood to her Beetle in the parking lot of a quaint little jazz club that's nestled into the city's arts district. She wheels Joe's chair around to the passenger side door that he has already swung open.

He had been oddly quiet on the drive over; she was worried that he was having second thoughts about coming with her.

"Here we go," she says, covering her inner murmurings with a smile as she parks the wheelchair next to the door and locks the wheels in place.

"Thanks," Joe replies as he places one hand on the far armrest of the chair, the other on his seat, and expertly transfers himself over—the training with T. J. paying off.

The two make their way to the open front door of the club in awkward silence.

The little nightclub is pretty packed. People fill booths along the walls and small tables surrounded by chairs that have been placed on the usually open dance floor.

The bar in the corner has a couple of flat screen televisions on the wall. They play in silence for the few patrons at the bar who can't force themselves to miss the final minutes of a basketball game.

A band on stage oozes out a mellow groove in the dimly lit environment.

Rachel makes her way through the crowded room, Joe doing his best to navigate his chair through the narrow spaces behind her.

The two arrive at a table close to the stage. A RESERVED sign sits atop it.

Rachel pulls out one of the two chairs there and slides it to the next table over. Joe rolls into the vacated spot.

"I need to go and check in," she informs Joe, leaning over the table toward him. "Will you be okay here?"

"Yeah, totally," Joe assures her, as best he can.

"You want something to drink?" she asks.

"God, yes," Joe answers, glancing around.

"Okay," Rachel replies, even more anxious now after his response. "I'll be right back," she tells him, again covering her thoughts with a smile.

Rachel slips back through the crowd. Her initial excitement about sharing this special evening with Joe is beginning to wane.

As Joe watches her disappear into the crowd, his thoughts hurriedly return to the same place they've been for the last forty-eight hours.

The meeting at the lodge had obviously not gone down at all as he had planned.

He had really thought that he could help repair the relationship between Cindy and Trace. He knew that Trace's friendship had meant a lot to Cindy, and he wanted to try and help to put that back together again.

He had expected bumps along the way, but the bomb that Cindy had dropped on him was one that he could never have anticipated.

Despite his ensuing conversations with Johnny and his call to Sarah, he hadn't been able to come to any kind of conclusion about what to do yet.

It seemed that getting back together with Cindy, no matter how much it could be touted as the right thing to do, was probably not even a possibility. She had refused to return any of the messages he had left her since she had bolted from the center. He also knew that, regardless of how much they had cared for each other, it was obvious that they were both now very conscious of the fact that they had never really been truly in love.

Cindy had made her feelings plain long ago about raising a child in that type of environment. She had been raised by parents who only stayed together for her sake until she left for college, and she was convinced that the biggest thing she had learned from their example was how to have a screwed up relationship.

Johnny, surprisingly, had informed Joe that his parents had separated when he was eleven. Despite how hard it had been on Johnny at the time, when he looked back on it now, he thought that it had probably been for the best.

"When they were under the same roof, they was always fightin' or sulkin' or pretendin' to love each other—hell maybe they was tryin' to," Johnny had said. "But udders just don't work on a bull. You can't force love," was the cowboy's assessment of it.

After the initial shock of the split had worn off, Johnny said life had improved. His parents worked better as friends, and each raised him with respect for the other and a sense of independence. He wasn't sure that would have been the case had the two stayed together.

Still, Joe wasn't sure. Heck, he wasn't even sure how he could be a father. And he caught himself constantly wondering if his kid would be embarrassed by his condition.

"How do you like the music?" Rachel's voice asks as she places a beer-filled glass in front of him and takes her seat at the little table.

Joe still stares off into space, a million miles away.

"Joe?" Rachel calls again.

"Huh?" Joe responds, finally pulling himself from the depths of his troubled mind.

He spots the beer in front of him as her previous question arrives through his scattered thoughts.

"Thanks," he responds, picking up the beer. "Yeah, the music's great," he answers.

He bobs his head off beat, trying a little too hard to emphasize his interest in an effort to cover his distraction.

Rachel smiles weakly in response.

Joe smiles back, then downs half of the beer he is holding.

"Joe, are you okay?" Rachel asks as he places the glass back on the table.

"What? Yeah, of course," Joe answers.

"Are you nervous about being out?" she questions him, definitely feeling at this point like this was a mistake. "We can leave if it's too much," she offers, the disappointment starting to show in her face.

"Leave? No," Joe quickly replies. "Look, I'm sorry, you're right. It's just...this is my first time out since...you know. But I'm okay," he tells her, only partially lying.

"Are you sure?" Rachel asks, not fully buying the explanation.

"I'm like this the first game every new season. It's no big deal, really," Joe assures her, with a grin.

"You're certain?" she asks one more time. It's obvious to her that Joe is still not comfortable here.

Joe realizes his lack of attention is not really fair to Rachel, with this being her debut. He regrets his selfishness; he does really want to be here with her and support her.

He takes a deep breath through his nose, trying T. J.'s pain-management technique to calm his impinging thoughts. He exhales slowly, succeeding at releasing at least some of the stress and focusing more on this moment.

He looks Rachel directly in the eyes. "There's no place I'd rather be," he tells her, surprising even himself. It's the most honest thing he's said since the conversation began. "Besides," he adds, grinning at her, "there's no way you're getting out of singing for me."

Rachel smiles back and gives a little nervous chuckle. She glances down, and then back up at Joe's soulful eyes. He's really looking at her for the first time since she picked him up at the center earlier tonight. The tension that had started to build in her stomach finally releases with the comfort he sends her in his gaze.

"I'm really glad Brian got me a tutor," Joe says, still grinning.

"Oh!" Rachel jokes, "So that is all I am to you?"

The two both laugh, and each relaxes a little bit more. Their eyes fully lock on each other for the first time without the impediment of the teacher-student relationship there to interfere—all the other barriers at least fading to the background for a moment.

The applause of the crowd interrupts the sparks between Rachel and Joe. The latest band number has just ended.

The piano player, Al Johnson, leans forward into his mic.

"Thank you, thank you," the old jazz veteran's voice rumbles as the applause dies down. "Ladies and gentlemen, we have a special treat here for you tonight," he adds.

"Wooohooo!" Joe calls from the crowd, knowing exactly what he is referring to.

The crowd laughs; Rachel blushes.

"I think this young man may already know something about it," old Al observes, playing along.

He winks down at Joe as he continues.

"We have a young lady making her debut here at the club this evening," he informs the crowd as Rachel rises from her seat and starts toward the side of the stage. "She is as talented as she is beautiful," he continues. "Please join me in welcoming Miss Raquel de los Rios."

The crowd applauds as Rachel crosses the stage to the mic.

Joe whistles from his seat, beaming up at her, forgetting his worries for the moment.

Although all eyes are now on Rachel, in the corner of the club, above the bar and behind Joe, one of the small flat screen televisions silently flashes images from *Sportsnews* into the dark room—the basketball game having ended a few moments previous.

The pretty sports reporter Jessica Drolet—who had last interviewed Joe after the Rattlers' terrific comeback to defeat the Bears—stands in front of a luxury hotel back in the Rattlers' home city.

She looks intently into the camera as she reports on a story involving the hotel.

A picture of Joe, in his Rattlers football uniform takes the place of her on screen.

"Thank you, *gracias.*" Rachel acknowledges the crowd's applause, on the stage in front of Joe, as she removes the mic from its stand.

She turns back to the band, says a few quick words off-mic, then takes a deep breath and faces the crowd once again.

"Butterflies," she admits to them with a big smile.

The crowd laughs, Joe with them, totally unaware that the television screen far behind him now shows Jennifer Ames—the gal who overdosed in the hotel room—speaking to a horde of reporters.

The keys of the piano begin softly emitting a melody, the Latin bolero *Solamente Una Vez*, beside Rachel on the stage.

"Solamenté una vez..." Rachel sings the opening lyrics in a smooth voice that pours into the audience. *"Amé*

en la vida," she continues as she conveys the traditional bolero about the rarity and power of the miracle that brings about the wonder of loving each other.

Rachel sings with passion and feeling the song she grew up hearing her father and uncles share so many times through her youth.

Her smooth energy enraptures the crowd. They get the passion and complete concept of the song, regardless of their lack of understanding of the Spanish lyrics.

Joe feels like he is the only one in the room. His mind is fully focused now on the incredible, beautiful woman in front of him.

The song ends and Rachel places the mic back on its stand as the crowd erupts with applause, Joe's "Wheeeeeww!" ringing loudest of all.

"Thank you, *gracias*," Rachel says into the mic, blushing at the raucous acknowledgment.

"Sing us another!" a man shouts from the back of the crowd.

The crowd all laughs and the piano player begins again, a big smile across his weathered face.

Rachel closes her eyes and leans into the mic as she begins the next ballad, the aesthetic of the moment taking her over as she pours out her soul once more into another storied song.

A jubilant Rachel and Joe exit the club into the crisp night air.

"Wow. You were incredible," Joe tells her as the pair head toward the parking lot and her car.

"*Gracias*," Rachel replies, still on cloud nine. "It was a lot of fun," she admits with a big smile.

"They should have laid out red carpets all the way to your car," Joe insists, grinning as well.

"Well, I don't think that my feet are touching the ground anyway," Rachel admits with a laugh.

Joe reaches out and grabs her arm, pulling her down into his lap.

"They aren't now," he says. "Sit tight, my lady," he adds in his best English accent.

Joe wheels for the car as Rachel hangs onto him, the two of them fully enjoying the exhilaration of how the night is turning out.

"Your chariot, Madame," Joe says with a flourish and a dramatic wave of his arm as they arrive at the red Beetle, both still grinning from ear to ear.

"Why thank you, kind sir," Rachel replies, playing along.

She starts to get up, but then stops and looks at Joe. Their smiles fade as they lean toward each other and their lips meet in a slow, soft, intimate kiss. Their hearts silently melt as the world around them fades away.

Their lips part, but their faces stay close. Rachel tenderly touches Joe's face as they look deeply into each other's eyes and then kiss again.

Joe sits in his wheelchair on the sidewalk in front of Agape Rehab, next to Rachel's car. Rachel, standing in front of him, leans down. They kiss once again.

The kiss is shorter in length than their first, but it is followed by the same intimate look into each other's eyes that only love can share.

Rachel straightens up, smiling at him.

"Good night, Joe Gilmore," she says softly before turning toward her car.

"*Buenas noches, señorita bonita,*" he utters. It's a phrase he's been working on translating from the English verbiage "good night, pretty lady," since she had asked him out.

Rachel laughs as she heads around her car, pleasantly surprised.

"*Gracias, senõr,*" she replies. "*Tu eres una sorpresa muy buena,*" she adds.

"Uhm, yeah, I'm going to need a dictionary for that one," Joe admits, grinning.

"You are a wonderful surprise," Rachel translates for him, her heart full.

"*Gracias, señorita,*" Joe replies, his heart bursting as well.

Rachel blows him a kiss as she gets into her car.

Joe watches her drive away with a smile spread across his face.

As the lights of the red Beetle disappear down the tree tunnel and into the dark, his smile begins to fade, his earlier worries returning once again.

"Shit," he says under his breath as his shoulders sink. He turns and rolls for the warmth of the lodge as his mind begins to swim with conflicting thoughts.

Chapter 24

Joe sits on the deck beyond the open doors of the sitting room, staring out at the lake inlet in the midmorning sun.

Brian comes walking into the lodge behind him.

"Joe?" he calls.

"On the deck," Joe calls back, still looking out at the water.

Brian makes his way through the room and out the doors. He walks up next to Joe and looks out at the water as well.

The two take in the serene setting in silence.

Finally, Brian speaks.

"I heard from Trace," he tells Joe—referring to Cindy's pregnancy—while still looking at the inlet.

"I figured," Joe slowly responds, keeping his gaze fixed as well.

Another moment passes in silence as each examines his thoughts.

"What are you going to do?" Brian asks quietly.

"Don't know yet," Joe admits. "Pretty sticky situation."

"Yeah," Brian acknowledges. He takes a deep breath. "Joe, I have to tell you something," he says.

Joe looks at him.

"The girl from the hotel talked to the press," Brian tells him.

Joe looks away. He can't believe the timing of this.

"Jesus," he says. "When it rains it pours."

"There's more," Brian informs him.

"Oh, well by all means, please share," Joe responds sarcastically.

"It's something that's been on my mind for a while," Brian begins, looking down at his feet. "Just couldn't find the right time…"

Joe looks back to him, waiting.

Brian takes another breath. He looks up at Joe.

"I'm the one that told Coach about the hotel room," he admits.

"You what?" Joe responds, his eyes immediately flashing with anger. He's shocked at the seeming betrayal of the one person he would never have expected it from.

"I had to, man. You were out of control, I didn't know who else to tell," Brian responds.

"Who else to tell?!" Joe fires back. "You don't tell anyone about that shit, Brian!"

"You didn't leave me any choice, Joe," Brian says, holding his ground. He believes in the rightness of his decisions and actions and knows in his heart that he was acting to protect his buddy and his team.

"Are you kidding me?!" Joe yells.

"Hey!" Brian yells back, "I had to clean up your mess, man! I brought the team doctor! I carried your drugs out of that hotel in your bag!"

"Yeah, you're a real hero." Joe seethes at him.

"You ever think about anyone but yourself, Joe?" Brian questions pointedly.

"You know what? Screw you," Joe responds. "We're done."

Joe rolls over to the screen doors and yanks one open, then wheels into the room.

Brian calls after him as Joe crosses the sitting room. "The reporters went after Cindy, man."

Joe stops, but doesn't turn back to him.

"Your mom, Coach, the team...me..." Brian adds.

Joe just stares ahead, trying to block out what Brian is telling him.

Not knowing what else to do, he grits his teeth and continues on through the sitting room and out the front of the lodge. He's not even sure where he's going, but he has to get away from Brian and this conversation—right now.

Brian stares after him, pained by the fight, but knowing he had to come clean to maintain their friendship. He could only hope the break would heal.

Sarah stands in front of a large desk in the office of Pastor Roman.

"My son is a good person; he's just confused," she emotionally insists to the pastor, who sits behind the desk.

"I'm not saying he isn't, Sarah," Pastor Roman replies, "but the Word is the Word."

"You keep saying that!" Sarah responds, her voice rising for the first time ever at her pastor. "He needs more than my prayers. He needs my support, my love," she continues, trying to get him to see her point. "The same unconditional love that our Savior has for us; that's what he needs, that's what he deserves."

She had rehearsed this conversation over and over in her head for days before showing up unannounced this morning.

She knew what she was going to do regardless of what Pastor Roman said, but, despite her own knowing, for some reason she still felt like she needed his permission—or at least his indifference. This sense of dependence on his approval made her angry. And no matter how many times she had promised herself that she was not going to get emotional, she was losing that battle just now as she fought for her right to care for her son without being condemned for it by the leader of her church.

"Sarah," Pastor Roman says in a seemingly empathetic tone, trying to calm her down. "Sarah, I truly don't disagree with that," he assures her, before adding, "But your actions must align with Scripture."

"By whose interpretation?" Sarah demands, shocking herself with her challenge of this man of God.

"By what it clearly states," Pastor Roman fires back indignantly, his own emotions getting the better of him.

Sarah just stands there, looking at him. This man had helped her through so much, but now she feels as if he is forcing her to choose between him and Joe. Her body is racked with emotion as she worries that God might strike her down at any moment for questioning one of the leaders of His flock. And then it hits her.

"Put your trust in the Lord within." She remembers the note she had seen written in the margin of James' Bible.

All of the stress begins to run out of her body.

Of course! She had read it in James' own handwriting. It had touched her at the time, but just now, at this exact moment, its full meaning finally sunk in.

She had been fighting against her own God-given instincts to love her child no matter what, to support her child no matter what. But she had believed that she must be wrong if this man in front of her didn't agree.

She had felt the presence of the Almighty before and the expansiveness of the embrace of His love in her darkest hours.

How could one who loves us so much that He gave his son, expect me to abandon mine in his greatest hour of need?

she thinks as a sense of peace washes over her. *It's simply not possible.*

And with that thought and the realizations that had just rolled through her mind like dominoes across a table, gone was her need for approval from outside sources.

It didn't mean that Pastor Roman hadn't helped before, or that he was always right or always wrong.

It simply meant, for Sarah, that no one and nothing should trump what she knew in her heart to be true, especially when what she knew matched her own experience and understanding of the Divine.

No doubt her pastor had been a help in expounding on that understanding in the past, but no one could supersede the connection to the Kingdom of Heaven that she sensed lying within her.

"I don't need you to interpret for me anymore, Pastor," she calmly states. "My actions are between me and the Lord now."

And with that she turns and walks out the office door.

"I'll be praying for you, Sarah," Pastor Roman calls from behind her in a condescending tone. "I'll be praying for you..."

Joe wheels down the hallway of the main building pissed and confused—but mostly pissed.

The events of recent days felt like a slap in the face for the effort he was making to change his life.

A door opens in the hall in front of him and the curious man steps out in full clown regalia, jovially grinning from ear to ear as the laughter behind him fades with the *click* of the closing door.

Joe rolls by, intent on ignoring him. But a few pushes of the wheel past the man he stops and spins back around.

"Is this a joke to you?" Joe demands. "My life? You having fun toying with me?"

"No," the man answers honestly as he loses his smile.

Joe looks over the man's outfit. "Perfect," he says. "You are a clown."

The man looks down at his floppy, oversized shoes. He raises the large toe of one of them.

Joe spins and continues rolling down the hall.

"I'm dressed," the man calls after him, referring to Joe's condition for any further conversations at their last meeting.

Joe continues huffing away, ignoring him.

The man takes off running after him. "I'll go with you," he calls, his shoes loudly flopping against the floor as he hurries after Joe.

Joe spins back around a second time.

"You told me to choose again," he states accusingly.

"I know," the man replies, arriving next to him, his shoes stopping a moment or two after he does.

"So I did," Joe insists, still angry.

"I know," the man responds with a smile. "Well done."

"Well done?" Joe questions emphatically. "If it's well done, then why the hell is everything so difficult, so complicated?" he demands.

"Have you ever cleaned the turkey pan after Thanksgiving dinner?" the man asks, totally serious.

"You're..." Joe begins before abruptly stopping, having no idea how to respond to the absurdity of the man's question.

He spins away again and furiously continues his path down the hall.

"You know, the pan that the turkey's cooked in, with the stuffing and all?" the man calls after him as Joe disappears around a corner.

The doors to the cafeteria swing open and a smoldering Joe comes rolling through.

The curious man stands to the side of the entrance in the empty room.

The momentary surprise of the character's new location causes Joe to stop. He stares at the man.

"While that turkey's cooking," the man continues, "all of the juices and the fats and the spices just keep burning right into the bottom of that pan, right?"

"You done?" Joe asks flatly.

"Hey, you asked the question," the man responds innocently. "I'm just trying to answer it."

Joe closes his eyes and shakes his head viciously, then grips his wheels and rolls for the kitchen area.

The man watches him go, then sits down at one of the tables.

Joe rolls all the way into the empty kitchen, looking for something but unable to find it.

"Peanut butter with bananas, right?" a familiar, calm voice asks.

Joe slowly turns to see James, who is also dressed in clown gear—complete with a red wig and nose—standing next to the man.

James holds a plate containing a piece of bread covered with peanut butter, slices of banana and honey.

A second plate, containing the same, sits in front of the man.

"What are you doing?" Joe asks his dad.

"Just clowning around," James responds nonchalantly, as he places his plate on the table, opposite the man.

Joe starts rolling toward him, but James turns for the door.

"Are you leaving again?" Joe questions.

"It's your moment, son," James responds as he reaches the door. He stops and turns back to Joe.

"Don't worry, Joey," he adds, "I'm putting money on seeing you again."

He grins, winks at Joe, and then disappears out the door.

Joe slowly looks from the door over to the man.

"It's crunchy, not smooth," the man assures him.

"The only person I've ever shared that snack with is my dad," Joe informs him. The appearance of his father has softened his mood somewhat, and increased his curiosity about the man, but he still holds his position across the room.

"I know," the man responds, looking back at him. His face is filled with compassion. "Would you mind having it with me?" he asks gently, reaching over and lifting the extra plate in his direction.

"How do you know him?" Joe questions, the familiarity between the man and his dad obvious.

"A friend from way back," he answers, smiling as he sets the plate back down on the table across from him.

Joe looks away. He exhales a deep, pent-up breath before looking back toward the man.

The man, having taken a bite of his treat, now chews heartily on the mixture of salty and sweet in his mouth.

"It's really good," he mumbles to Joe over the sticky mass in his mouth.

Joe shakes his head and begins rolling toward him, giving in to the food, at least.

As Joe arrives at the table the man holds out a fork to him, which he grudgingly takes.

The man looks down at his plate, his face lighting up again. "Ooooh man do I looooove peanut butter," he says, cutting off a very large piece this time and stuffing the whole thing into his mouth.

Joe watches him, trying to figure out his continual odd behavior.

He looks like an overgrown child as he tries to chew the oversized glob of peanut butter, banana, and bread in his completely stuffed mouth.

"Mmmmmm-mmmm," the man exclaims. "Tha' es goo'," he adds, barely choking out the syllables over the food.

"You sure are…" Joe begins.

"What?" the man questions innocently, the side of his cheek looking like a chipmunk's from the mush he has momentarily shoved to one side with his tongue.

"Nothing," Joe responds, his fingers rubbing the scalp beneath his hair as he exhales again. "Nothing," he repeats as he takes his fork to his own food, cutting off a much more reasonably-sized bite.

"Okay," the man responds, finally swallowing his load. He starts to cut off another bite and then stops, looking up at Joe.

"Hey, can I ask you a question?" he queries.

"Why not," Joe responds before popping his bite into his mouth.

"After cooking all day, then sitting there while everyone is eating off of it, what's left of that turkey and dressing in the pan is stuck pretty good, wouldn't you say?" the man asks as though they had never left the subject.

"Oh wow," Joe responds, between chews. "You gotta be kidding me. Don't you ever stop?

"Hu-uh," the man replies, shaking his head no. "It would be stuck pretty good, wouldn't it?" he questions again.

"I don't know, man," Joe says, dropping his head and rubbing his eyes. "I guess so," he answers with frustration, lifting his head back up and cutting off another bite as he swallows what's in his mouth.

"What happens when your mom puts that pan in the sink and fills it with soap and water?" the man asks, as though he's trying to figure it out as well.

"You just...you're going to take this all the way, aren't you?" Joe asks, momentarily pausing with his work on the plate.

"Uh-huh" the man responds, shaking his head yes.

"Okay, fine," Joe says, putting down his fork and finally giving in to the conversation. "It's...it starts...the water gets, like, dirty, then the stuff starts floating to the top." He picks up his fork again. "You happy now?" he questions sarcastically.

The man grins, emphatically shaking his head yes, before quickly asking a follow-up question. "Does it look better or worse than when she first put the water in it?"

"It looks worse!" Joe exclaims. "It looks worse. The water's all nasty, all the crap is floating in it—" He stops, dropping his fork as it hits him. "Wait a second, are you saying that all this stuff happening is the crap floating to the top because I'm cleaning my *turkey pan* life?" Joe questions pointedly.

"Uh-huh," the man responds, starting to cut off another huge bite. "Happens every time."

"Well that sucks," Joe responds.

The man chuckles.

"Well it does," Joe insists.

"Just the process of cleaning anything up," he assures Joe. He decides to forgo the cutting and instead folds what is left of his bread in half so that it will fit into his mouth. "From a closet to a country to a life," he adds with a shrug of his shoulders and a grin. "As long as you keep scrubbing, it'll come clean." He winks at Joe. "Tell you what—you wash, I'll dry," he adds before turning his attention back to his food.

The man grabs what's left on his plate and stuffs the entire bite into his mouth. He begins chewing as Joe stares at his plate trying to process this new tidbit of crazy that seems so simple he knows it has to be true, regardless of how much he doesn't like it.

"Hey," the man calls through the stuffing in his cheeks.

Joe looks up at him.

"Aaaaahhh," the man says, opening his mouth and showing him his mushed-up food. His eyes dance like a third grader's at the lunch table.

Joe laughs despite himself. "So much for dignity," he observes.

"It's highly overrated," the man assures him, busting into a laugh of his own.

A piece of the mashed-up food falls out of his mouth and onto his plate as he guffaws. He immediately reaches down and grabs it with his hand, then pops it back into his mouth again.

This sends Joe over the edge. He howls with laughter at the completely undignified character across from him.

The man roars too as he fights to keep the remnants of the sticky snack behind his lips.

They both wipe tears from their eyes at the same time and with the same hand, mirror images of each other.

"The best part is..." the man says after he manages to swallow at least a chunk of the food in his mouth and the laughter begins to die down. "The best part is," he repeats, pretty much under control once again, "if you made the turkey pan dirty, then obviously you have the ability to make it clean again."

"Yeah, but it still sucks," Joe insists, his laughter starting again.

"I know!" the man agrees, laughing again as well. "But such is life on planet earth!"

And they are both off again...

Chapter 25

Johnny rolls into the bedroom, feeling like a nap. His experiment with less and less sleep for the body is not quite working out as he had planned.

Joe sits in his wheelchair at the foot of his bed, listening intently to the phone pressed to his ear.

"Yeah, I'd love to," he says into the mobile device with a grin. "Great, great...I'll see you then," he adds, ending the call.

Joe lowers the phone and the corners of his mouth simultaneously.

"What's up?" Johnny asks him.

"Dinner with Rachel," Joe responds, his mind chewing on something else.

"Well I'd've expected to see a much bigger grin on your face than that," Johnny tells him.

"Yeah, I know," Joe responds. "But apparently my turkey pan isn't clean yet."

"Your what?" Johnny questions.

"Oh, long story," Joe answers. "Just trying to go with the crazy."

"There you go," Johnny says with a big smile, pointing at him.

Joe grins back, but is still obviously mulling over whatever was on his mind—the burnt remnants of turkey and stuffing, apparently.

He looks down at the phone and swipes the screen until he gets to another number. He presses it with his thumb and places the phone to his ear once more.

"Cindy?" he says, shocked that she actually picked up this time. "Hello?" he tries as the phone goes silent. "Damn it."

He pulls the phone away and sees the "call ended" on the screen.

"She hung up again," he informs Johnny.

"That sucks," Johnny astutely observes.

Joe thinks for a second, then shoves the phone in his pocket and rolls for the door.

"Keep climbin' back on," Johnny tells him as he slides from his wheelchair up onto the bed. "You'll get that bronc rode yet, partner."

Joe chuckles as he exits the room.

"Whatever that means," he mumbles to himself.

A white transport van with AGAPE REHAB written on its side is parked in front of a luxury apartment building. The side doors are open and the lift gate sits on the ground.

Gary leans against the front of the van, his face scrunched against the afternoon sun as he peers up at the exterior of the building.

Joe sits in the building's elevator, intently rehearsing the coming conversation in his mind as it rises.

The *ding* announcing the next floor interrupts his internal conversation; he glances up at the number—seventeen.

He grabs his wheels. This is the floor.

The elevator doors open, and Joe rolls out into the familiar hall. He makes a natural turn to the right and heads down the hall, arriving at a familiar door.

He sits there for a moment or two, trying to steady his nerves and quiet the rapid thoughts that have suddenly begun shooting through his mind, as well as the beat of his heart which has risen to match the pace of his mind.

What if she's not here? What if she is? What if she's already had the baby? How far along was she, anyway? What if her dad is here? What if...

Screw it. Joe cuts off the thoughts, reaches out, and rings the bell before he loses his nerve.

"Coming." Joe hears a voice call from inside.

He exhales sharply, trying to blow his nerves away.

The door swings open.

Cindy's eyes drop down to Joe's level, her face immediately following.

"Joe, I don't have time for this," she tells him as she starts to close the door.

"I have to talk to you," Joe pleads.

"There's nothing left to say," she responds. The door is almost shut now.

"I'm trying to...Listen, I want to help, Cindy," Joe cries, desperate.

Cindy flings the door back open.

"You arrogant son of a bitch!" she barks. "I don't need your help, Joe. If there is one thing this baby has helped me to realize, it's that."

"You're right, you're right. I'm sorry, that came out wrong," Joe tries.

Cindy takes a deep breath and attempts to calm herself, for the baby's sake if not for her own.

"Look, I get it, okay?" she says to him, the hurt still evident in her eyes. "I was the model and you were the star quarterback. It was comfortable, but it wasn't real and it wasn't love. But still—my *best friend*, Joe?"

"I—" Joe tries to start, but is cut off.

"And I find out about that other girl from a reporter?" Cindy continues, her voice rising once again. "With a mic stuck in my face? How many more were there?!"

A couple of concerned neighbors venture into the hall at the sound of Cindy's ascending tone.

Joe glances in their direction, then back at Cindy.

"Cindy, can I come in, please?" he asks quietly, obviously embarrassed by the public display.

"No," Cindy says, crossing her arms over her bulging belly. "If you have something to say to me, you can say it from right there," she tells him with a small sense of satisfaction as she watches Joe squirm.

"Cindy..." Joe tries once more.

Cindy cocks her head to one side in response, waiting.

"Okay, fine," Joe says. "Fine." He tries to find a way to begin. "Look, I..."

The pressure of the onlookers is too much. He turns to one particularly bold neighbor, an older woman who is peering down at him disapprovingly through her bifocals.

"Do you mind?!" Joe demands.

"Well excuse me!" the woman retorts as she and the other neighbors retreat back into their abodes.

Joe turns back to Cindy, trying to regain his focus, to remember any of the statements that he had so carefully rehearsed.

"Okay..." he begins. He stops, rubs his face with his hands. Nothing he practiced comes to mind, so he simply begins again.

"Okay look, I'm...I'm not here to try and explain myself. It's unexplainable," he says sincerely, having probably made the best decision he could to just spill his guts in whatever way they came out. "All I can say is, I'm sorry. Regardless of how things were, you deserved better. I'm sorry for how I treated you, I'm sorry for what I did, I'm sorry for how you found out. And I'm sorry for the media…I'm just…sorry," he tells her. The true regret is evident in his mournful eyes.

Cindy is still standing there with her arms crossed, but she is at least listening now. She's surprised by the vulnerable honesty that Joe is displaying; his ability to apologize had not been a particular strength for him in their previous time together.

"The point is. I came to tell you thank you," Joe continues. "Thank you for not telling me earlier. If you had, I probably would've tried to talk you out of having the baby…not that I would have succeeded," he quickly adds, "but I know I would have tried."

"Well that's part of the reason I didn't," Cindy admits, showing a small chink in her armor. "I'm not sure what my response would have been."

"And who could blame you?" Joe observes supportively. "With someone like me on the other end of the situation."

Cindy appreciates the acknowledgment and the responsibility that Joe seems to be taking for the hurt he has caused her. She appreciates it, but it still doesn't fix things for her. She's still on her own. Although she is finding that—much to her surprise—she doesn't hate it so much, that perhaps she is a lot stronger than she had previously given herself credit for.

It was amazing how much this baby had already changed her. She had come to gratefully realize that being responsible for someone besides herself, who was totally dependent upon her, caused her to find strength she didn't even know she had. And, having begun to find it, Cindy was hesitant to let this man who had made her feel weak, stupid, and replaceable be part of what she and her baby had going.

So the two just sat there in silence for a moment, as past lovers and friends often do in awkward moments of repair or transition.

"I've screwed up a lot of things in my life," Joe finally says, breaking the momentary silence, the sorrow on his face revealing the honesty behind the statement. He looks down at his lap. "But..." he continues, "but there's going to be a baby here." He glances up at her belly. "Really soon, I'm betting," he smiles, meaning it as a compliment. "I just want to find a way past all this so that I can be part of its life...part of your life. We could at least be friends again..."

Cindy looks at him. Part of her is relieved. Part of her wants to cry, but she has no more tears for this.

"Please leave, Joe," she quietly requests.

"Can you at least think about it?" Joe asks.

"I don't know..." Cindy responds honestly.

She softly closes the door.

Joe is left alone in the hall; not at all sure what effect this conversation has had on Cindy, if any.

Chapter 26

Joe nervously rolls down the hall of the main house at Agape Rehab. He wears a nice button-up shirt and V-neck sweater, dressed for his dinner with Rachel.

He absently passes by an open door in the hall before stopping a few spins of the wheels past it.

"You've got to be kidding me," he says to himself regarding what he just saw out of the corner of his eye.

He reverses his path back to the door and slowly rolls through it.

An incredibly elaborate set for model trains is spread out before him. It literally fills the entire room.

There's an old small town with live townspeople hurrying here and there, an enormous mountain range with animals roaming around on it, and even a large desert-like Grand Canyon area with Native American peoples camped out in tepees along the edge of the cavernous ravine.

Several sets of different trains run around the tracks, disappearing into mountain tunnels and coming out again, crossing over streams, and stopping in the town to pick up passengers.

The curious man is running around this world, wearing pinstriped overalls, an engineer's cap, and an ear-to-ear grin.

"Ain't it cool, man?!" he exclaims to Joe like a little boy enjoying the best Christmas present ever.

"What are you doing?" Joe asks.

"Playing," the man explains with a wink. "Watch this," he tells Joe, turning back to one of the tracks running across the landscape in front of him.

A little steam engine locomotive passes by him, billowing out white smoke.

The man beams.

"Look at the little wheels," he says, grinning and pointing at them as they go by.

As the train passes Joe, who has now parked himself next to the man, a little gray-bearded engineer sticks his head out of the engine and pulls the cord for the whistle.

The curious man is in ecstasy as the whistle rings out across the magical world.

Joe follows the train down the tracks and continues past it, following the long trajectory of the winding track's path through the countryside and out into the desert.

The rails lead up to the edge of the Grand Canyon area, but there is no bridge to carry the train across to the other side, only jutting rails that hang out over the edge of the massive ravine.

"Uhm, I think you forgot something," Joe observes. He indicates the missing track.

"Oh," the man replies, "I should see if he's done."

The man steps back to the front part of the room and eases around behind the scenery. He ducks down toward the back of it, disappearing from view.

Joe waits for a moment or two as the little train continues to make progress toward the dangerous gap in the tracks.

"Hey, you coming back?" Joe calls, beginning to worry about the little rosy-faced engineer.

The man doesn't answer.

Joe rolls over to the control switches. He looks them over, trying to figure out how he can stop the small engine.

"Hey, it's going to crash," Joe calls, more urgently now.

Still no response.

Joe cautiously throws one of the switches on the panel.

The little wheels on the train continue to carry it toward its doom, the happy engineer seemingly oblivious to the peril that awaits him and his passengers.

Joe throws another switch.

The train continues on, just seconds from the edge of the canyon now.

The Native American figurines next to the canyon pause their activities and turn to look toward the oncoming train.

The townspeople also take a break from their busyness and look in the general direction of the ravine as they sense something pivotal to their world is impending.

The wheels of the train spin toward the track's edge, the plunge inevitable.

Joe is throwing switches like mad.

"HEY!" he calls in desperation.

At the last possible second, the man pops up from behind the tracks and plops an elaborate suspension bridge down over the canyon, connecting the two sides of the train tracks.

The little train scoots across the bridge, the bearded engineer still all smiles.

The Native Americans break into a celebratory dance, beating their drums as they weave a path around their campfire.

The townspeople shake off their momentary feeling of worry and go back to their usual rushing about.

"Man, that little dude wasn't stopping!" Joe exclaims.

"He knew the bridge would be there when it was time to cross over," the man responds matter-of-factly, as though it was no big deal.

The man leans toward the bridge.

Atop it sits a little red-haired figurine, wearing big black cowboy boots.

The character waves up to the man, smiling.

"Nice work, friend," the man calls down to him, waving back.

"Did he build that?" Joe questions.

"They were big boots, but somebody had to wear them," the man answers with a grin. He winks at Joe. "Everyone needs a little help from their friends," he adds.

Joe chuckles, shaking his head at the absurdity of it all.

"So what's up?" the man asks, seemingly out of the blue.

"Huh?" Joe responds.

"What's up?" the man asks again, indicating Joe's attire.

"Oh," Joe says, "I uhm, I have a date with Raquel."

"Niiiiiice," the man responds, rubbing his knuckles up and down across his chest like a buffoon as he nods his head and wiggles his eyebrows.

"You're such a dork," he tells the man, with a smile.

The man smiles back.

"It's way more fun," he responds. "So what's there to be nervous about?" he asks, having picked up on Joe's emotions, probably even before Joe entered the room.

"Well…" Joe begins, not really sure himself. "I guess I'm kind of nervous about my date with Raquel," he admits. "It's just…I don't know."

"I see," the man responds, his brows furrowing in concern. "Hey, what do you love about football?" he suddenly questions.

Joe slumps back in his chair and smiles.

"Here we go again," he sighs, starting to get used to the man's seemingly random questions that always, somehow, have a way of actually being totally relevant.

He considers the question for a moment.

"In one sentence?" he asks.

"Sure," the man responds.

"I lose myself in it," Joe answers.

"Wow," the man replies, genuinely impressed. "You don't hold anything back, worry about what the other guys are going to do, or whether or not they'll show up when you need them?" he asks, sincerely interested.

"No way, man," Joe says. "You don't think, you just play the game. You...ah..." he ends, getting the point.

Joe cracks a smile. He exhales audibly. The man has gotten him again.

"Yooouuuuuu," Joe says, pointing at the man.

"Yooouuuuuu," the man says, pointing back with a big grin.

He winks at Joe. His eyes flash, twinkling with light.

"You'll have to show me how to do that some time," Joe tells him.

"It's a deal," the man replies.

Joe looks at his watch.

"I'll see you later, then," he tells the man who is becoming more and more a trusted confidant.

Joe releases the breaks on his chair and starts for the door.

"I'll be around," the man replies, turning back to his trains as Joe exits the room.

"Okay," he calls to the miniature world, rubbing his hands together. "Who's ready for round two?"

Joe and Rachel sit at her dining table, finishing up the *Buñuelos de Viento* desert—light as air Spanish fritters—that Rachel had served following her home-cooked meal.

Rachel's apartment is a cozy, loft-style abode. It has a very open and flowing feel to it—much like its owner.

The dining room opens onto the living area, where an electronic waterfall runs in the corner. An ancient-looking eight-point cross adorns one of the walls in the peaceful space. A Native American dream catcher hangs next to a sliding glass door. Lit candles are scattered about. A coffee table holds a stack of books: Dr. Wayne Dyer's *Wisdom of the Ages*, *Friendship with God* by Neale Donald Walsch, *A Course in Miracles* from the Foundation for Inner Peace, and the Dalai Lama's *An Open Heart*.

Joe takes the last bite of his powdered-sugar dusted, egg-custard-filled treat.

"That was amazing, Raquel," he tells her.

"*Gracias*," she responds. "I have always loved cooking," she adds, rising and taking the empty plates back to the kitchen.

"My *abuela*," she calls. "Grandmother," she clarifies, poking her head back into the dining room before disappearing again and continuing the thought. "She always said that love was the secret to great cooking. It was her key ingredient in every family meal."

"Sounds like good advice," Joe acknowledges.

"For everything," Rachel observes.

Joe looks around the room as Rachel rinses off the dishes. He takes a deep breath. The effect of the curious man's pep talk is wearing off and his nerves are beginning to return.

Rachel reenters from the kitchen, drying her hands on a towel.

"I would like to go and sit on the balcony," she tells him. "Would you care to join me?" she asks with a smile.

"Yes, I would," Joe responds. He loves her directness.

Rachel tosses the towel onto a counter in the kitchen and turns toward the sliding glass door.

Joe doesn't move.

Aware that she isn't being accompanied, Rachel turns back to him.

"Would you like to do it now, or were you waiting for more dessert?" she questions, grinning at him.

"I have to tell you something," Joe says to her. He's completely lost his nerve and his live-for-the-moment footballesque feeling, but he's trying to steel himself to do the right thing here. Regardless of the outcome.

"Okay," Rachel responds.

"I'm not sure how you're going to take it," he adds, nervously.

Rachel pulls out a chair from the table and sits directly in front of him, sensing his apprehension as she begins to worry herself.

"Well, why don't you just tell me, and we'll find out together," she says, offering a gentle smile to cover her own nerves. She wants to be supportive; she sees how difficult a time he is having.

"Okay...It's just, uh..." Joe begins, stumbling over his words. "I really like you, Raquel. Maybe more than like."

Rachel smiles, her stomach relaxing. *Definitely a good beginning*, she thinks.

"I...I want to be honest with you. I don't want to have any secrets," he says, looking directly at her despite the fear in his belly.

Rachel reaches out and takes his hand; she wants to connect with him, make it safe for him to express what's in his heart.

"Joe," she says, softly, "Just tell me."

Joe looks down. He exhales again, looks back up.

"My ex-girlfriend, Cindy?" he says.

"Yes?" Rachel responds, her stomach immediately launching into flip-flops.

"She's pregnant...very pregnant," Joe tells her.

Rachel slowly sits back in her chair, doing her best to cover the immediate shock she is experiencing. She looks away, trying to process the information.

"We're not getting back together," Joe assures her. "But I'm going to be a dad, and..." he trails off. Rachel is still looking away. "I just thought you should know," he finishes.

"That's a lot to take in," she finally responds, her mind suddenly full.

"I know," Joe acknowledges., "It was for me too," he admits, his heart dropping from the effect he sees the news is having on Rachel, regardless of how much he comprehends her response. "If you want me to leave, I'll understand," he tells her. "I can call a cab or something."

Rachel stands.

"I need some fresh air," she tells him, turning for the balcony.

Rachel walks through the living room, trying to keep her knees from buckling before she makes it outside.

She opens the sliding glass door and steps onto the balcony; the dream catcher waves in the light breeze created by her exit.

Joe looks down at his lap, not sure what to do. He lets out a long exhale, assuming the invitation to join her has now been withdrawn.

Rachel plops down on her wooden bench on the balcony, feeling like she wants to cry.

She looks out over the railing toward the sound of a bubbling brook that runs alongside the apartment building, in the darkness of the evening. She takes a deep breath, trying to focus her thoughts and to examine the situation rationally instead of emotionally.

Joe's face drops as he figures that Rachel's absence must be her response to his offer to leave.

He unlocks the brakes on his chair and slowly rolls toward the front door, his face filled with sadness.

His hand reaches up and grabs the doorknob.

"Hey," Rachel's voice calls softly from across the room.

Joe looks over to the glass door and sees Rachel standing in its open doorway.

"Come here," she instructs, and then steps back outside.

Joe sits there for a second longer, his hand still on the doorknob as he debates whether this is a good or bad indicator of her feelings. Unable to decipher her request, he finally releases the handle and pushes his wheels across the living room.

Joe cautiously rolls out onto the balcony.

Rachel is sitting again, gazing out. She appears calmer now, more together.

Joe stops next to the bench. He nervously waits for Rachel to say something as he stares off the balcony as well.

Rachel slowly slides down the bench, arriving next to Joe.

Still looking out across the balcony, she reaches over and takes his hand in hers.

"You're an amazing man, Joe Gilmore," she tells him.

"Huh?" Joe responds. It's absolutely the last thing he expected to come out of her mouth.

"This all happened before me," she continues. "And even though I'm not sure how to handle it—or if I can—I know I have to find out." She turns and faces him. "No one has ever had the courage to be that honest with me," she says with love in her eyes.

Rachel leans toward him.

The two share a long, slow, intimate kiss that eases their fears and releases their heartfelt passion for each other.

They pull apart, their relieved faces close once more.

"Every time I kiss you, I feel like I can't breathe," Joe tells her softly. "I'm scared."

"Of what?" Rachel asks, squeezing his hands tightly.

"Of you, of us, of this," Joe says, his chest pounding. "I've never felt this way before, Raquel," he confides, the honesty continuing to spill out of him in the safety of her open gaze.

"What way?" she asks, her pulse now racing as well.

"Like I want to place my heart in your hands," he says. "Like I want to breathe you in and never exhale."

He squeezes her hands, looking directly into her beautiful eyes.

"*Tu eres mi amor, Raquel de los Rios.* I love you."

Rachel's heart explodes as she looks back into the soulful, hazel eyes staring at her with piercing and loving clarity.

Everything outside of their gazes fades as glowing silhouettes of their ethereal bodies rise up out of their sitting human forms.

In the soft light of her bedroom, Joe and Rachel are still staring into the windows of each other's souls.

Their transparent bodies glow in the moonlight that streams in through her billowing, sheer curtains.

Rachel stands in front of Joe. Joe *stands* opposite her.

Her fingers tenderly reach for the softness of Joe's sweater, grasp the fabric, and pull it over his head.

Their love-filled eyes lock as Joe's hands find the buttons that run the length of Rachel's red dress, hers connecting with those on Joe's black, collared shirt.

They slowly release the buttons as each stares deep into the heart of the other.

Rachel pushes Joe's shirt over his broad shoulders. His arms drop to his side and the shirt floats to the floor.

Joe follows her lead, opening her dress and gently sliding it up and over the top of her small frame. Her hot skin burns under the touch of his strong hands.

The dress crumples onto the floor beside her toes.

Rachel unlatches his jeans, causing them to find the floor as well.

Joe pulls her in close. The skin of their bodies melds together as their hearts beat in unison. Their lips are inches from each other; their eyes are wide in the cascading beams of the moonlight.

Joe unclasps her bra from behind, releasing the veil from over her breasts and pressing them against his strong chest as the lacy fabric joins the crumpled clothes below.

Rachel's fingers dance across his abs, reaching down to his tight boxers just as Joe's fingers slide under the straps of the delicate silk of her white thong.

They step out of their undergarments—their passions freed—and fall into the bed in the unison of the truly naked embrace they share.

Rachel's light, aesthetic body stretches across the top of Joe's muscled frame.

He rolls her over and softly connects his lips to hers as his fingers lightly caress the round flesh of her perfectly shaped breast. He parts from her mouth and his lips press against the curve of her neck. His tongue finds her skin as he savors every moment of the pleasure his touch brings her.

His mouth replaces his hand on her breast and his hands gently trace the contours of her body. Rachel melts into his every touch, their love present in every treasured moment of caress.

His lips continue down the line of her stomach, his tongue lightly touching the wispy, fine fuzz of her delicate body hair, which stands on end as he finds her navel.

Rachel's face turns to ecstasy and her fingers grip the sheets as Joe continues his enraptured trek down her trembling body.

She rolls her head back into the bed, her back arching—she can take it no longer.

She reaches down and pulls Joe's lips back up to her open mouth. They kiss as deeply as a sun-parched man drinks in the water of an oasis in the desert, as they consume the love each has for the other.

Rachel rolls Joe over and slides on top of him. She feels him enter her physically, the emotional and spiritual oneness they share expressed through human form.

They move together as they make love, each delighting in the other's pleasure far more than their own.

Their eyes never close. Their faces stay close as they share this magic; mouths open, breathing each other in.

The lovers' bodies explode in ecstasy as they climax together, still looking into each other's eyes.

A tear escapes from Joe's as his body relaxes.

He simply can't believe the beauty of this experience or the amazing love he feels for the incredible woman wrapped in his embrace.

Joe inhales sharply, on the balcony of Rachel's apartment. A tear trickles from his moist eyes.

The two still stare into the windows of each other's soul, Rachel now sitting in Joe's lap.

"God likes me," Rachel tells Joe with a smile stretching across her beautiful face. "She really, really likes me," she assures him, the grin breaking into a laugh as her eyes sparkle with delight.

"You 'ave no idea mon," Joe replies, in his best Jamaican accent, laughing as well.

Rachel wipes away his tear. The two kiss again as she savors the love she has found in the man finally real enough to be honest and he cherishes the wholeness he sees reflected in her eyes.

Chapter 27

Joe comes rolling out of the cafeteria. The sound of his fellow patients and the staff enjoying Chef Robert's morning nourishment is replaced by the chirping of springtime birds as the cafeteria doors close behind him.

He heads toward the lodge, his face no longer showing the troubled concern of recent days.

There was something about the way that Rachel looked at him that just freed him. It made him want to get better, to be better.

It was like she saw him for who he could be, and as though he was that man already. She wasn't trying to put some projected image out there for him to live up to or grow into. No, it was more like how he remembered his grandmother looking at him. You'd have thought he personally went out and hung up the moon each night, the way she admired him. And, interestingly enough, when he was around her he almost felt like he *could* hang that moon in the sky.

It was a good feeling.

Joe reaches the lodge and turns onto the worn path at its side to make his way around the building.

He arrives at the back, looking out toward the lake inlet, when he spots his new friend, the curious man.

The man is in his fishing gear again—he always dresses the part. He sits at his usual spot in his folding chair, trying to untangle the line on his pole.

Joe begins rolling over toward him.

Hearing him coming, the man glances up. He offers a grin and a friendly wave in his direction.

"Hello, Noble One," he mumbles, more to himself than loud enough for Joe to hear.

"I thought you might be out here," Joe calls as he gets closer to him.

"And so I am," the man responds, still working the line.

"Little tangled?" Joe asks.

"Yeah it was," the man answers. "But it seems to be straightening out alright," he adds. "Just a few last knots left to be undone."

He reaches down next to his chair, grabs another rod and tosses it to Joe.

Joe catches it, looks at him.

"I was saving it for a friend," he says, winking at Joe.

"I guess I'll have to suffice," Joe retorts, grinning back at him.

Joe releases the lure from one of the rings on the pole and casts the line out into the water.

He looks out at the little red-and-white bobber floating on top of the inlet.

His mind drifts back to his dream of his father. He smiles.

"This *is* a beautiful moment," Joe admits, almost to himself, as he gazes out at the serene setting. He takes in the peace that radiates from Mother Nature's aesthetic display.

"Summer is almost here," the man observes, looking to the sky just above the reeds across the inlet.

Joe looks in that direction as well. A beautiful swan skims over the top of them and gracefully comes to rest on the water's glassy surface.

"Hmm," Joe replies, admiring.

Johnny rolls out from the back of the lodge, behind Joe. He peers out toward the water, spots his bunkmate, and begins rolling his way.

Joe turns his gaze from the swan back to his bobber. A couple of dragonflies dance around it. He grins.

It's amazing how much life can be around you and you don't even notice it, he thinks.

Johnny comes rolling up behind him.

"Catch anything?" the cowboy asks.

"Not yet," Joe and the man respond in unison.

"Still don't get no better," Johnny observes, looking out at the placid inlet.

"You can say that again, partner," Joe tells him.

"Still don't get no better," Johnny obliges with a grin. "Hey Joe, you left your phone on your bed. It keeps going off. Figured you'd wanna know," he informs the chuckling Joe.

"Guess I better go check it," Joe responds. "Want to hold my spot?" he asks, offering the rod and reel.

"Don't mind if I do," Johnny replies, taking up the pole and Joe's watch over the water.

"What kind of lure you slingin'?" Johnny asks as Joe starts rolling back to the lodge.

"Whatever was on it," Joe calls over his shoulder, continuing toward his room.

"Hmmm," Johnny ponders as he begins reeling in the line to check.

As Joe reaches the lodge, he glances back out toward the fishing spot. Johnny sits alone, casting the line back out into the water.

That's odd, Joe thinks, looking around for the man but not spotting him. "Wonder where he disappeared to," he voices to himself, before shrugging it off and rolling through the doors.

Big Salt, Larry, Johnny, Coach Osborne, Sarah, and Brian—along with his beautiful wife, Melissa—are all in a waiting room at Park Memorial Hospital once again.

But, unlike their last visit, this one is filled with excited anticipation. The group anxiously glances around at each other with big smiles plastered across their faces.

"Uncle Salt," Big Salt announces to the group. "I like the sound of that."

Everyone laughs.

Sarah exhales a nervous breath. Brian, sitting next to her, hears it, reaches over, and takes her hand.

Sarah looks over to him and smiles over her anxiety—she's about to become a grandmother.

She squeezes Brian's hand, glad he's here for support.

Brian smiles and squeezes back, anxious to become a surrogate uncle himself.

Another set of hands clenches in a delivery room; these belonging to Cindy and Joe.

Cindy lies on the bed, her legs in stirrups; the attentive Dr. Pollack, in soft-colored scrubs, squats between them. Joe sits by Cindy's side in his wheelchair.

Cindy strains with a quiet grunt as she pushes to get their baby into the softly lit world of the delivery room.

"Good, Cindy," Dr. Pollack coaches. "Now breathe again, the baby's almost out...Okay, now puuuussshhhhh."

"Hhhhhhnnnggggghhhhh," Cindy responds as she tightens her body.

Joe's face lights up in anticipation as he looks expectantly toward the doctor, his hand turning white in the vise of Cindy's grip.

"Veeerrry goooood. Keep pushiiiiing...and she's out," Dr. Pollack announces, as she catches the little baby girl in her hands. A smiling nurse quickly steps over to help.

"She's a girl?" Joe asks with tears in his eyes, his heart already bursting with love for her.

Dr. Pollack smiles at him. As the nurse sucks the fluid out of the baby's mouth and nose, her adorable little cry finally fills the air.

"Yes she is," Dr. Pollack responds as Joe and Cindy listen to the most beautiful sound they've ever heard, while their eyes and hearts spill over.

Dr. Pollack glances up at the clock on the wall. "Time of birth: nine p.m. exactly," she announces for the hospital records.

"Would you like to cut the cord?" she asks Joe, looking toward him and extending her medical shears.

Joe glances at Cindy, grateful that she decided to include him to this point and hesitant to overstep his bounds.

"Go ahead," Cindy says, beaming through her exhaustion and tears. "It should be cut by her daddy."

Joe squeezes her hand and rolls down toward the doctor and the new love of his life.

He takes the shears from her, reaching over Cindy's leg and beholding the most beautiful thing he's ever seen.

He has to wipe away his tears of joy and awe just to be able to adjust his focus from his daughter and actually see the cord.

He chuckles at himself as he clears his eyes with the back of his hand. Dr. Pollack smiles at him understandingly.

Joe places the shears around the cord and cuts it in two. The nurse immediately wraps the baby in a large towel, and Dr. Pollack places her on Cindy's chest.

"My baby," Cindy quietly chokes out through her tears as she wraps her arms around the greatest gift she has ever received.

She looks up at Joe, who is making his way back to her side. He looks back at her. Their eyes meet.

They may not be getting back together, but their mutual respect and admiration now far exceeds any pain they had inflicted on each other. They share this treasure together. In this moment, they both know that they will be good, supportive parents, and that this little gal will never have to worry about whether or not she is loved and adored by either of her parents; they both know it to their core.

The anxious group from the waiting room all shuffles in, their faces filled with the wonder and anticipation of a group of four-year-old children approaching the tree on Christmas morning.

"Oohs" and "aahs" quietly fill the room as Sarah leads the charge forward.

She stops next to the bed, then turns back to the group. With the same instincts as a mother bear guarding her young, she pulls out a small bottle of hand sanitizer and hands it off, insisting everyone use it before they even come near the bed.

The group all obliges as Joe and Cindy chuckle at the protective grandmother.

"Better get used to that," Joe tells Cindy.

"I know," Cindy replies, smiling. "It's one of the many reasons I love her," she says.

Sarah turns around to her and squeezes her hand and then her cheeks. But before she can turn her freshly sanitized hands to the treasure on Cindy's chest, Brian's voice calls out from across the room.

"What did you name her?" he asks, still standing next to the door with Melissa.

Everyone stops.

Joe looks up at Brian. Their eyes meet for the first time since their fight.

"Grace," Joe answers. One look is enough to repair their strong friendship in an instant.

"Awwwww," Coach Osborne leaks out.

The group laughs as Coach Osborne sniffles. The big guy is all heart.

Coach Osborne, Brian, Big Salt, and Larry all sit next to each other in the waiting room once again. This time Joe sits opposite them.

He had called this most recent Rattlers family huddle, and was using it to try and repair the damage he had done to his brothers in arms.

"I'm sorry I brought that on you, Coach...guys," Joe continues, referring to the scandal.

He looks to Larry, truly remorseful. "Especially you, man. No excuses. I screwed up. I'm sorry," Joe tells him, his voice cracking.

"Appreciate that, QB," Larry responds.

Joe nods to him and turns to Coach Osborne. "I want to come and talk to the team too, Coach. If that's alright with you."

"I think it's a good idea, son," Coach replies.

"Yeah," Brian agrees, proud of his buddy.

Big Salt nods his head in agreement as well.

"You can still slip your hands under my funny business anytime, QB," he says with a wink, humorously referring to their pre-snap positions on the field.

The boys all share a good laugh.

Coach Osborne stands, then steps toward Joe. He places one of his large hands on Joe's shoulder as the laughter dies down.

"I'm proud of you," he tells the leader of his team. "Your father would be proud of you too."

"Thanks," Joe responds, looking up at him, really appreciating the sentiment.

Joe and Sarah are in front of the nursery window, watching Grace receive her bath.

"She is so beautiful," Sarah observes to her son, her face glowing.

"Yeah, she is," Joe agrees, smiling.

He slowly drops his eyes from his daughter to his lap, before turning them to Sarah.

"Thanks for coming, Mom," he tells her.

She puts her hand on his shoulder and squeezes, her eyes still on Grace.

"Mom..." Joe says.

"It's okay, Joey," Sarah answers, still watching her grandbaby as she fights back her emotions, knowing where Joe is going.

"No. It's not," Joe tells her.

Sarah finally turns to him.

"I'm sorry, Mom," he says, his voice breaking again.

"No, I'm sorry," Sarah blurts, bursting into tears too, as she bends down and squeezes him tight.

The two sniffle on each other's shoulders, their embrace repairing their wounds.

They release their hug, smiling and wiping tears, relieved to be firmly and fully in each other's corners once again.

They both turn back to Grace, smiling through the tears that have yet to dry up.

Sarah puts her arm around Joe.

"I think maybe it's time to move on," she softly tells her son.

"You think Dad would want that?" Joe asks.

"I think *she* deserves that," Sarah responds, staring at Grace.

Joe smiles, agreeing completely.

"And yes," Sarah continues, "I most definitely think he would want that."

She wipes away another tear, then notices the smeared mascara on her hand.

"Oh, Lord, I'm a mess," she observes.

"Well, go clean up," Joe says, smiling up at her. "We're not going anywhere."

"Okay, okay," Sarah responds. "I'll be right back." She stops. "Just, just...I don't want to miss anything," she tells him.

"You've got a lifetime, grandma," Joe tells her.

Sarah beams.

Another tear runs down her cheek.

"Oh my word," Sarah exclaims in exasperation, as she turns away again. "I'm leaking like a water hose today."

Joe laughs, as she continues down the hall, before turning his attention back to Grace.

The nurse is wrapping her up in a fresh blanket.

Joe stares at his beautiful baby girl. He can't imagine what he has ever done to deserve to be so lucky.

It's extraordinary how much you can love someone from the first moment they enter your life, he thinks.

Lost in his thoughts about Grace, he doesn't even notice the pair of legs clad in green scrubs that step up to the window next to him.

"Hello, Noble Ones," says the curious man who wears the scrubs as he looks into the nursery at the little bundles of joy all wrapped up and lying in their see-though, plexiglass cribs.

Joe looks over at him, checking out his attire.

"So you're a doctor now?" Joe questions.

"A surgeon," the man clarifies. "Heard some of them think they are God, wanted to find out what that was like."

Joe laughs.

The man winks at him. His eyes flash, twinkling with light. He looks back into the nursery.

"She's beautiful," he tells Joe. "They all are."

"Yeah," Joe agrees, looking back as well, "They are."

They both just stand there, watching the joy of new life squirm and snooze and cry in the tiny beds before them.

"She's the most beautiful, of course," Joe offers to the man with a grin.

The man is the one who laughs this time.

"Of course," he admits to the proud poppa. "Hey, can I ask you a question along that line?" he asks.

"Shoot," Joe answers, still grinning.

"How do you feel about Grace?" he questions.

Joe laughs, figuring he has just answered that question with his last statement, but the man's expression doesn't change. He wants to know more.

"What, are you serious?" Joe questions.

"Never," the man responds. "But I do really want to know."

"Okay," Joe replies, examining the feelings of his heart a little more deeply. "You know," he begins, "it's weird. She just showed up but..."

He turns to look at her again before continuing.

"I don't know if I could really put into words how I feel about her. I love her, of course, but it's more than that. You know?" he finishes, looking back to the man.

"Yeah," the man responds tenderly, his eyes filled with an understanding of that magical bond.

He turns and looks back to Grace, Joe joining him.

"But she can't *do* anything," the man oddly interjects into the beautiful moment.

Joe laughs, figuring the statement to be another of the man's jokes.

"Well, I'm just saying," the man continues, "I mean, don't you realize how much sleep you're going to lose over her?"

"What? Are you messing with me?" Joe questions him, getting the feeling that this isn't one of the man's light-hearted observations.

"You know, right now she can't feed herself, she can't clean herself," the man plows on with the laundry list of care the little gal is going to require. "She even needs help to regulate her own body temperature!" he exclaims.

"What the hell's wrong with you?" Joe fires at him, grabbing his wrist and spinning the man to face him. "I don't care about any of that," Joe declares as he stares up at him, defending his feelings for his daughter.

"Yeah, but she doesn't even know how to love you back," the man insists.

"I don't care about any of that!" Joe declares again, his voice and his passion rising. "She doesn't have to know how. She doesn't have to be perfect. I don't care how much sleep I lose or how much she'll make me worry. I just want to be near her, to share her life with her, I love her—no matter what," Joe finishes, his face flushed.

"And what will she ever do to deserve that?" the man asks, shaking his head down at Joe.

"She doesn't have to *do* anything," Joe answers flatly. "She's here. And that's enough."

The man stands opposite Joe, a knowing smile slowly returning to his face.

"Bingo," the man says, grinning once again.

Joe's heartbeat slowly returns to normal as a smile gradually spreads across his face, the realization of what he has just said fully sinking in.

A tear escapes out of Joe's right eye just as one also breaks through from the man's left.

The tears simultaneously roll down each man's grinning cheeks, as if in a mirror, while they share an understanding look.

Chapter 28

The deep black eye of the Buffalo on the Colorado University banner peers out over the football stadium at Joe's old college.

Joe sits in his wheelchair on a stage that has been erected in the middle of the football field, staring up at section number ten, where the school mascot-flag hangs.

IT'S BUFFALO TIME!! the banner reads.

Joe smiles, the college war cry bringing back fond memories.

Family members and friends of the graduating students are scattered throughout the stands. The honorees sit in folding chairs in front of the stage. They wear caps and gowns, as does the graduating Joe.

On the stage with Joe are faculty and administration members and the valedictorian. Reporters' cameras line the front of the stage, documenting the event.

The dean stands at the mic, wrapping up his opening speech.

While he speaks, Joe scans the crowd and finds Sarah, who holds the little bundle of joy Grace. The still recovering Cindy sits to her right, along with Brian, Melissa, Larry, Trace, Big Salt, and Coach Osborne.

"I know that this is a little unusual," the dean acknowledges to the crowd, "but the university feels that this man's recovery and academic perseverance set a great example for our current students and all those who will follow the tradition of excellence here at CU."

"CUuuuuuuuu!" the students cry in unison.

The dean smiles and continues. "With much-deserved recognition, I give you your quarterback, Joe Gilmore."

The crowd goes nuts as Joe rolls to the mic, glancing into the crowd once more and finally spotting Rachel.

He smiles up at her as she pumps her arm in a circle and yells out his name with the throng in the stands.

The dean finishes lowering the mic for Joe. He shakes his hand, congratulating him, and steps to his seat.

Joe takes his position in front of the mic as the applause dies down.

"Thank you," Joe says, looking out over the crowd and taking in the individuals looking back at him, as opposed to the collective group of fans he used to see them as. "I know that most of you remember me as your quarterback," he continues.

The crowd cheers again. Joe waits for them to quiet down; he appreciates the acknowledgment, but has more to say.

"But I hope that today you can see me—" he stops.

Something at the foot of the stage catches his eye. It's the *Sportsnews* cameraman, turning his cap around and zooming his lens in for a close-up.

"That you can see me as just..." Joe tries again before his voice trails off, distracted by the movement of the camera once more.

He looks down at the large lens pointing up at him.

His heart skips a beat as he leans forward, trying to confirm what he sees in its reflection.

Finally the image comes completely into focus for Joe, who now sees himself *standing* in front of the mic.

Before he can even think his next thought, he hears James' voice.

"It's just a moment, son," his father says.

Joe jumps back from the mic. Everything goes silent. He spins around, but there is no wheelchair in sight, no James Gilmore on the stage for him to find.

"None of this is real, anyway," he hears James' voice continue from another place.

The scene from the red planet flashes in front of Joe, the disturbing jumbotron and its holographic images disappearing from the sky with the wave of James' arm.

Then the entire scene fades from before Joe, who stands on the stage in confusion.

Joe looks up into the stands searchingly, but only empty seats stare back. He looks out onto the field to find that the entire student body has been replaced by a single person: his younger self.

"It's time to wake up," Young Joe calls up to him, then his eyes flash/twinkle with light, and he is gone.

Joe's heart pounds as he turns to his left, sensing someone else on the empty stage with him.

His eyes find the curious man sitting in what was just previously his own wheelchair. The man grins up at him, as Joe hears the voice of his Agape Rehab roommate.

"Don't worry, cowboy, you'll have your moment when you find Grace..." Johnny's voice assures him.

The image of himself sitting in front of the nursery, looking at his daughter, flashes before him, before being replaced by the one of him sitting on the deck outside the lodge with Johnny.

"And then *wham*," Johnny's voice continues, "it'll be like you're wakin' up for the first time."

The cowboy looks at Joe, winks, and the image vanishes.

Joe finds himself standing to the side of the stage now, where the curious man was just sitting. He looks back toward the mic.

The man is there, sitting in Joe's wheelchair. He leans into the mic.

"But I hope today that you can see me…" he voices through the stadium speakers before pausing and turning his gaze toward Joe. "As just a friend." He finishes the line Joe had been trying to complete when he found himself whole once more in the reflection of the probing camera.

The man's eyes flash, twinkling with light, as he looks over to Joe.

"Keeee-aaaaaaaaa!" Joe hears the hawk's magical cry from behind and above him.

He turns to see the hawk leap from its perch atop the field goal post in the end zone behind him and spread its wings as it arches through the sky, coming toward him.

Joe looks back to the man.

The man grins at him.

"Just so you know," he says as the hawk continues through the sky toward Joe.

"I'll be around," Joe hears himself saying in unison with the man across from him, who begins to morph into Joe's own current likeness.

"If you feel like talking…" the two Joes finish together, the metamorphosis complete.

Joe stands, looking at himself sitting in the wheelchair, while simultaneously looking back at himself standing on the side of the stage.

"Keeeeeee-aaaaaaaa" the hawk cries behind the standing Joe as it crashes into the upper part of his back, just beneath his shoulder blades.

Joe's arms extend out. White light pours out through his chest, then out his fingers, and finally his face and eyes.

The light flashes throughout the whole stadium.

The massive flash of light retracts back into Joe as he finds himself standing on the red planet. The hospital gown he wears moves gently in the calm breeze sweeping across the landscape. The red dirt feels soft and cool beneath his bare feet.

The stadium and the football field are gone, the demons, reporters, and screens as well.

Joe looks out over the horizon. James stands alone atop the crest of a hill in his ancient robe, staring back at him.

"Was it worth the fight?" James calls to Joe with that Gilmore grin.

Joe smiles back at him.

"Every second of it," Joe calls back.

"And what does it all mean, my son?" James questions him.

Joe chuckles.

"Whatever I want it to," he replies with sparkling eyes.

James laughs. His eyes flash as they twinkle with light.

Joe laughs as well.

And, *finally*, Joe's own eyes flash and then twinkle with light as his laughter echoes across the hills of red dirt.

Joe's eyes blink slowly open as the light above his bed comes into focus, in the Park Memorial ICU unit he lies in.

His head slowly turns to the right, where his eyes find a room filled with balloons and flowers and signs, all wishing him well.

His eyes travel across his bed and down his legs, finally landing on Sarah.

Sarah stares up at him as she holds a wet sponge on his leg, tears streaming down her smiling face.

Joe glances up as the nurse stops in the door.

"Rachel," her name tag reads.

Joe's eyes find Raquel's and she smiles her big, beautiful smile at him, her eyes dancing.

Joe smiles back, his eyes dancing as well.

He catches a movement out of the corner of his eye that pulls his attention and his gaze to the window.

The hawk stands on the balcony railing outside Joe's window, looking in on him.

Joe laughs as he stares at the hawk.

The hawk bobs its head up and down in its own expression of joy. Joe is sure he sees a smile play across its beak.

The two share a knowing look, the hawk now certain that the message he came to deliver had found its way home.

Joe smiles as he watches the majestic bird turn and leap from the railing, taking to the sky once again.

Its powerful wings press against the air as it rises higher and higher, toward the clouds.

As it breaks through the white, fluffy ceiling its magical cry rings out across the sky.

"Keeeeeee-aaaaaaaaaaaaaaa..."

The entire sky flashes with light.

Q&A WITH THE AUTHOR ABOUT THE HIDDEN GEMS IN *freedom for joe*

Reporter: Tell us about the hidden religious themes within the story.

Lee: *Well the Christianity is probably obvious, but there are many and I wouldn't want to give them all away. Hopefully part of the fun is discovering them for yourself and sharing with others, but if you are a student of a number of the world's religions you will find specific teachings, just below the surface of Joe's journey, interwoven into the storyline.*

Reporter: Well at least give us one example.

Lee: *Haha. Sorry, yeah, I'll give you a few. If you know about Native American Spirituality, for instance, obviously the meaning of the hawk is explained by Johnny. However, what's not explained is that actually every single animal that Joe sees or is associated with or says the name of has very specific spiritual meaning, even the mascots of the football teams. His team is the Rattlers, because the snake is the symbol for rebirth. It sheds it's skin and becomes new. And his first opponent is the Bears. Because the bear is the symbol for introspection. It goes into its cave to hybernate, or goes within, and when it comes out again, it's to the Spring of a new world. This is symbolic also of what Joe's journey is about. And of course when Joe is injured he is playing the Coyotes. The coyote is considered to be the great trickster.*

Essentially he plays tricks on himself and gets himself in all sorts of "Wyle E. Coyote" type situations, but generally ends up coming out unscathed on the other side, with the opportunity to have learned from his adventure, which, of course, is what happens to Joe. So those are some examples, but like I said, there is definitely more.

Reporter: What are some of the other religions present in the story?
Lee: *I think that whatever religion one follows, you are going to find some gems that you relate to from the tenents of your faith. That's one of the fun things about the story for me. After the ebook came out I had a friend call me and say that she couldn't believe how much of the religion she adhered to was in there, and then we spent about an hour discussing it. Then the very next day I had another friend call me and tell me the same thing about an entirely different religion and we discussed that one at length. Personally, in my own study of religions, I've found a lot more similarities than differences. I should tell you, one of the lesser known religions that I had a lot of fun fitting into the story is Numerology.*

Reporter: Wait. There's numerology in *freedom for joe*?!
Lee: *There is. To go in depth on Numerology one would need to study it, but MY real quick, overall take on the part of it that is being explored in 'freedom for joe' is that the numbers in one's life end up adding up to where one is at in a*

particular spiritual evolution. The numbers run one through nine, because one would then reach ten, which added together (one plus zero) is a new one, or a new, higher spirtual plane than the person was previously operating on. So in 'freedom for joe' every number that Joe directly sees or says, thoughout the entire novel, adds up to where he is at in his current, spiritual evolution. If you look at the numbers he is saying in the play calls on the football field, they each add up to four. Well all of them except one. Before he scores the touchdown in the first game, part of his call is "Buffalo 19." This actually combines Native American symbology and Numerology. One and nine would be ten, or a new, higher 'one' – and the Buffalo is the symbol for thanksgiving and abundance. Besides the more immediate experience of the celebration of the coming touchdown, this is actually a kind of foreshadowing of what's coming later in the story. In chapter twenty-eight, (the last chapter, which does add up to ten, or a new, higher one, by the way), Joe is seated at his college graduation and looks up to see the Buffalo banner hanging in – you guessed it – section ten.

Reporter: Wow! Well what else?
Lee: *Haha. Well, I could go on and on, but like I said in the beginning, I'd prefer to leave it up to the discovery of the reader for now. I'm sure we will do something on the dvd for revealing more of this stuff, but I'd rather not cloud the reader's experience any further. Part of the whole point of 'freedom for joe' has always been that it's up to the*

interpretation of the reader to decide what so many things mean. We are all 'joe' on our own journey to freedom, and in the end, as Joe says to his father in the last chapter, it all means "whatever I want it to mean."

ABOUT THE AUTHOR

Lee Burns is an actor, a writer, a producer, an acting teacher and career consultant.

More information on Lee is available at www.leeburns.net and on the internet movie database (imdb) at http://www.imdb.com/name/nm0122759/.

Or connect with him on Facebook on the Actor/Director page for Lee Burns and follow him on Twitter at @theleeburns.

ABOUT *freedom for joe* THE FILM

freedom for joe is currently in the works to become a major motion picture. For more information please visit www.freedomforjoethemovie.com, or on imdb at http://www.imdb.com/title/tt1241215/, or Lee's Production Co, Awareness Entertainment, website www.awarenessentertainment.com.

Made in the USA
Middletown, DE
08 January 2023

21681081R00205